LOCKED IN PURSUIT

ALSO BY ASHLEY WEAVER

LOCKED IN PURSUIT

An Electra McDonnell Novel

ASHLEY WEAVER

MINOTAUR
BOOKS
NEW YORK

First published in the United States by Minotaur Books, an imprint of St. Martin's Publishing Group

www.minotaurbooks.com

Designed by Omar Chapa

Library of Congress Cataloging-in-Publication Data

Names: Weaver, Ashley, author.
Title: Locked in pursuit / Ashley Weaver.
Description: First edition. | New York : Minotaur Books, 2024. |
    Series: Electra McDonnell series ; 4
Identifiers: LCCN 2023058013 | ISBN 9781250885906 (hardcover) |
    ISBN 9781250885913 (ebook)
Subjects: LCSH: Safecrackers—Fiction. | World War, 1939–1945—
    England—London—Fiction. | LCGFT: Detective and mystery
    fiction. | Spy fiction. | Novels.
Classification: LCC PS3623.E3828 L63 2024 | DDC 813/.6—
    dc23/eng/20240104
LC record available at https://lccn.loc.gov/2023058013

Our books may be purchased in bulk for promotional, educational, or business use. Please contact your local bookseller or the Macmillan Corporate and Premium Sales Department at 1-800-221-7945, extension 5442, or by email at MacmillanSpecialMarkets@macmillan.com.

First Edition: 2024

10 9 8 7 6 5 4 3 2 1

Once again, for Ann Collette,
with heartfelt thanks for everything

LOCKED IN PURSUIT

CHAPTER ONE

LONDON
JANUARY 1941

In the last war, your father was spying for the Germans.

They were not the sort of words one wanted to hear in the midst of a war with Germany. Indeed, they were not words one wanted to hear at the best of times. They had been haunting me since my mother's closest friend had uttered them in October, and they were on my mind as I sat at the breakfast table on this frigid January morning.

My grim family history was the sort of thing worthy of Shakespearean tragedy—or perhaps a Greek tragedy like the one that shared my name. My father had been murdered before I was born. My mother, convicted of the crime and condemned to death, had given birth to me in prison. She'd been sentenced to hang, but the influenza had claimed her instead.

She'd died proclaiming her innocence, and I'd grown to adulthood determined to prove it. That was why I had gone to see her friend. I'd hoped she would be able to aid in my quest to clear my mother's name. Instead, I'd opened a Pandora's box of long-hidden secrets and lies.

My father had been passing information to Germany and had likely been, for reasons still unknown, killed because of it. The who and exactly why were still a mystery. Whatever the case, my mother had kept his secret, willing to go to the gallows rather than reveal that her husband had been a traitor to his country, rather than put the rest of her family at risk.

It was a secret that had weighed heavily on me ever since. Because what was I to do with this information? Should I pursue what I had learned, attempt to find my father's true killer in the face of what I now knew? Should I attempt to clear my mother's name at the expense of blackening my father's?

I knew there was a trunk of my father's belongings in the cellar, but I'd had yet to work up the fortitude to search it for the clues I suspected might be there. In truth, I was afraid of what I might find.

Because, if my mother hadn't murdered my father, it meant someone else had. But who—and why? Had the English killed him because of what he was doing, or had it, perhaps, been the Germans because of something he knew?

We were in our own war with Germany now; it didn't seem like the ideal time to bring up mysteries from the last one. I was caught in a sort of quagmire of indecision.

At least the Germans had stopped dropping bombs on our heads every evening. After fifty-seven consecutive nights of bombings, we'd had a brief holiday reprieve. No bombs had fallen on England on Christmas or Boxing Day. It was difficult to be grateful to the Germans for anything, but I was thankful for the chance to celebrate in peace.

Celebrate being a relative term. Christmas, which had always been my favorite holiday, had been a challenge this year. It wasn't the lack of the usual festive foods, the shortage of new decorations, or the makeshift presents that made the holiday feel empty. None of those things mattered in the least.

It was that my cousins were gone. Raised practically as siblings, the boys and I had never before spent Christmas apart. This year, Colm was in Torquay, a mechanic at the RAF base there. And Toby was . . . well, we still didn't know where Toby was. Every day that passed without word chiseled away a little bit of our store of hope that he had survived at Dunkirk.

We had all tried to be merry in their honor. Nacy, the housekeeper who had raised us with as much love as any mother ever had for her own children, prepared her famous spiced punch and Christmas pudding. We sang carols, Uncle Mick's lovely baritone ringing cheerfully through the house. We'd even played a few games as we sat around the fire, and there had been a rousing speech from the king on the wireless. But it had been difficult, all the same, and a part of me was glad it was over.

Perhaps next year, the boys would be home. Perhaps next year, the war would be over and we could truly celebrate.

All these thoughts weighed on me as I listlessly stirred the porridge Nacy had made for breakfast that morning. She made the best porridge in all the world—even with the tightness of rationing—but I'd found the turmoil of my emotions had left me with very little appetite the past few weeks. I'd done my best to hide this from Nacy, but she was not an easy woman to fool.

Wasting food was a sin in our family, even before the war, so I had tried to conceal my decreased appetite by taking smaller portions and eating as much of them as I could.

I was chewing a small bite and glancing listlessly at Uncle Mick's paper across the table when a headline caught my eye: DARING DINNER PARTY ROBBERY.

My interest piqued, I read the article across the table.

A dinner party at the Mayfair home of diplomat, nightclub owner, and noted man-about-town Nico Lazaro was the scene of a surprising incident this past Friday. The

meal—luxurious by all accounts—was disturbed, not by
Luftwaffe bombers, but by a gang of hold-up men who
stormed into the house demanding valuables from the
startled guests. Present at the feast were such notables as
the Countess of Molford, who was relieved of an emerald
necklace, and acclaimed actor Daniel West, who is now
short one pair of gold cuff links. Scotland Yard is investigating and intends to quickly take the thieves into custody:
"Society cannot be allowed to crumble during wartime.
After all, when we have prevailed and our country is once
again free of the threat of tyranny, citizens must be assured that law and order will prevail."

I frowned, read the article again. That was odd. Not the robbery in itself, though something about it did seem a bit strange.
What struck me as curious was that, while we were certainly not
friendly with every criminal in London, we should have heard
rumors of something along this scale. We knew most of the best
thieves in London, being among the best ourselves.

Criminals were not, of course, wont to take one another into
their confidence, but rumors spread. The theft of jewelry from a
countess and a famous actor was the type of thing people in our
circles would talk about.

"Did you hear anything about that?" I asked Uncle Mick,
pointing at the paper.

He folded the newspaper and looked at the article. "I read
about it."

"No, I mean did you hear anything about it. Through the . . .
usual channels?"

"Can't say that I did, Ellie girl." He looked up at me with a
grin. "I'm not exactly in the center of things at the moment. Word
has spread that your old Uncle Mick has taken to the straight and

narrow, and it's brought me down a bit in the estimation of some of our associates."

We hadn't committed a burglary—indeed, a major crime of any kind—since we'd begun working with military intelligence. My involvement in the dangers of espionage work had given me the thrills that thieving had once provided, but I sometimes wondered if Uncle Mick missed his old way of life. He'd been at it for a lot longer than I had, after all. He had longtime associates—even close friends—in that world. For the first time, it occurred to me how difficult it must have been for him to turn his back on all of it.

"Do you miss it, Uncle Mick?" I asked.

"It's hard for a leopard to change its spots," he said. "But even a leopard grows gray with old age."

"Does it?" I asked. "I thought them spotted until the end."

"I didn't say the spots were gone, lass." He winked at me and then rose from the table. "I'll be in my workshop if you need me."

"All right."

He left, and my gaze returned to the newspaper on the table. I couldn't shake the feeling that something felt off about the whole thing.

But perhaps it was just that I, too, was a leopard who missed flaunting my spots a bit.

I stirred my cold porridge.

"Are you sick, Ellie?" Nacy asked, coming from the kitchen and moving to my side to press the back of her hand against my forehead.

"No, I'm quite well." I gave her my best imitation of a cheery smile. "I'm just a bit tired this morning."

"And what's been the reason for the rest of the food you haven't been eating these past few weeks?"

I ought to have known she had noticed my lack of appetite. Nacy never missed a thing.

"I'm fine," I said. "Really! Just not hungry."

She looked down at me, her expression suddenly both intent and gentle. "Ellie . . . You and Felix . . . you aren't . . . expecting a little surprise, are you?"

Felix Lacey was my closest friend and confidant, and something a bit more besides. We'd been hovering at the intersection between camaraderie and romance for the past few months, neither of us anxious to give a definite name to our relationship. But it seemed Nacy had drawn her own conclusions.

It took me a moment to understand what she was asking, and when I did, I gasped in shock. "Nacy!"

"These things happen, Ellie. If there's anything you want to tell me, you needn't be afraid to do so. It will all come out all right in the end."

"'These things' may happen, but they haven't happened to me," I protested.

"All right, all right," she said. "No need to get your feathers ruffled. I only meant it wouldn't be the first time a baby's come along a mite before it was expected. I just wanted you to know that you can always come to me if you're in trouble."

"Thank you," I said. "But I don't anticipate I shall ever come to you with that particular dilemma."

"Well, thank goodness for that," she said, patting my shoulder. "I'm still not entirely sure Felix is the right fellow for you. Of course, you're old enough to make up your mind on that score. But, whatever man you choose, it's best to buy the ring before needing the cradle."

"Yes, thank you, Nacy," I said, now thoroughly uncomfortable. "I will certainly remember that."

She went off to the kitchen, and I forced myself to finish the bowl of cold porridge, as though that would put the matter to rest.

I had never imagined she might make such an assumption. Granted, Felix was often at my flat late into the night, and she'd once seen him leave in the morning after he'd fallen asleep on my sofa. Despite appearances, however, we'd done nothing more than while away the evenings kissing to the strains of orchestra music on the gramophone.

And, truth be told, I'd been less encouraging of Felix's kisses the past few months, ever since the events of my last assignment and the information about my father that followed hot on its heels. He seemed to understand my inner turmoil and hadn't pressed the issue, but I knew we'd need to discuss things sooner or later.

There were so many things unresolved in my life. Of course, my personal problems were minor on the scale of what was going on in the world, of what was going on in my own city. We'd been bombed night after night for weeks, and thousands of people had lost their homes, their families, and their very lives. Despite my uncertainties, I knew I had a great deal to be thankful for.

Nevertheless, I was beginning to get that restless feeling again, the feeling that I should be doing more to help. I hadn't heard from Major Ramsey, the military intelligence officer who had recruited us as skilled thieves in service of our country, in nearly three months. Our mission in Sunderland in October, while technically a success, had had some unforeseen outcomes that I suspected were the reason for his silence. Or perhaps he'd just had no need of thieves since then.

Thieves . . .

I looked back down at the article in the newspaper.

Was it possible . . . ? I wondered suddenly if Major Ramsey had found some other set of criminals to do his bidding. Did this robbery have something to do with espionage? If so, perhaps there was a way that I could help. If nothing else, it could prove to be just the distraction I needed.

There was only one way to find out.

CHAPTER TWO

I left the house before I could think better of it, but the doubts began to sink in faster than the chill from the icy gusts of wind that
enveloped me on my way to the Tube.

This winter was the coldest I could remember. It seemed unfair, somehow, that we should have to contend with both the Nazis
and this weather. Perhaps the Germans had brought it with them.
Perhaps it swept down from the Alps and followed in their wake as
they marched across Europe.

As I caught my thoughts rambling on about the weather, I was
forced to admit, if only to myself, that I was nervous about visiting
with Major Ramsey. Things had been rather emotionally fraught
the last time we'd been together. Our mission in Sunderland had
ended with his being shot four times. In fact, we'd both come per-
ilously close to dying.

Shortly before that, we'd shared an ill-advised but extremely
passionate kiss, which we'd agreed should not be repeated.

We'd said goodbye in a hospital room, and the major had made
it clear we'd not be seeing each other again unless it became necessary. Even the influence of morphia had not prevented him from
nixing the possibility of a romance.

No, that door was closed. And rightly so. Attraction aside, we were ill-suited in almost every conceivable way.

Nevertheless, there were clearly some unresolved feelings there that were likely to lend our reunion an added layer of discomfort. There was also the added weight of the secret I was carrying about my father's work for the Germans.

I certainly couldn't confide this bit of information to the major, couldn't let him know that my family had past ties to Germany. I'd proved myself to him time and time again, but some part of me still suspected he didn't entirely trust me. I was a thief, after all. A thief from a family of thieves. And also a family of spies, it turned out.

But none of that was relevant to why I was going to see him today. This was strictly a professional visit, and I meant to keep it that way.

I reached his Belgravia residence—a lovely town house in keeping with his posh roots—which served as his office, and rang the bell. I was pleased to see the street was still undamaged by recent bombings, though the ever-present sandbags were a reminder of the imminent threat. A moment later the door was opened by Constance Brown, the major's secretary.

"Miss McDonnell," she said in her customary pleasant-yet-professional tone. "How nice to see you again. Won't you come in?"

I stepped inside, glad to be out of the cold. If this unusually frigid winter persisted, I was going to need a warmer coat. My boots also left something to be desired, I realized as I tried to wiggle some feeling back into my numb toes. I had never been keen on clothes shopping, but now I wished I'd been a bit more extravagant before the war started.

"What can I do for you?" Constance asked, turning to me in the foyer. She did not ask to take my coat.

"Is Major Ramsey in? If he has a moment, I'd like to speak to him." I didn't like the vaguely uncertain note in my voice.

I was sure I didn't imagine the slightest pause as Constance considered her answer. Ever efficient, however, she didn't hesitate for long.

"I believe his schedule is rather full today," she said. "But I'll just check in with him."

"I should have rung up first, but I was in the neighborhood . . ." I had not, of course, been in the neighborhood. Before meeting Major Ramsey, I'd never been in Belgravia unless it was to commit a burglary.

"I won't be a moment," she said, turning down that once-familiar hallway in the direction of his office.

It didn't escape my notice that she had made no guarantees. I wondered if he'd told her to ward me off if I happened to come begging to see him. The thought stiffened my spine, and I decided that I would not be put off, even if I had to barge into his office uninvited.

Such dramatics proved unnecessary, however, as, a moment later, she was back, her smile still in place. "He says please come back, Miss McDonnell. May I take your coat?"

"Thank you."

My coat discarded, I pressed aside my nerves and, chin up, made my way to the major's office. There was no reason I should be hesitant to speak with him. We'd moved beyond the kiss even before we'd parted ways; it was practically ancient history.

The door to his office was slightly ajar, but I tapped on it.

"Come in," he said.

I pushed the door open and stepped inside. He was standing on the other side of the desk. For just a moment, we studied each other.

I ought to have expected that he wouldn't look quite as hale and hearty as he had in the past. He'd had four holes in him three months ago, after all. Still, it was a bit surprising to see him paler than usual and dark beneath the eyes. He'd lost a bit of weight, too, though his height and well-built frame helped to conceal it.

He was still rather ridiculously good looking, of course. Perfectly put together in his spotless uniform, every blond hair in place. Sometimes I had to fight the urge to salute, even more so now that he greeted me with no noticeable change in expression.

"Miss McDonnell. This is a pleasant surprise," he said, breaking the silence with what seemed a rather obvious falsehood.

"Hello, Major. I'm sorry to drop in unannounced."

"No trouble at all. How are you?"

"I'm very well. How are you? I hope your recovery is going well?"

"Yes. Thank you."

There was a pause.

Why must it be like this? Why must things feel so awkward just because we happened to have kissed once?

"Would you like to sit down?" he asked, motioning to the chair I usually sat in when visiting his office.

"Thank you. I know you're busy; I won't take much of your time." I walked to the chair and took a seat. He sat, too, a carefulness to his movements that would not have been noticeable to a casual observer. I wondered how much his wounds still pained him, and it made me sad I didn't feel comfortable enough to ask.

"What brings you here?" he asked when we were settled. His tone was polite, though not particularly warm.

What *had* brought me here? That was a good question, wasn't it? He seemed to assume it was not a social call, and I was very glad I had two excuses for coming.

"I happened to see this in the paper this morning," I said, pulling the folded-up scrap of newspaper from my pocket. I had torn it from the paper, taking a chance that Uncle Mick had been finished reading the article printed on the other side.

I handed it to him across the desk, and he unfolded it, his eyes scanning the text before coming back up to me. "Do you know something about this?"

"No," I said. "I thought perhaps you did."

"I'd heard about it, of course. Lazaro is influential in diplomatic circles, and this was something for people to talk about besides the war. But I know nothing more than what is written here, if that's what you're asking."

"Oh," I said. "Well, I thought it was odd."

"In what way?"

"That's the thing," I said. "I'm not exactly sure. Something about it strikes me as strange, though I haven't yet put my finger on it."

He said nothing, waiting.

"It's so brazen, for one thing," I ventured. "They might have got away with a better haul by simply doing a quiet robbery of an unoccupied house."

He still didn't reply, and I had the impression he was not overly interested in my theory.

Unsure of what else to say, I offered him a smile. "Oh, well. Perhaps I'm overthinking it. I thought it couldn't hurt to ask you." And then, because I could not quite let the matter go, I said, "Perhaps I merely wanted to be sure you hadn't replaced us with a better band of thieves." The words didn't come out quite as light as I'd intended them to, and I was annoyed that he might be able to sense my uncertainty.

"I would be hard-pressed, I think, to find better recruits than the McDonnells," he said, with the slightest smile.

"I'm glad to hear it," I said, flushing a little. "Then there hasn't been any other work for us to do?"

"No," he said. And then, perhaps thinking better of his brusqueness, he added, "Not at the moment. Things have been a bit slow on that front."

I had no idea if he was telling me the truth. It was usually impossible to tell with him. I suspected that he might be, however, as he'd probably been forced to spend some time recuperating after his injuries. No doubt his workload had significantly decreased the past three months.

Then that, it seemed, was that.

"Well, you know where to find us if something comes up," I said with a cheeriness I didn't feel.

"Your family is doing well?" he asked, the politeness of his society breeding overriding his desire to be rid of me.

"Oh, yes. Everyone is fine. We had rather a lovely Christmas, all things considered."

"I'm glad to hear it."

Another pause before we finalized this goodbye.

"Oh, I also wanted to give this back to you," I said, suddenly remembering my second excuse for visiting.

I reached back into the pocket of my woolen jumper and pulled out a handkerchief. I unfolded it carefully. Inside it was the large diamond ring I had worn as a part of a cover story on a previous job. It was the ring he had bought to give to his former fiancée once upon a time, and it made me uncomfortable to have so valuable and personal an object in my possession.

I held it out across the desk, and he reached to take it. Stupidly, the mere brush of his fingers against mine sent a little jolt through me.

Our eyes met.

"Gabriel Ramsey, Betts tells me you didn't eat your breakfast. Again."

The words came from the hallway right before the still-slightly-ajar door opened and a woman came in. To say she charged into the room would be inaccurate; it was done much more elegantly than that. Even at a glance, I could tell at once this was the sort of woman who did everything elegantly.

She was tall, fair, and very beautiful, and she wore a burgundy suit that I was fairly certain had cost more than my entire wardrobe. I didn't like the little lurch of dismay that hit me as I combined all this with her apparent intimacy with the major.

Major Ramsey rose from his seat even as the woman spotted me and stopped in the doorway.

"Oh, I beg your pardon," she said, her eyes darting from me to the major. "I didn't know you had a visitor."

Her gaze came back to me and was assessing me with interest now. I was glad that I'd taken more care than usual with my appearance this morning. I was wearing a dark gray wool skirt with a thick, dark green jumper over my white blouse. Not exactly stylish, but neat. And the green of the jumper matched my eyes. Even my notoriously wayward black curls had been pinned into an orderly chignon.

"Close the door on your way out," the major said pointedly. I noticed the ring had disappeared, presumably into his pocket. "And tell Betts she can dashed well mind her own business."

The woman was unfazed. "I'm Noelle Edgemont," she said to me.

"My sister," Major Ramsey said. Now that he'd been forced into it, politeness demanded he finish introductions, and he did so tersely. "Noelle, this is Miss Electra McDonnell. A colleague."

His sister. I could see it, now that he said it. There was a strong resemblance, though the major's chiseled masculinity was softened into cool beauty in his sister. Her eyes were the same violet-blue that his were.

"I'm so pleased to meet you," she said. "Have you offered her tea, Gabriel? Never mind, I can see you haven't. Would you like some tea, Miss McDonnell?"

"Oh, that won't be necessary."

"Noelle . . ." Major Ramsey said. I recognized the warning note in his voice, but she took no notice.

"I'll have a pot sent in. It's such a cold day. It won't take a moment."

She smiled at me, ignored the major completely, and then turned and left the room, closing the door behind her.

It was clear that she knew nothing about me. Of course, Major Ramsey would not be likely to discuss his work with his sister.

And that was the only part of his life in which I was involved. *A colleague,* he had told her. That summed it up very neatly.

"I apologize for the interruption," he said as he took his seat again. "She is visiting me for the holidays and has taken to riding roughshod over my household."

I smiled, both at this clearly accurate description and at the feeling that a bit of his formality had thawed.

"She seems lovely," I said. "And I'm glad to hear you've had someone to look after you during your recovery."

I immediately felt self-conscious about saying this, but the major didn't seem to mind.

"She's been very helpful on occasion, though apt to fuss."

"How are you feeling, really?" I asked, while I was feeling brave.

"Fine. The wounds have healed nicely."

"You've lost weight," I said.

"So have you."

I was surprised he had noticed, and I fumbled for an excuse. "Things have just been rather hectic lately. Perhaps I've been getting more exercise than usual."

I was avoiding his eyes, but I could feel his gaze on my face. "You haven't been greatly troubled about what happened in that cave in Sunderland? Nightmares, that sort of thing?"

"No," I said, though I had been troubled lately by several dreams about my father and mother, filled with shadowy spies and knives dripping blood.

It seemed as though he was about to say something else, but, thankfully, Mrs. Edgemont returned then with a tray in hand. "Betts had just finished making a tray, isn't that a lucky thing?"

"Lucky indeed," Major Ramsey said without enthusiasm.

"How do you take your tea, Miss McDonnell?" she asked, setting the tray down on the corner of Major Ramsey's desk.

"I . . . a bit of sugar, please."

"A lot of sugar," Major Ramsey said.

I looked up at him and smiled at his recollection of my sweet tooth. Sugar was the most difficult part of rationing for me. When the war was over, I wouldn't toast our victory with champagne. I would have a cup of tea with heaps of sugar in it.

Mrs. Edgemont took his word for it and put two large spoonfuls of sugar into the cup. "There you are," she said, setting it in front of me.

"Thank you." I took a sip, appreciating the warmth and the sweetness. I hadn't realized that I was still cold until I felt the heat of the cup seeping into my chilled fingers.

"Do you live in London?" I asked politely, as the silence seemed to be lengthening.

"No, I just came for the holidays," she said as she poured Major Ramsey's tea—black, naturally—and set it in front of him. I wondered if she would pour herself a cup and sit down for a chat. "Gabriel and I always spend Christmas together. It's our birthday."

"Your birthday . . ." I began, confused. And then it hit me. "Oh, you're twins!"

She smiled. "Yes. We were born on Christmas, the most extravagant gift our mother ever received, I daresay. We've spent every birthday together, except for last year when he was in North Africa."

Twins born on Christmas. Gabriel and Noelle. It was all so impossibly adorable that I wanted to laugh with delight. One glance at Major Ramsey's face, however, and I realized that he was not finding this conversation amusing.

"I don't know any twins," I said. "It must have been nice to grow up with someone exactly your age."

"Oh, it was great fun," Mrs. Edgemont said. "Wasn't it, Gabriel?"

"It had its moments." He did not elaborate, and he hadn't touched his tea. I realized he was hoping to bring things to a close. His next words confirmed it. "Miss McDonnell did not come here on a social call, Noelle, and I'm sure she does not need our family history."

She sighed. "All right. I'm going. It's just not very often you have visitors."

He did not reply, but his expression seemed to be reminding her that I was not, technically, a visitor.

"So nice to have met you, Miss McDonnell," she told me.

"You, too, Mrs. Edgemont."

She left again, and I turned back to Major Ramsey. I felt the distance creep back between us again, and now I wanted only to be on my way. Perhaps coming here had been a bad idea, but now at least I knew it.

I took a final sip of the tea then set the cup down on the saucer. "Well, I won't take up any more of your time."

I rose, and he followed suit. "Thank you for coming by, Miss McDonnell. I'll certainly be in touch if any work comes up for you and your uncle."

"Thank you." We looked at each other, and then, because there was nothing else to say, I said, "Goodbye, Major."

Now that the ring was returned, I doubted my path would cross again with Major Ramsey's anytime soon. I couldn't help but feel a bit gloomy as I left.

CHAPTER THREE

My sense of disappointment was somewhat relieved by the fact that there was a letter from Felix waiting for me when I got home.

I took it to my flat, a small building behind the main house that Uncle Mick had given me when he'd thought I could use a bit of independence. I loved having a little place of my own just a walk through the kitchen garden away from my family.

Sitting on the sofa, I slid my finger under the flap without bothering to find the letter opener. I pulled the letter out and unfolded it.

It was only one sheet of paper, and not even completely covered, at that. Felix had always been an indifferent correspondent at best. Even when he had been in the navy, I had never known when to expect a letter.

Felix was gone again on one of his frequent and mysterious trips to Scotland, and the letters were really only short notes he dashed off at sporadic intervals. It was nice, I supposed, that he was thinking of me, but the irregular contact was also frustrating. Felix was the only other person who knew the secret about my father. There was no one else with whom I could discuss the matter, and I wished him home.

I read the letter.

Ellie, my sweet,

I am jotting you a note because there is a beautiful evergreen outside my window, and every time I take a moment to glance at it, I think of your eyes.

There is nothing here to remind me of your lips, but I think of them constantly nonetheless.

I hope to be back soon so that I can do away with remembering and resume enjoying.

You will tell me I am scandalous, no doubt, but I am saving the most scandalous of my thoughts to tell you in person.

Until then, I remain,

Yours,
Felix

xx

Despite my general exasperation at his flippancy, I couldn't help but smile at this rather outrageous letter. Felix enjoyed making me blush. He was flirtatious and provocative, but in a way that was respectful and all in good fun. I missed him, I realized, and not just as a confidant.

I had hoped that he would be with us for Christmas, but he had been away. He'd left me gifts: some expensive and divine-smelling French soap, which I didn't know how he'd managed to acquire; some equally difficult-to-acquire silk stockings, which had caused Nacy to raise her eyebrows; and a lovely silver bracelet. They were not the sort of homemade and inexpensive gifts that most of us had given one another, and I knew they clearly indicated that Felix and I were more than friends.

Oddly enough, he'd not yet formally asked me to be his girl. I hadn't pushed the matter—especially now that I had conflicted feelings. All the same, a part of me wondered why Felix had not tried to make things official. Nor, despite Nacy's suspicions, had Felix pressed for physical intimacies beyond the kissing we frequently engaged in.

Perhaps there was something—or someone—in Scotland that was dividing his attention.

I didn't know what he was up to in Scotland, and the lack of knowledge left me uneasy. Felix was not prone to keeping secrets from me. Even before there had been anything romantic between us, we had shared confidences. But whatever was happening in Scotland was something he refused to speak about.

Whenever I brought up the topic, he always deflected. When deflection didn't work, he outright refused to tell me what it was all about.

I determined that when he returned we must have a serious discussion. I needed to know why he was being so secretive.

I assumed he was working on something of an illegal nature. Felix was a master forger. I had never seen anyone with a more natural aptitude for the craft. He could replicate the handwriting of the king himself and convince him to believe it.

I worried that he was involved in something dangerous. It was the sort of thing he would do as much because it amused him as for financial gain. One thing that could be said of Felix: there was never a dull moment with him.

I let out a loud sigh. Everywhere I looked there were closed doors or more questions.

Well, perhaps, if I really wanted answers, it was time to stop avoiding my father's trunk and see if there was something to be found within it.

Taking a deep breath, I set aside Felix's letter, left my little flat, and walked through the kitchen garden toward the house. It was time to search for some answers.

Nacy was away at the shops, and Uncle Mick was on a locksmithing job, so I was able to venture down into the cellar without calling attention to my activities.

I went slowly down the wooden stairs. Perhaps needless to say, I had mixed feelings about this part of the house these days. It was associated with the terrors of constant bombing, but it was also the shelter that had kept us secure. It was both a safe haven and a place I would like never to visit again when the war was over.

The trunk of family artifacts was stashed in one corner. It had been in the attic until the Blitz had started, tucked away under the eaves and covered with dust and cobwebs. Yet it was one of the first things Uncle Mick had hauled down to the cellar after the first night of bombing.

It held family objects dating back generations, but I knew for a fact that some of my father's things were in it. Uncle Mick had shown them to me once when I was a child.

If there was something in this house that might give me more of a clue as to what my father had been involved in, and perhaps what had led to his murder, it would be inside this trunk.

It was locked, though I wasn't certain why, as the lock wasn't likely to keep anyone in our family out. Perhaps it was just force of habit. I wondered if Uncle Mick even knew where the key was.

Whatever the case, it took only a few twists from a hairpin and it was done.

I knelt down before the ancient trunk and unfastened the straps, lifting the heavy lid. Dust floated up to tickle my nose, and I wiped it on my sleeve before I surveyed the contents.

As I had remembered, there were several objects related to our family history: a worn, faded quilt made by my great-grandmother;

a family Bible, too delicate for further use, wrapped carefully in a cloth; a small box that held my grandmother's rosary and my grandfather's pocket watch.

One corner of the trunk seemed to hold slightly newer items, and it was there I spotted a stack of letters. A glance at the envelopes told me they were from my mother to my father. Uncle Mick had never shown these to me.

I opened one envelope and saw the date at the top of the letter. It was dated before my parents were married. Undoubtedly love letters. I set them aside to read later.

It felt like an invasion of privacy, but I realized that this was a part of my history, that whatever was in them involved me, too, now that my parents were gone. I had never had the chance to know either of them. I'd been robbed of my parents by an unknown assailant and a series of injustices. I had to piece together a legacy wherever and however I could.

Toward the bottom of that side of the trunk, I found a short, flat cardboard box filled with yellowed newspaper clippings. I sifted through them and realized they were all related to the case. Uncle Mick had apparently cut them out to keep for posterity but had been disgusted enough with all of it not to bother pasting them in a scrapbook.

I'd seen the articles before, in local papers I'd rummaged through at the library. There had been a phase in my adolescence when I'd wanted to know all I could about my parents and had set about researching on my own. So none of the clippings in the box were a surprise to me.

There were several of them, arranged chronologically, the progression showing how the case had devolved into sensationalism.

HENDON MAN FOUND SLAIN, the earliest of them read. It recounted how my father had been found by his brother, Uncle Mick, dead in his own house from several stab wounds. The crime had been vicious, and even the early articles had speculated that it might be a crime of passion, as it appeared that nothing was missing from the house.

The next headline, HENDON MAN STABBED TO DEATH, WIFE ARRESTED, related how my mother had been found wandering with the knife, questioned, and eventually arrested and charged with the crime.

TRIAL DATE SET IN MCDONNELL MURDER, read the next.

IS BEAUTY A BEAST? an article asked, a large photograph of my mother front and center. It was a photo she'd had taken at some point after her marriage, for her wedding ring was visible. She was wearing a chic silk and lace dress and smiling happily, her eyes bright, her glossy black hair gleaming even in the colorless photo. She really had been beautiful. It was largely the reason the case had aroused such interest.

I reached the final article in the stack: MARGO MCDONNELL FOUND GUILTY, SENTENCED TO HANG.

He hadn't kept any beyond that, not the ones that detailed her appeal, the discovery that she was pregnant with her murdered husband's child, the fact that she had died in prison of the influenza that had decimated the world.

I set the lid back on the box with a sigh. It was all so terribly tragic. But, of course, my tragedy was not particularly noteworthy in this time of great tragedy. People were suffering losses every day.

That didn't mean, of course, that I didn't intend to find out what had happened to my father. It only meant that I wouldn't feel too sorry for myself while I did it.

There was a faded leather photo album beneath the box, and I flipped through it. I'd seen most of these before. Uncle Mick had brought them out for me to look at when I'd been old enough to start asking questions. It was likely he had returned the album to its place in this trunk rather than keep it in the family sitting room because the memories it evoked were more painful than happy. Most of the photos had my mother in them, after all.

Mrs. Maynard, the friend of my mother's who had told me about my father's espionage, had given me a different photo of my parents, a photo my mother had sent her for safekeeping. It was a picture of my father and mother in front of a cottage with mountains behind them. I had failed to see the significance of the photo or why my mother would want to hide it, but Mrs. Maynard's other revelation had made that clear.

The photo had apparently been taken in Germany. But when had my parents been there? And how was it that my father had got entangled with the German cause? My father had been born and raised in Ireland, and, like Uncle Mick, I'd assumed he'd been a County Galway man, through and through.

I supposed Uncle Mick might know about the visit to Germany, and it would make the most sense to ask him. He'd even told me, when he'd discovered that I'd written to Mrs. Maynard, that he would tell me anything I wanted to know about my mother. But I couldn't ask him, not yet.

Not when it might mean revealing to him what his brother had been involved in. I knew how much Uncle Mick had loved my father. Knew it as certain as I knew he loved me. And to find out that his brother had been an enemy spy would be to break his heart all over again.

There was a book of Greek mythology at the bottom of the trunk. I wondered why it had been left here, among my parents' things, rather than put on the shelf with the other books. I had a few of my mother's mythology books already. They were great favorites of mine.

My mother had named me Electra, and it had always felt like a connection to her, like something valuable passed down along with her collection of books. After I was old enough to understand the character of Electra, how she had avenged her father's murder, I had begun to see it as a sign, as a message from my mother to me, that perhaps someday I would be able to avenge my father's death.

I wasn't sure what to believe about that now.

I flipped open the cover of the book. There was an inscription handwritten on the title page:

Niall,

κλείνω τα μάτια μου και βλέπω το πρόσωπό σο.
  Σ΄αγαπώ,
Margo

I hadn't known my mother knew Greek. I wondered what the words meant.

I traced my finger over the elegant, unfamiliar swirls. I'd seen few samples of her handwriting, and when I came across them I felt closer to her somehow. I wished for the millionth time in my short life that I had known her.

I had been taken from her at the prison when I was a few months old and given to Uncle Mick and Nacy's care. I'd had the best upbringing a girl could ask for—family of thieves or no—and I had never wanted for love or affection or familial support.

But one always misses one's parents, doesn't one?

I flipped through the pages of the book. I saw now that there were notes in the margins. They weren't my mother's handwriting, so perhaps they were my father's? I had seen less of his writing. It seemed that, like Uncle Mick, he had not been much of one to keep written records of things. It had been up to me almost since I could form neat letters to keep records straight for Uncle Mick's locksmithing business.

So why had my father been interested enough in this book of mythology to write in the margins? I leaned close to look at the notes and realized suddenly they weren't definable words—not English words, anyway. And not Greek either. Nor German, for that matter.

I flipped through a few more chapters to see if it was all the same and stopped when I came across a folded sheet of paper. I took it out and opened it.

It was more of the same but written in a different hand. A note my father had received, perhaps? But from whom?

I looked down at the book and felt a sharp stab of surprise at the chapter heading: "Electra."

Did this mean something? It had to mean something, didn't it?

It must be a code of some sort. And perhaps my name was part of the key.

A wave of various emotions hit me all at once: elation, consternation, worry at what it meant.

But I already knew the worst, didn't I? My father had been spying for the enemy. If it were this war, we would have been working for opposite sides.

How deeply had my mother been involved in it all? It seemed there must have been some reason she had decided to keep the secret, that she had felt it was worth her life to protect my family.

But, if my father had been dead when I was born, who had she named me to pass a message to?

"Ellie?"

I jumped at the sound of Nacy calling my name upstairs. I'd been so engrossed I hadn't even heard her come into the house.

"In the cellar, Nacy!" I called. "I'll be right up."

Setting the things I'd removed carefully back into the trunk, I closed the lid behind me and relocked it with my hairpin.

Everything was as I'd left it—well, almost everything.

I slipped the Greek mythology book with the letter inside it into the pocket of my jumper before going upstairs to greet Nacy.

CHAPTER FOUR

I went with Uncle Mick on a locksmithing job the next morning, after I'd been sure to eat every bite of the breakfast Nacy had served.

My mind had been churning over the possibilities of what I'd discovered in the mythology book. Not that I'd had much chance to study it. The Germans had come back again at twilight, and we'd been forced to spend the night in the cellar.

Luckily, the locksmithing job today provided ample distraction for my tumultuous thoughts. We opened three safes that a gentleman had inherited in the dusty cellar of an old apothecary shop he had purchased. There was nothing of too much interest in them, but the opening of the safes was diverting enough. Besides, the contents didn't really matter when we weren't sneaking home with them.

Uncle Mick did the bulk of the work. He was so adept at opening safes that he didn't require a pencil and paper to graph the points as I did. The math just clicked together in his head. I had always marveled at this innate skill, at the talent for numbers that he had been born with. Watching Uncle Mick work was like watching a virtuoso play a concerto.

I had trained long and hard to be able to open safes. It was the difference between someone who could read music well and someone who felt that music in their bones.

For me, there was the satisfaction of solving a complex problem. It was nice to have a job to do, and I knew that the money would be useful as well. We hadn't exactly been flush with cash lately. The government had paid us for the work we had done, but that meant the recent lack of official business had put a strain on things financially.

I had worried more than once in the past months that we would run out of work and be forced to resort to thievery once again. I had surprised myself by thinking of it in terms of an unwanted necessity. Not long ago, I would have relished the thought of planning a job, would have thought nothing of taking what we found to supplement our income. Now it felt as though my view of the world and my place in it had shifted drastically.

Sometimes I wondered what I would do when the war was over. The future lay stretched before me, so blurry and indistinct I sometimes got vertigo looking at it.

"Are you all right, Ellie girl?" Uncle Mick asked me as we walked home from the Tube station.

"Of course. Why do you ask?" Just like Nacy, Uncle Mick knew me so well it was difficult to hide things from him. Unlike Nacy, he wasn't one to press, but he was always there if I needed a shoulder to lean on. That's what made it so difficult that I had to keep what I had learned about my father from him.

I knew how Uncle Mick felt about this adopted homeland. I knew how he would feel if he learned his brother had been spying for the Germans. He couldn't find out. I would do everything in my power to make sure he didn't.

"You've been quiet lately. It's not like you."

"No, I suppose it's not," I said with a smile. "I've just had a lot on my mind."

"With what happened in Sunderland?"

I hadn't been able to tell him the full scope of our work there, but he knew that things had got thorny and that Major Ramsey had been injured. I had come home shaken from the experience—and from what I had learned about my father. And I had been unable to discuss any of it. In so many ways, war was putting up walls that hadn't been there in peacetime.

"Yes, in part," I said. "I'm still working a lot of things out."

He put his arm around my shoulders and gave me a little squeeze. "Well, you're more than capable of that, love. But don't forget that I'm here if you need me."

"Thank you, Uncle Mick."

When we got back to the house, Nacy beamed at me. "You've had a message," she said. "From Major Ramsey."

Nacy adored Major Ramsey. Granted, he had been more than usually charming with her. He was not, as a general rule, the sort of man I would consider charming, but he could turn it on when it suited him, and he had always been unfailingly courteous to Nacy. As a result, she was ready to plan my wedding to him at a moment's notice. My telling her she would be waiting in vain had no effect whatsoever.

Despite myself, I felt a jolt of excitement at her words; I had been so sure from his manner that he planned to go on avoiding me. What had caused him to change his mind?

I tried not to appear too interested as I asked, "Oh? What did he say?"

"He asked if you would come back to his office this afternoon." Her eyes twinkled mischievously. "You didn't tell us you had been to see him."

"I went to return that ring to him," I said. I had never been able to lie convincingly to Nacy, but half-truths sometimes did the trick.

"Well, it seems the visit made him realize how much he missed you. He wants to see you again."

I gave her a skeptical look, but my heart rate had increased. What was it that he wanted to see me about?

I looked over at Uncle Mick. "Can you do without me for the rest of the afternoon?"

He grinned. "If the major wants you, who am I to say no?"

I took the Tube to Sloane Square, my mind turning over the possible reasons the major had asked me to return to his office.

It was nothing of a personal nature, that much was certain. He'd rarely been more formal with me than he had been yesterday. Any sense of camaraderie that we'd built up over the earlier part of our Sunderland mission had been obliterated by that stupid kiss, and we were back to where we'd started when the major had first recruited me: cool civility and strict officialness.

I sighed. This was all a waste of reflection. A distraction from what really mattered. It was why the major had said that we could not be involved romantically. Because it was a breach of protocol and would no doubt prove a detriment to any sort of work we could do together. And if there was any choice to be made between his personal inclinations and his duty to his country, there was no doubt whatsoever which Major Ramsey would choose.

As for myself, I thought there could possibly be room for both duty and personal inclination, but the point stood. We had agreed that nothing else would happen, and that was that. I didn't have Nacy's unerring sense of romanticism.

Constance let me in again, taking my coat immediately this time with brisk efficiency. "He's waiting for you," she said. Constance had a knack for conveying the major's frame of mind without saying anything, and I sensed from her tone that he was in one of his more snappish moods.

I walked back down the hallway and found that the door to his office was open. He was indeed waiting for me, then.

"Good afternoon, Miss McDonnell," he said, beckoning me into the room in a gesture that veered more toward impatience than politeness.

"Good afternoon."

"Thank you for coming back again at such short notice."

It never ceased to amaze me how he could maintain this level of formality after all we'd been through together. After the way he'd kissed me senseless.

"You're quite welcome," I replied in the same punctilious tone. His gaze caught mine for just a second; he'd discerned that I was being facetious. He decided to ignore it.

He motioned for me to take a seat, and then he sat. It appeared he was in no mood to dally with false pleasantries.

"Your instincts have proved good once again, Miss McDonnell."

Then this was about the robbery I had brought to his attention. I felt a surge of excitement I was careful to suppress. I had learned it was best not to appear too enthusiastic about anything thievery-related in the major's presence.

"I asked around yesterday about the article you showed me," he said. "And it seems there is more to it than meets the eye."

A dozen questions immediately sprang to mind, but I waited for him to tell me more.

"You're sure you don't know anything about this?" His eyes fastened on me, and I realized he was wondering if I had deceived him yesterday.

"No," I said, meeting his gaze steadily. "I don't know anything about it. I only thought something in it seemed . . . odd."

"You don't know who might have done it? Anyone who works this way?"

I shook my head. "That's another thing that struck me. We don't know every thief in London, of course, but Uncle Mick usually hears a thing or two about the bigger jobs. Especially jobs like this. You might not hear about it when it was being planned, but you'd hear things about the valuables they were trying to sell, who was thinking of buying. These things get around. People brag, especially about big scores. The criminal world is its own community, in a way. So the very fact we've heard nothing is unusual."

He considered what I'd told him. Then he nodded. "That fits in with what we're thinking."

He opened his desk drawer and took out a sheet of paper. I watched him as he did so and found that he didn't look particularly well rested. He had always given the appearance of being indefatigable, but now he looked tired. It was on the tip of my tongue to ask him if he'd got any sleep since I'd been here yesterday, but I knew he would not appreciate it.

At least I knew his sister was here; I was sure he would be more receptive to her scolding than to mine.

He looked up at me from the sheet of paper in his hand. "In the past two weeks, there have been three robberies reported in London at the residences of politically influential individuals."

"Three?" This was a surprise. "Were the others in the paper as well?"

Had I missed them? Uncle Mick read the paper from front to back, so I knew he would have seen them and likely mentioned them to me when we discussed the article.

"No," Major Ramsey said. "Only the one you noticed was in the paper. Two of the robberies were kept out of the papers deliberately. The third was the one you brought to my attention. Let me lay out the details for you."

I nodded, the familiar focus that came during jobs settling over me. I realized how much I had missed this feeling, missed the sensation of being involved in important work that required concentration and skill.

"The first robbery was ten days ago at the Savoy. Miguel Perez, a Spanish diplomat, reported to the police that several items were stolen from his hotel room." He glanced at the paper in his hand. "A gold cigarette case, a diamond tiepin, and things of that nature. I have a complete list of the items reported stolen that I will show you in a moment. Perez was here on diplomatic business but was sharing the hotel room with a female companion who was not his wife. He was anxious the matter be handled quietly, and the hotel was as anxious to hush it up as he was."

I nodded my comprehension of the facts, and he continued.

"The second was Germaine Arnaud, a Frenchwoman who worked in the Paris government before she was forced to flee as the Germans approached. She was allegedly in possession of some jewelry that had belonged to several high-placed persons and brought it with her for safekeeping."

"And it was stolen?"

"Some of it was stolen. A week ago. She was visiting a friend until quite late and arrived back at her hotel to find her room had been broken into. There was a small jewelry box in one of her drawers that was taken, but she had secreted the bulk of it beneath her mattress, and the thieves did not find it."

I frowned. Any thief worth his salt knew to look beneath a mattress.

"She rang the police when she discovered the jewelry box missing, but asked that the matter be kept quiet," he said. "She is hoping that the jewelry can be recovered before its absence is a matter of public knowledge."

"She doesn't want the owners to know it's gone unless it's necessary," I said.

"Presumably."

"What about the robbery in the article?" I asked. "Are those facts correct?"

"Relatively so, it seems. Lazaro was hosting a dinner party when three masked intruders entered the house. One of them took the valuables of the guests, one of them held the staff at gunpoint, and one of them searched the house. A few other valuables were taken: Lazaro mentioned a gold cigarette lighter, some silver, and a valuable vase."

"A vase?" I repeated. What an odd thing to grab when one was taking jewelry from dinner party guests.

"So he says. This matter, too, would likely have been hushed up, but it happens that one of the guests mentioned it to the wrong person and it ended up in the newspaper."

I shrugged. "It's not so very bad for it to be in the newspaper, is it? It's not as though Mr. Lazaro did anything wrong."

He said nothing to this.

"Can you be sure that all of these crimes were committed by the same person or persons?" I asked at last. "After all, the methods are very different. Usually a thief prefers either stealth or an armed robbery, but it's rare that someone uses both. It's odd that they would have snuck into an empty hotel room on two occasions and then came in with guns at a dinner party on another."

He nodded. "That's what the police thought, too. It appeared it was just a rash of unfortunate robberies. But then we looked a bit closer."

I looked up at him, knowing a reveal was coming. Major Ramsey was the most phlegmatic person I knew, but he did enjoy a bit of the dramatic on occasion.

He set the sheet of paper on the desk and pushed it across toward me. "This is the full list of the items that were reported stolen from the three robberies. What do you make of it?"

I ran my eyes over the list. It was as he had said. There were the usual things, the things one would expect a thief to take: necklaces, pocket watches, cuff links. Then there were a few things that struck me as strange. The vase, of course. There was also a porcelain figurine that was part of the Savoy's décor and a decorative cigar box that belonged to Miguel Perez.

Without a comprehensive list of what had been in each of the locations, I couldn't tell if anything important had been overlooked by the thieves. But something struck me as unusual about the list of items that had been taken.

"It's all very haphazard. It's almost as if . . ." The idea clicked suddenly into place, and I looked up at the major. "As if the robbery wasn't the main goal—as if someone was looking for something in particular."

His eyes took on that approving glint they sometimes got when my guesses were correct.

"A quick check told me these people have one thing in common," he said. "Each of them was on the same flight from Lisbon a fortnight ago."

My brows went up. "And you think one of them brought something back with them. Something that someone else wants."

He nodded. "Yes, I'm quite sure that has been the motive behind these robberies. While valuables have been taken, it is my impression that the stolen items are somewhat random in nature."

I considered what he was telling me. It was obvious from the list of stolen items that these were not, in fact, professional thieves. Or, at least, not professional the way my family and I were. These people were looking for something, not burglars out to take the most valuable items they could get. That meant that Major Ramsey was very likely correct in his assumption that they were committing robberies with a specific goal in mind.

"It would be difficult, I suppose, to determine what they're after just by looking at this small list of items, and the people from whom they've stolen them," I said. "Do you have any more information you could share with me?"

"I don't really have any information at present, Miss McDonnell," he said, and I sensed he was telling me the truth. There was the slightest note of weariness in his voice that I had never heard there before. "All I know is that something is clearly going on here, and, given the connection with Lisbon and the rampant espionage activities there, it is probably in our best interest to figure out what it is."

"Does this mean you are offering me this job?" My heart thudded heavily as I awaited his answer.

His response was noncommittal. In fact, his entire reaction was less enthusiastic than I would have hoped.

"I don't even know what this job might entail as of yet," he said. "But I think that your intuition is good, and you were clearly onto something when this came to your attention. I'm of the opinion it's something we should pursue. I've spoken to my superior, Colonel Radburn, and he agrees. He told me I should make use of your expertise."

Ah. It had been an order, then. I kept my expression neutral, determined not to show the silly way this knowledge stung.

I offered him a polite smile. "Colonel Radburn has good sense, it seems."

His eyes met mine, and I could feel everything we were leaving unsaid hanging in the air between us. Did he think I might be worried he would pursue a physical relationship? Or did he think I might throw myself at him? Perhaps he just thought the past would affect how we worked together.

Whatever the case, orders were orders, and Major Ramsey was nothing if not a rule-follower.

He gave a brisk nod. "Then, yes. I am offering you a job. At the very least, we can look into these robberies and rule out the espionage angle."

I smiled, a bit more genuinely this time. "Excellent. So what's the plan?"

"The plan," he said, his eyes on mine, "is to try to determine where, assuming these thieves are after something in particular, they might strike next and prevent it. Or catch them in the act, if possible. To do that, we need to discover what it is they're looking for and why it's so important they get it back."

I nodded. The fact that they were going to such lengths to retrieve whatever it was indicated we didn't want them to have it. But we were working with such a vague idea of what our nemeses' motives might be. It was going to be an uphill battle.

I considered. "It seems that the Germans believe whatever it is they're searching for was on that plane. You'll want to talk to the people who were on it. Do you know who else, besides the robbery victims, came to England on that flight?"

"Oh, yes," he said. "That was easy enough. I've been able to obtain the passenger lists."

That had been quick work. No wonder he looked as though he hadn't slept.

"There are only a few of the passengers still in London. The others have moved on to other locations. Which leads me to believe the thieves have narrowed it down to the London residents as well."

"Then they know that *someone* brought *something* back to London, but they don't know who any more than we do."

"So it seems."

"Do you have any contacts in Lisbon?" I asked.

He gave a brief nod. "I've sent inquiries through the usual channels, but it may take time to get any leads."

I sighed. "This is a monumental task. You think this is important enough to go to all this effort?"

"Colonel Radburn thinks so, and I'm inclined to agree with him. There is something that these people have deemed worth taking great risks for. It is best that we get it before they do."

"Fair enough," I said. "What do we do first?"

He gave the appearance of considering, though I had no doubt that the plan was already neatly laid out in his head. What he was considering was likely how much of that plan he wanted to lay out for me.

"I've been over the list of the people who were on that flight and gathered what information I could on them."

He had accomplished a lot since my last visit. Not exactly surprising; when Major Ramsey set his mind to something, very little could stand in his way.

"And you've decided who we should talk to first?"

"We may as well proceed in an orderly fashion, visit the earlier robbery victims and proceed from there. Miguel Perez has, unfortunately, left the country for the time being, but Germaine Arnaud is still here."

"Does she have a flat in London?" I asked.

"No. She was robbed in her hotel suite. She's since moved to the Ritz, thinking it might be safer."

"Ah, so she's that type of refugee, is she?"

He looked over at me, his brows raised slightly.

"A rich one, I mean. There're a lot of people who've fled the Continent who don't have enough to eat. This woman sounds like the type I wouldn't have minded lifting a few valuables from myself."

"Don't get any ideas," he said darkly.

I narrowed my eyes at him but did not respond to this remark. "When do we go to see her?" I asked.

He looked at his watch. "Would now suit you?"

CHAPTER FIVE

I tried to force any thoughts of awkwardness aside as the major helped me into my coat in the foyer.

"Miss Brown, if Colonel Radburn phones, tell him I'll be back this afternoon," the major told Constance. And then we exited the town house.

It felt good to be assigned a new case. It felt good that he had decided to involve me. I couldn't help but think that if he had been adamant about his desire not to work with me, Colonel Radburn would not have pressed the issue. So I could only conclude that the major was not entirely opposed to my help.

Whatever the reason I had been recruited, I was no less prone to feeling pride in my accomplishments than anyone else. There was a sense of satisfaction in knowing they had not been able to replace me.

I had rather been hoping we would take the Tube, as it prevented excessive conversation—or lack thereof—on the way. Alas, the major ushered me to the big black government car parked at the curb.

I was pleased to see it was being driven by his usual driver, Jakub. Jakub was an immigrant from Poland, and we shared the burden of both having someone we loved missing after a battle.

Jakub's son had been missing for a bit longer than Toby, and we often discussed if there had been any news about our boys. I hoped that one day we would both have a positive update to share.

I greeted him warmly.

"Hello, Miss Ellie," he said. My attempts to get him to call me simply "Ellie" had so far been futile.

"How is everything, Jakub?"

"Well enough," he said. He did not mention his son, so I didn't ask. I knew that if he had news he wished to share he would have done so.

It was a big car, but it felt small sitting next to the major in the backseat. I noticed that he was very careful to sit far enough away so that we didn't actually touch. No doubt he didn't want to give me any undue encouragement.

I knew that, to some extent, I was being unfair to him. The boundaries of our working relationship were clear, and we could proceed as we had always done.

It had been only one kiss, after all. It wasn't technically his fault that it had been the most electric kiss of my life.

I sighed. I didn't realize I had done it until he looked over at me.

Jakub spoke up from the front seat then, sparing me the necessity of explaining my heavy sigh. "A bit of rough road ahead."

That was not an unusual thing now, not with German bombs dropping from the sky night after night. I sometimes marveled that there was anything left of London at all.

The car began to bump over the rutted section of road, the wheels grinding over rubble, jostling the backseat heavily. I leaned away from the major so I wouldn't fall against him. Then one of the back tires dropped into a hole, jarring us both, and I saw the major's jaw clench.

Jakub guided the car through the bad stretch of road, and a moment later it smoothed out again.

I resettled myself on the seat and looked over at the major. His jaw was still tight, his body tense.

"You're hurting quite a bit, aren't you?" I said before I could think better of it.

"The pain is manageable," he said without looking at me.

It was just the sort of thing I would expect him to say. The sort of thing he would no doubt still say if a lion had ripped off his arm.

"Are you taking something for the pain?" It wasn't my place to ask, but the urge to care for those around me that I'd inherited from Nacy was hard to ignore.

"Occasionally," he said. I knew what that meant; he wasn't taking anything.

"No one will think less of you for taking medication." I was well beyond the bounds of polite concern now, so I felt I might as well do a proper job of it.

A slight frown appeared between his eyebrows, a signal he was thinking of giving me a dressing down. But he didn't. Instead, he rubbed his fingers across his forehead. The gesture was telling. In all our time together, I had seldom seen him give any indication of how he was feeling. He must be feeling bad indeed to let this indication of discomfort past his armor of self-control.

Or, just perhaps, he was growing a bit more comfortable with me now that I had broached the topic of his health. Whatever the case, he said, "The morphine dulls my senses. And I can't afford that in this line of work."

So he was suffering through the pain for the good of his country. No wonder he looked exhausted.

"How much do you know about what is happening in Lisbon?" he asked. His posture straightened and his expression turned impassive; he was clearly closing the conversation about his health for the time being.

"Not much," I admitted. "I know they've chosen to remain

neutral, of course. And that a great many refugees are ending up there, trying to get to the United States or elsewhere."

He nodded.

"That's the public face of it. And because of that, the situation in Lisbon right now is a hotbed of espionage. We have agents there, of course. And so does the Gestapo. Additionally, there is the PVDE—Polícia de Vigilância e Defesa do Estado—Portugal's own secret police. They are keeping a tight watch on everything that happens in the city, and there's little that escapes their notice. They are often influential in finding out the background of the refugees there and helping to determine who gets visas, and who does not."

"It sounds like a proper mess," I said, glumly. "How does one even make headway in such a situation when there are so many forces opposing each other?" Even as I said the words, I knew the sort of people who would take such a job, people who relished the challenge, and who would do everything in their power to make sure that they succeeded. People like Major Ramsey.

"It is a mess," he acknowledged. "The city is awash in spies. Often members of rival spy rings will have dinner at tables beside each other in the more popular restaurants, hotel bars, and nightclubs. Spies, refugees, and assassins stand shoulder to shoulder at the casinos' tables. One thing Lisbon has going for it: there are no blackouts."

I had to tamp down the part of me that thought it sounded rather glamorous. I had learned the hard way that being a spy was not an easy job, and I couldn't imagine the additional pressures of operating in territories swarming with enemy agents. All the same, there was a little piece of me that was jealous of the opportunity to mingle and listen and learn.

I looked up to see that Major Ramsey was watching me, and I flushed as I had the uncanny sensation that he had been able to read my thoughts. "It . . . sounds rather exciting," I admitted.

"Your actions in Sunderland have proved that you no doubt

have what it takes to work in high-pressure situations," he said. "But we need you here at present."

We, he'd said. Not *I.* Well, I hadn't expected a declaration.

I gave a short nod. "Of course."

"With that level of activity, there is potential for any number of important articles to have been smuggled out with one of the people on our list. It's imperative that we get as much information as we can before the situation escalates."

I nodded, not wanting to press him on what escalation might entail.

"Do you have any theories about what they're looking for?" I asked.

"It won't do any good to speculate at this point," he said tersely.

I turned to look out the window so he wouldn't see me roll my eyes. The pain was making him irritable, it seemed.

The Ritz was as glamorous inside as one might suppose. I was tempted to let out a low whistle like Uncle Mick might have done, but I realized it would only put me more out of place than I already was.

The major, of course, strode across the lobby as though he owned the place. And people moved out of his way. It was impressive, I had to admit. Having myself come from a group who strove to avoid notice, to remain in the shadows, watching him take command of the rooms he entered was a study in the sort of poise and self-assurance that is born and bred into the upper classes.

Not that my family had ever been lacking in confidence. But there was a different kind of confidence that came with the major's military authority, not to mention his heritage and breeding. It wasn't the empty bravado I'd seen in other well-to-do men; it was grounded in his certainty that he was in command of every situation in which he found himself.

That was what I found attractive in men, I realized. Competence. Unfortunately, Major Ramsey had it in spades.

While I was thinking all of this, he was getting the information we needed and having the concierge ring Madame Arnaud's room to inform her we were coming up.

As we reached the lift and got inside, I glanced at the major, whose ramrod posture and granite expression told me now was not the time to ask questions.

We exited the lift, walked down the hall, and the major knocked at the door. I wasn't certain what role he wanted me to play, so I decided to just follow his cues.

The door was opened by a maid in uniform. Her gaze raked over us in a decidedly French manner, and, dismissing me, she looked at the major for a long moment before she pulled the door open to let us in.

We were ushered into the main room of the suite. It was decorated in cream and pastels, under an enormous glittering chandelier. My first thought was how much damage it could cause if a German bomb sent it crashing down.

The lady did not rise to meet us. Germaine Arnaud was a slim, regal-looking woman in what I estimated to be her late forties. She had auburn hair without a hint of gray and a sharp, pointed face with large emerald eyes. She was striking and exceptionally chic.

She also looked annoyed that she was having to speak with us. It seemed to me that she would be glad to have someone looking into the robbery so she might get the items back. Unless there was something she was hiding.

The major said something I assumed to be an introduction and perhaps an explanation in what sounded like impeccable French.

"We are in England, Major. I don't mind speaking to you in English." Her voice was as haughty as her manner, low and only lightly accented.

He tipped his head. "As you wish, Madame. As I said, we won't take more than a few minutes of your time."

She inclined her hand graciously to the pair of chairs across from the sofa on which she sat. Major Ramsey motioned for me to take a seat, and I sat down in one. Madame Arnaud's eyes flicked to me for just a moment, and she dismissed me just as quickly.

She was clearly impressed by Major Ramsey, however. Her eyes seemed to gleam a bit as she watched him make his way to the other chair. I had noticed often enough that his impressive good looks lent him an advantage where women were concerned. He generally reined that element in, but he occasionally used it to his advantage.

And today would be one of those days, it seemed, for he smiled at her as he removed his service cap and ran a hand over his hair.

Though her expression hadn't much changed, I saw her eyes soften slightly, and her tone had lost some of its coolness when she said, "I don't know what I can tell you that I didn't tell the police, but I will do what I can."

"Thank you. You left Lisbon on the BOAC flight on the seventeenth of December, I believe?" he said.

"Yes. I was only too glad to be out of Lisbon," she said. "It was so very crowded. I had to stay in a very inferior room in a hotel that was not at all up to my personal standards."

She was overplaying the high society role a bit, and I had to assume that it was for the major's benefit. Even his years in the military had not been able to dull the sheen of aristocracy on him, and I knew she could sense it. Whatever else she might be, Germaine Arnaud was a sharp woman.

"We have, of course, the general information about the robbery at your hotel, but I have a few questions about the flight. Is there anything you can tell us that was unusual about any of the passengers?"

Her thin brows rose ever so slightly. "Unusual? They were all unusual."

Major Ramsey gave the faintest smile at this assessment. "In what way?"

Madame Arnaud shrugged. "It was a disparate group of people fleeing their countries and trying to find safe harbor. It was bound to be an odd assortment."

"Was there anyone in particular that caught your notice?" He was all politeness and patience now. It was a side of him I had rarely ever seen, but I could tell it was having the desired effect.

She wanted to answer him but was determined not to look too eager to do it. So she took her time about considering, reaching into the lacquered box on the table and removing a cigarette. The major dutifully picked up the lighter from the table and lit the cigarette for her.

She took a deep drag and then slowly blew out the smoke. "There are, of course, certain people who draw one's attention more than others. I sat beside a young Belgian woman who seemed exceptionally anxious. That could have been the situation, of course. We were, naturally, all anxious to leave Lisbon and there is always the threat of the Luftwaffe when crossing near France. But she kept looking out the window and then wiping her brow with a handkerchief, as though she was afraid at any moment that someone would come to haul her from the plane."

"Did she appear less anxious once the flight was in the air?"

"Much more so. She was somewhat talkative, even friendly, with the other passengers."

"Did you happen to catch her name?"

"I did not catch it. She gave it to me. Her name was Anna Gillard."

Major Ramsey gave a short nod. "Was there anything else?"

She paused, seemed to be pondering if there was additional information she could relate. She had been irritated by our visit at first, I think, but now she was beginning to enjoy herself and wasn't eager to bring her conversation with the major to a close. I could not exactly blame her. With Paris in the hands of the Nazis, her entire life turned upside down, it must be nice to be sitting in the London Ritz drinking tea and chatting with a handsome officer.

"There is, perhaps, one thing that might be of interest to you," she said at last. "She was composing a letter during the flight, and

I happened to see a few of the words written on it. It said: 'I am bringing it to you, at great risk to myself.'"

I glanced at Major Ramsey. His expression was bland, nothing more than polite interest on his features.

"And did you see to whom the letter was addressed?" he asked.

She shook her head. "No. It was only a quick glance, you understand. It was not my intent to read her letter, and I looked away at once. I just happen to have the sort of mind that remembers."

He smiled at her. "Very good."

"It could, perhaps, have been a letter to her sister. She mentioned that she was going to be reunited with her. She wore a necklace, which she said she and her sister both wore. She seemed an excessively sentimental sort of person."

"You have been very helpful, Madame. And is there anything else?"

"No, I think that is all."

Major Ramsey rose from his chair then, and I followed suit. "Thank you, Madame Arnaud."

She inclined her head in acknowledgment. "Fifi will see you out."

"There's no need. We'll see ourselves out," he said, motioning for me to precede him. "Good afternoon."

We made our way from the suite, Madame Arnaud and I never having spoken a word to each other.

The major said nothing in the lift on the way down, nor as we made our way across the lobby.

I was able to hold my tongue that long, but as we left the hotel, I turned to him. "It seems like the next person we need to talk to is Anna Gillard."

"Yes," he agreed.

"Do you know where Miss Gillard is staying?"

"Yes," he said again. "I've gathered the locations of everyone on the list. If she hasn't changed locations in the past twenty-four hours, we should be able to find her."

I wanted to suggest that we visit Anna Gillard right away, but instead I waited to see what Major Ramsey would say. I was trying to learn patience, and I hoped he would appreciate it.

He looked at me, not fooled by my show of restraint. "You want to go there directly, of course. As it happens, I agree with you."

I couldn't help but smile. "I was hoping you'd say that."

"Yes. I thought you might be."

We arrived at the little hotel, the Valencia, not half an hour later. It was a lovely Victoria-era building in Chelsea that had thus far escaped the Luftwaffe. At a glance, I would have guessed it catered to those who were wealth-adjacent, but didn't necessarily have the spare funds to put up in one of the swankier London hotels. It certainly wasn't the Ritz, but I would've been more comfortable staying here.

This impression was increased as we entered the high-ceilinged, marble-floored lobby. The rugs were just the slightest bit faded and the furniture was perhaps a decade old, but everything was sparkling clean, and the guests who wandered across the lobby were well dressed and elegant looking. There were potted plants in large brass planters in the corners of the room, and several of the big windows had the blackout curtains pulled up for the day to let in the sunlight.

The major didn't appear to care about taking stock of our surroundings but made his way straight toward the front desk. I followed along.

There was a tall dark-haired girl behind the counter who gave us her most professional smile as we approached, though I thought it wavered a bit at the perpetually stern expression on the major's face.

"Good afternoon," she said. "Welcome to the Valencia. Do you have a reservation?"

The major spoke before I could. "I'm looking for one of your guests, Anna Gillard." He had apparently used up his daily allot-

ment of patience on Madame Arnaud. He said this in that author-
itative way he had that brooked no argument, and, indeed, the
woman behind the desk asked no questions. She merely consulted
the hotel register in front of her. I saw the frown wrinkle her brow
as she perused the list.

"What's wrong?" Major Ramsey asked. His tone was edging
toward snappish, and I could tell this particular young woman was
overawed by his looks and uniform rather than intrigued by them.
I stepped forward and smiled reassuringly at her.

"We have an appointment with Miss Gillard," I said. "Is she
not a guest here? I'm sure this was the hotel she mentioned."

"Well, that's the thing," she said, darting a nervous glance
at the major before looking back at me. "She only had the room
reserved through yesterday, but I don't see that she's checked out.
But perhaps she decided to stay an extra night. That happens sometimes. We're somewhat short-staffed at the moment. One of our
girls is unreliable, and—"

"What room is Miss Gillard in?" Major Ramsey cut in.

"I . . . I'm not really supposed to give out room numbers," she
stammered. "It's against hotel policy."

Major Ramsey was about to reply, but I reached out and put
a hand on his wrist below the level of the desk, where she couldn't
see it. He glanced at me, impatience clear in his expression, but he
pressed his lips together.

"Since she's expecting us, can't you just give us the room number?" I asked. "In fact, I believe she gave it to us already; I've just
forgotten what she said. I'm afraid I don't have a head for numbers."

I gave her what I hoped was a cheerfully dim smile, and the
woman nodded, her expression giving the impression she was relieved to have an excuse to do as the major asked. "It's room 214."

"Thank you," I said, even as Major Ramsey turned without
comment and strode toward the lift.

I hurried to catch up with him. "You ought to trot out your charm in situations like these, rather than scaring people half to death," I said in a low voice.

"We don't have time for niceties," he said.

"No, Watson; the game is afoot!"

He shot me a disapproving look as we got into the lift.

"I suppose *I'm* meant to be Watson," I said.

Unsurprisingly, he didn't answer.

The lift opened on an empty hallway, and the major led the way down the worn green carpet to the door of room 214.

The major rapped sharply on the wood. There was no sound from inside. After a short pause, he knocked again. Again, it went unanswered.

"Open it," he commanded curtly, gesturing at the door.

I hesitated. "Are you sure? She probably left as intended and forgot to check out. It's not likely she left anything of value."

"Open the door, please."

Sensing now was not the time to argue with him, I pulled my ever-present lockpicking kit from my pocket and removed a suitable pick. It took only a moment to disengage the lock.

The major was, I think, about to move past me to enter, but I didn't give him the chance. I opened the door and slipped into the room.

"Wait," he said.

But I had already switched on the light and then recoiled as both the sight and the smell hit me.

My eyes took in the scene, realization flashing through my brain like lightning. There was a body on the bed, the sheets around it soaked in blood, the metallic tang of it like a slap to the face.

CHAPTER SIX

I gasped and turned instinctively, my body moving on its own to get away, and I ran directly into the major. His arm came around me, steadying me.

For just a moment, we stood still. I was trying to gather my composure, and I assumed the major was taking in the state of the room.

"When the woman at the desk said she hadn't checked out, I . . . I didn't even think she might be . . ." I whispered into his chest. The words trailed off as I realized why he had been so impatient to get into the room. "You knew?"

"I suspected," he admitted. "Why don't you wait outside?"

"No," I said, taking a deep breath. "I'm all right."

But I didn't move away, and he didn't release me as I continued to lean against him, my eyes closed. I was certain that if I stepped back, I would do something embarrassing like fall or be sick. If I had just a moment to collect myself, I could overcome it.

"You don't need to see this," he said. "Wait outside, and I'll do a quick search."

I shook my head. "I'm all right," I said again. I drew in one more deep breath then forced myself to look up at him. "Really."

He studied me, as though to determine if I was telling the truth, and my chin tipped up a bit with determination. I wasn't going to be left out of this, no matter how unpleasant it was.

At last he gave a little nod. I'd passed muster, it seemed.

I stepped back, out of his arms, and turned to face the scene once again. Major Ramsey's warm hand rested against my back for just a moment, as if to be certain I wasn't going to fall to pieces, and I appreciated the gesture.

It was even worse than my first glance had told me.

The person on the bed was a woman, but it was difficult to tell from the state of her face. She had clearly been killed by being struck repeatedly with some heavy object. There was blood everywhere: splattered on the walls, seeping across the bedclothes, dripping down to puddle in the rug beneath the bed.

I was determined to be stoic, but it was quite the worst thing I'd ever seen, and I had to clench my teeth against the rising nausea at the sight and the stench of blood in the air.

"Don't touch anything," the major said. It was an unnecessary directive; I had absolutely no intention of touching anything.

He moved past me toward the bed. Quite out of the blue, I had a sudden flash of what had happened to us in Sunderland. Of his lying there on the floor of that dimly lit cave, shot, covered in blood. Of the absolute terror I had felt. I was almost dizzy remembering it, and I reached out a hand and steadied myself against the wall for just a moment, pushing the memories away.

Then, summoning all my resolve, I followed him farther into the room and forced myself to look at the figure on the bed. Almost immediately, I had to look away again.

I focused instead on the major. I watched him as he surveyed the woman's injuries with an expressionless face. His eyes moved over the scene with a calm efficiency I couldn't possibly hope to emulate.

"She hasn't been dead long," he said.

I would take his word for it.

He moved next to the window, drawing back the blood-splattered curtain. "Unlatched," he said. "They probably came in and out this way."

He looked back at me, his eyes moving over my face, and then nodded toward the wall behind me. "Check the desk and bureau, will you?" I knew he was giving me a task to take my mind off things, but I was relieved and not insulted.

I nodded, turning toward the wall where the bureau rested. There was an inferior painting to one side and a small writing desk beneath it.

My legs felt rubbery as I moved to the wall, and my hands were shaking as I reached out to open the desk drawer. This was not the sort of reaction I ought to be having. I ought to be brave and unaffected. But I couldn't seem to pull myself together. The body behind me on the bed felt like a weight pressing down on me, and I was short of breath.

I had been in dangerous situations before this. I had faced death more than once. So why did this particular scene feel like almost too much to bear?

I clenched my teeth and concentrated on my task. There was nothing in the drawer but some hotel stationery. I sifted through it, but it was all unused.

I moved to the bureau. I didn't look behind me to see what Major Ramsey was doing, but I heard movement and the light shifting of fabric. I assumed he was searching the bed.

There were a few clothes hanging in the bureau. I concentrated on examining them, thinking of nothing but getting through this without embarrassing myself.

There was nothing. Everything was in order, but there was not so much as a spare receipt or loose coins in any of the pockets.

I had forced myself to focus to such a degree that I jumped when the major appeared at my side.

"Anything?" he asked.

"No." The single word came out sounding hoarse and breathless.

His eyes were on my face again. I tried to keep my expression as bland as his, but I doubted I was successful.

"Come along," he said, taking my elbow. "There's nothing else to be done here."

"The . . . police?" I asked.

"She'll be discovered soon enough. We don't want to be here when she is."

I didn't have the energy to argue with him, even if I'd wanted to.

He opened the door and looked out before hustling me into the hallway and leading me back toward the lift, his grip on my elbow reassuring.

My legs were still trembling, and my head felt a bit foggy as the door closed behind us.

Inside the lift, he turned to face me. "I know that was hard, but I need you to behave as normally as possible until we're out of the hotel. Can you do that?"

"Of course," I said, my slight irritation at the question doing much to rouse me from my stupor.

He nodded, and I wondered if it had been his intention.

The lift door opened, and we stepped out into the lobby. It was disorienting to be back in that bright, cheery space after what we had just seen. I thought we would leave directly, but the major walked back toward the front desk instead.

"We knocked, but there was no answer," he told the girl at the front desk. "If you see her, will you tell her to please telephone John Grey? She has the number."

"Yes, of course," she said.

He didn't let go of my arm as we left the building and began walking down the street. A short distance from the hotel, he stopped and pulled me into the shadowy doorway of a vacant building.

He turned to face me then, still holding on to my arms. "Take slow, deep breaths."

"I'm fine," I said, though, in truth, I felt wretched, and it was taking all my resolve to keep from being sick as I had the first time we'd come across a body.

"I'm sorry you had to see that," he said.

"I don't know if I'll ever grow used to it, to seeing the ugliness of murder," I said, tears threatening to overflow despite my best efforts to repress them.

"You don't need to grow used to it," he said.

"This is so useless," I said, wiping my eyes. "I thought I was past this."

"Look at me," he said, and the gentleness in his voice was almost enough to push me into full-fledged crying. I managed to push back the tears, though, and looked up at him.

"There's no reason for you to feel as though you can't be upset at what we've just seen."

"This job . . ."

"This job does not require you to remain stoic in the face of unexpected violence."

I said nothing, and he raised his brows slightly. "Understood?"

I sighed, a bit of the weight in my chest lifting, and nodded. "Understood."

"Good."

I was still looking up into those clear violet-blue eyes, and I felt the wall between us waver.

Then he turned and nodded toward the tea shop across the street.

"Come along. I'll get you some tea."

"Oh, that's not necessary," I said, as he took my arm and began leading me in that direction. All things considered, I would much rather return home and have a good cry.

He didn't release my arm, nor did he break stride. "You're pale and trembling. I'm not going to leave you until you're feeling better."

I was feeling just better enough to be slightly incensed at this high-handedness, but not better enough to argue with him.

"Besides, we need to discuss what we're going to do next," he said, mollifying me.

We went into the tea shop and found an empty table. A moment later the waitress came, and the major ordered a pot of tea and a plate of scones and biscuits.

"I don't want anything to eat," I said.

"It doesn't matter if you want it. You'll feel better if you eat a bit of something."

I doubted it. My stomach felt sick, and every time I thought of the horrific way that woman had been killed, of the way her face had been . . . obliterated, my nausea welled up again.

"Why . . . why was she killed?" I whispered. "Do you think she had the object and refused to tell them where it was until they . . . made her?"

"No. This wasn't torture. If I had to guess, I'd say she was unlucky enough to be in the room when they broke in. Perhaps they were afraid she would raise the cry. Or that she might identify them."

"It was so . . . brutal."

"Convenience. She was killed with a heavy bronze statuette, presumably part of the room's décor. It was on the floor on the other side of the bed."

I shuddered.

"Despite the way it looked, it was probably quick," he said. "The first blow or two would have knocked her unconscious."

I knew he meant this as a comfort of sorts, but my vision swam a little at the words. Thankfully, I was spared having to formulate a reply by the appearance of the waitress with our tea.

"There's something else," Major Ramsey said when she had gone.

"What is it?"

He looked a bit reluctant, as though he was debating on whether to share it with me. But he had mentioned it, so it was too late to turn back now.

He reached into his pocket and took something out, setting it on the table between us. "This was in the ashtray on the table by the bed."

It was a scrap of paper no bigger than a matchbox with ragged edges, as though from a letter or other document that had been torn up. It had also been mostly burned. The edges were blackened so thoroughly they were crumbling into ash, and even the middle of the scrap had been darkened by flame. Gingerly, I picked it up. It was dry and fragile-feeling beneath my fingers, but I could still read the words written on the center of the scrap in dark ink: *with Lazaro.*

There had been other words, of course, but these were all that were legible.

I looked up at the major. "Then he is involved."

"It appears there is some connection, yes," he said, as he poured a cup of tea.

"Do you suppose the thieves saw this?"

He began to spoon a liberal amount of sugar into the cup. "I doubt it. It was beneath a good deal of ash and several cigarette butts. It seems to have escaped their notice."

Leave it to Major Ramsey to have thought of sifting through the ashtray.

"Then we have a lead they don't have," I said.

"Perhaps." He pushed the cup of tea toward me. "The sugar is good for shock. We may as well lean into your natural inclinations when it's useful."

I managed a smile. I handed him back the slip of paper and took a sip of the tea. It did taste wonderful. I took a second deep sip.

"They've already been to his flat," I mused. "Perhaps he does have what they're looking for and they missed it. There might be time for us to discover what it is."

"It's possible." He pushed the plate of biscuits toward me. "And now one of these."

I didn't argue, though I found it a bit irritating how he was refusing to discuss the clue with me.

"You need to eat something, too," I said, taking a bite of the biscuit.

"I'm not hungry."

"I believe that doesn't matter," I said archly. "You're clearly not eating enough." I remembered how his sister had chided him for skipping breakfast.

He swore beneath his breath, but I knew him well enough now to know it was good-natured.

I pointed at the plate. "If you please."

With an expression of supreme annoyance, he picked up a scone and took a bite of it.

"Is the pain constant?" I asked. I hadn't really meant to ask the question, but it had come out anyway.

He didn't pause in his chewing. "It's worse some times than others."

"I don't mean to pry. But I . . ." I shrugged. "I suppose it's none of my business."

"I appreciate your concern," he said. The words sounded genuine enough, but something also told me he'd had enough of this particular discussion.

I took a bite of the biscuit, and we sat quietly for a moment, the comfortable sounds of the tearoom around us.

"Your color's come back," he said as I finished the biscuit and reached for a second. Major Ramsey did not take a second scone, but at least he had eaten one of them.

I was feeling recovered enough to be embarrassed about my

reaction to the body, but, in a way, it had made things better between us. He had been so kind, and I was comfortable with him again. The coolness that had existed since Sunderland seemed to have thawed, and it felt like we were on our way back to familiar footing.

"So, what now?" I asked, pushing these thoughts aside.

"They're growing more desperate, it seems. And they're obviously willing to kill in the course of their pursuit. So we need to find out what they're looking for before someone else is killed."

The words sent a chill through me.

"How are we going to do that?"

He sighed. "It seems the first step is going to be to question Nico Lazaro."

He did not sound particularly enthusiastic about this.

"Do you know him?" I asked.

"I've met him," he said, his tone giving nothing away and, consequently, making me assume that he was keeping something from me.

"Why don't you like him?" I asked.

I thought he would deny this accusation of dislike, but he surprised me by giving an honest answer. Or half of one, anyway. "You won't like him either," he said. "You'll see."

Major Ramsey was often disapproving, so I wasn't at all sure I would agree with him on Lazaro. After all, Major Ramsey would disapprove of the vast majority of my associates.

Thinking of my associates, I wondered if there was anyone I could contact who might know something about what had happened. If someone had been stealing jewelry, they would be anxious to off-load it. It might be possible for me to contact some of the fences we'd done business with in the past. There might be a lead that way.

"Feeling a bit better now?" he asked, looking at my empty cup.

"Yes. Thank you."

Our eyes met for a long moment, and then the major pushed back from the table.

"Come along, Miss McDonnell. I'll take you home."

CHAPTER SEVEN

I didn't sleep well that night. I tossed and turned before sinking into a fitful sleep plagued by ugly dreams.

When I woke from a particularly gruesome nightmare shortly before dawn, I got up and put the kettle on. I didn't know why I had been so affected by what we had seen yesterday. It had been horrible, yes, but it was not the first horrible scene I'd stumbled upon.

So why was it that I still felt shaken and uneasy? The only conclusion I could reach was that what had happened in Sunderland had affected me more than I had believed. I wanted to think that I had set aside that harrowing experience, but perhaps such things clung a bit more tightly than one realized.

I pushed the glum thoughts aside. If I was going to be awake at this hour, I might as well be productive.

I retrieved the mythology book I had found among my father's things. I didn't know if I was exactly in the right frame of mind for cracking the code, but it couldn't hurt to give it a try.

It seemed logical to me that someone with experience as a safe-cracker should also be competent at cracking codes. After all, they were similar types of puzzles, when one really considered it; both required a systematic examination of the components and the patience to work out how those components fit together.

I took the folded letter that was tucked into the book under the chapter titled "Electra" and spread it out on the table. Taking a clean sheet of paper, I copied out the coded message with wide spaces between each line for me to attempt to work out what the coded message might be.

It quickly became apparent that this was no beginner's code. None of the arrangements of letters I could seem to work out yielded any sort of coherent sentences. I arranged and rearranged the letters until my teapot was empty, and my eyes had begun to cross, but I was still none the wiser about what the letter said as the birds began to chirp outside the windows, alerting me that dawn had arrived.

It occurred to me suddenly that I might know just the person to help me. Frank Doyle was a fellow who lived a few streets over. He was known for being something of an eccentric genius, a mathematician of the highest order, and a dedicated curmudgeon. As children we had dared one another to see who was brave enough to approach his house—the ultimate feat to knock on his front door before running away. Inevitably, he would spot us through the window before we reached the porch, and he would shout at us as we fled at full speed.

The memory brought a smile to my lips. I hadn't ventured into Frank Doyle's yard in more than a decade, and I hoped he wouldn't shout at me through the window if I ventured to do so now.

I didn't know how likely it was that he would be willing to help me. Frankly, the odds felt low, but it couldn't hurt to ask, could it? I determined I would pay him a visit today while I waited to hear whether Major Ramsey had been able to arrange our visit to Nico Lazaro, the diplomat.

This plan to speak to Frank Doyle had the other benefit of the fact that, as he had few friends and associates and generally disliked everyone, there would not be anyone he would be likely to tell if he did decode the message.

He seemed the ideal candidate to help me in this matter. If, that is, I could convince him to do it. But I had faith in my persuasive abilities, and, if he was not charmed by me, perhaps he could be bribed.

I set off after breakfast, telling Nacy that I had a few errands to run. She didn't ask questions, as she was distracted by her least favorite task: dusting.

On the walk to Mr. Doyle's house, I practiced what I would say to him.

His house was not on my usual route, so I hadn't been past it in quite some time. I wasn't surprised, however, to find that it looked much the same.

The house was in the same state of indifferent repair as it had been a decade ago, no better and no worse. I noticed, however, that the walk had been cleared of snow, and there was a greenery wreath hung on the door.

I felt, for a moment, that sense of nervousness that had beset me as a child preparing to sneak up to knock on his door.

Don't be ridiculous, Ellie, I chided myself. *You're not a child anymore.*

And so I went up the slippery walk and stepped onto the stoop. Drawing in a steadying breath as the long-ago echoes of my cousins' taunts floated through my mind, I lifted a hand to knock.

Before I could, however, the door swung open, and I was face-to-face with the man himself.

He glowered at me from under bushy white eyebrows. "Who are you?"

His house hadn't changed in the past decade, and Mr. Doyle didn't seem to have changed much either. He was tall and slightly stooped with a high dome of a forehead. His wispy white hair floated around his head, and his eyes, a cold, sharp blue, stared at me.

"Hello, Mr. Doyle. I don't suppose you remember me. My name is Ellie McDonnell, and . . ."

"Mick McDonnell's girl," he said. There was nothing in his tone to indicate whether this was a positive or a negative, but, either way, I would never deny it.

"Yes."

He grunted. The door remained open, so I took this as tacit permission to continue.

"It's rather a long story, but I recently came into possession of an old letter that seems to be written in some sort of code."

There was no reply.

"I know that you're a mathematician, and it occurred to me that you might be just the person to look at this. Not that mathematics and codes are the same, but there are similarities, I think."

I forced myself to stop rambling and met his gaze. He looked at me for a very long time, and I was tempted to turn and flee as ten-year-old me would have done. But I held my ground.

At last, he said, "If I did have a look at it, would you be able to do something for me in return?"

I hadn't expected this, but it certainly wasn't unfair of him to ask. "Such as?"

He shrugged. "Sometimes a man needs a favor. Can't hurt to be owed one."

Some little part of me questioned whether this was a good idea, but where else was I to go to have a code broken? I certainly couldn't confide this part of my life's story to Major Ramsey.

At last, I nodded. "All right. I'd owe you a favor."

He gave me another hard look. "Then I'll take a look."

I let out a breath. "Thank you. I have the paper here . . ." I reached into my pocket to retrieve the book and the copy of the letter I'd written out.

He didn't invite me in. Instead, he extended a hand through the crack in the door. I handed him the book.

"May be two or three days," he said. "I'll be in touch."

Before I could answer, he closed the door.

As so often seemed the case in my life since the war began, I currently had many more questions than answers. But at least I was taking steps to make sense of what information I did have. My code was in the hands of Mr. Doyle, and the major had said he would make an appointment for us to see Nico Lazaro today, if possible.

From the sound of things, Lazaro was a busy man, but I had confidence in the major's ability to have his way.

My confidence, it turned out, was not misplaced.

I was helping Nacy fold some freshly washed linens when the telephone rang.

"Hello," I said as I picked it up.

"Miss McDonnell?"

"Yes."

"This is Constance Brown calling on behalf of Major Ramsey. He said he has confirmed your appointment for this afternoon and asks if you could come to his office at one o'clock."

I looked at my wristwatch. It was nearly noon. That didn't leave me much time.

The major's secretary was always so polite, and I knew she sugarcoated the major's lack of courtesy when impatient. He'd summon people like a king, and Constance would make it sound like we were doing him a personal favor.

Whatever way he'd relayed the message, I was glad he'd been successful at getting the interview with Mr. Lazaro. I hoped we would be able to learn something from the man. With any luck, we would be able to find what the thieves were looking for and catch whoever was responsible for poor Anna Gillard's brutal murder.

I was at the major's office well before one o'clock, and I had to wait for a bit in the little parlor off the entryway, as he was on a telephone call when I arrived.

At last, Constance poked her head into the room. "He's ready for you now, Miss McDonnell."

"Thank you. And, please, call me Ellie."

She smiled. "All right."

I made my way to the major's office and found the door ajar.

"Come in," he called before I could knock.

He was standing looking at a map on the wall. He turned when I came into the room.

"I've made contact with one of my people in Lisbon," he said without preamble. "There are several rumors, as of yet unsubstantiated, that there was an attaché case stolen from a man at the casino there."

"What was in it?" I asked.

"Whatever it was, it has the Germans scrambling. I'm told there was a slew of intercepted communications relating to the event, though they were all very vague."

I sighed. "That doesn't provide us with many answers, does it?"

"Not yet," he said. "But at last, we know that we're on the right track."

"We knew that already. As soon as we saw Anna Gillard's body." I couldn't help but cringe a bit at the memory.

I felt his eyes on me. "Are you all right?"

"I couldn't sleep," I said, and then was immediately angry at myself for admitting it. But the words were out now, so I might as well confess the whole of it. "I kept dreaming about her."

"I'm sorry you had to see that," he said. "I should have kept you out of the room."

"No," I said firmly. "I don't need to be sheltered. It was just a shock."

He was studying me, and I had the uneasy feeling he was wondering if I was up to snuff.

"War isn't easy on any of us, but we'll get by," I said in an attempt to dismiss his concern. "You were able to make an appointment with Mr. Lazaro?"

He was still looking at me in a way I couldn't quite interpret, but at last he nodded. "Yes. You told me once that you could take shorthand, I believe."

With a sinking feeling, I remembered that steel-trap memory of his. From now on, I could mention only things I wanted him to know. "Yes," I said warily.

"Good. You can pose as my secretary and take notes while I question him."

This was rather a demotion, as I had always previously posed as his girlfriend or wife. I was not, of course, going to make this joke to him aloud. I suppose I should be grateful he was allowing me to take part in the investigation at all. It was clear he valued my contributions; if he did not, I certainly would not have been invited along.

"All right," I said, trying to sound more game than I felt. "When do we go?"

His eyes swept over me. "What you're wearing is a sufficient costume for a secretary. We'll go now."

It was Nacy who had suggested I dress up a bit in order to pay my visit to the major. I had, naturally, rolled my eyes at the suggestion, but in the end I had given in because I knew we were going to see Mr. Lazaro.

I had chosen a dark-blue wool suit, one of the few suits I owned. It was not exactly the sort of thing Noelle Edgemont would have worn, and had probably cost about ten times less, but I left smart enough and now I was glad that I was well prepared for the visit we were about to pay.

The big black government car was parked in front of the house as we emerged.

"Doesn't Nico Lazaro live in Mayfair?" I asked. "I thought that's what it said in the article. We could walk from here."

"We could," he agreed. "But Lazaro is best dealt with using all the pomp and circumstance at our disposal. The more important he feels his information is, the more likely he will be to share it with us. He is the sort of gentleman who enjoys a bit of the theatrical."

I had wondered why he had not chosen to go in civilian clothes, perhaps posing as a policeman or some such official. Now I understood that, in his capacity as a member of military intelligence, he would be most impressive to our interviewee.

He opened the door for me, and I exchanged pleasantries with Jakub as I settled into the leather seat. The major slid in beside me, and the car pulled away from the curb.

We lapsed into silence for the few minutes that the trip took, both of us no doubt lost in our own thoughts. At last, we pulled up before what seemed to have once been a Georgian manor that had been converted into a building of very swanky flats. It seemed it had thus far escaped any bombing damage. I suppose that was why Lazaro had felt confident enough to host a dinner party.

"It goes without saying that you're to remain quiet and do as instructed, like a proper secretary," Major Ramsey said.

I tried to quell the smile that crept up at the corners of my mouth. "Yes, Major."

He got out of the car, and I met Jakub's eyes in the mirror. I gave him a wink before the major opened my door.

CHAPTER EIGHT

The doorman, suitably impressed by the major's uniform and the posh car, let us in without question and directed us to the lift.

We took the lift to the second floor and stopped outside the door to Lazaro's flat. I could hear music coming from within, a languid jazz tune. Someone had the gramophone up rather loud somewhere inside.

I glanced at Major Ramsey; he looked more grim than usual as he rang the buzzer.

"Remember what I've told you," he said. "Behave yourself."

"Yes, sir," I responded like a good secretary.

His scowl deepened, but he didn't reply.

A few moments later the door was opened by a solemn-faced man in a suit who wore an expression of long-suffering if ever I'd seen one. Not our man, I realized. A butler or valet, the put-upon manservant.

"Good morning," the major said. "Major Ramsey to see Mr. Lazaro."

"Very good, sir," the man said. "Please come in."

He didn't address me. It seemed the butler recognized me as one of the serving class. Between his behavior and Madame Arnaud's, one might develop an inferiority complex—if one thought of oneself as inferior, that was. Luckily, I didn't.

"May I take your coats?" he asked as we stepped inside, and he closed the door behind us.

Major Ramsey helped me off with mine and then handed the butler his own greatcoat and his service cap.

I looked around. It was a fairly large, marble-floored foyer, but the first thing to which the eye was drawn was the lifelike marble statue of a naked woman directly across from the front door. She was taller than me and noticeably voluptuous, her arms outstretched in a languorous and rather carefree posture.

Behind me, I heard Major Ramsey sigh.

"Not Grecian in style, that much is certain," I said in a low voice.

I turned my eyes from the statue and took in the rest of the décor. The walls were papered in black, an alternate pattern of glossy and matte stripes, and there was a black velvet sofa and a table that was configured in black and gold and glass. The naked woman aside, it was all very chic and modern. And expensive.

The butler appeared at our side, having magically divested himself of our coats without my having seen him do it, and inclined his head ever so slightly. "This way, if you please."

He led us past the naked lady—averting his eyes from it, it seemed to me—and into the large main rooms of the flat, then down a corridor. This flat was massive, I realized. It probably took up half of the floor. What must a place like this cost?

The music grew louder as we approached an open door to the left, and the butler led us inside. It was a sitting room, decorated in the same sleek art deco style of the foyer and what I had seen of the rest of the flat. A cloud of bluish smoke hung in the air.

There was a man in a black brocade dressing gown lounging on a sofa, folded newspaper in one hand, cigarette in the other.

"Major Ramsey to see you, sir." The butler nearly had to shout to be heard over the music, but the disapproval in his tone came through loudly enough.

Nico Lazaro glanced up from his newspaper then rose with a sort of indolent elegance, tossing the newspaper aside. He sauntered to the gramophone on the table near the window and turned it down, though not off, and stubbed out his cigarette in a jade ashtray.

Only then did he turn to us. His dark eyes swept over me first, and I recognized the practiced assessment of a first-class lecher. So he was that sort, was he? Our naked friend in the foyer ought to have been the first clue. I remembered just in time to keep my expression bland, my eyes slightly averted.

"Ramsey," he said then, turning his attention to the major. "Good to see you again, old boy. How is your uncle? I haven't seen him in town lately."

"He's well," Major Ramsey said. I noticed he did not return the pleasantry, nor volunteer any additional information about his uncle, the Earl of Overbrook.

While the gentlemen were exchanging greetings, I took the opportunity to study Mr. Lazaro a bit more closely. He was probably around forty but contrived to look younger with his bronzed skin and jet-black hair. He was undeniably attractive, but in a way I found distasteful. He was too sleek, too polished; there was an air of insincerity about him. I could see why Major Ramsey didn't like him.

"Thank you for agreeing to see me today," the major was saying. "I won't take much of your time; I merely want to ask you a few questions. I've brought my secretary along to take notes."

"By all means." He gestured to the pair of chairs across from the sofa. "Have a seat, will you?"

He returned to the sofa and sat, crossing one leg over the other. He reached toward the black enamel box on the glass table between us and flipped it open. "Cigarette?" he asked, his dark eyes on me.

"No, thank you."

"Major?"

"No."

He reached for a book of matches then, striking one. "So tiresome, matches. But my lighter was among the things stolen. A pretty thing, gold with my initials engraved on it."

He lit a cigarette for himself, waving out the match before tossing it into the ashtray, then sat back against the sofa. Only then did I notice the paintings behind his head. Framed in brass, they were both portraits of naked women. Though these two looked much less at ease than the woman in the foyer, their bodies strangely contorted and disproportioned. Picassos, I realized.

His gaze followed mine, and he grinned. "Admiring my ladies, are you?" he said. "You have good taste, Miss . . ."

"Donaldson," I said, giving him my usual alias.

"I don't know if you've heard of him, but Picasso is rather popular in Paris. Or was, before the Germans marched in. I don't suppose he's particularly lauded at the moment. They're not fond of *deviants*." He grinned. "I'm glad I got my hands on these."

I smiled but did not comment. I knew all about Picasso; one of Uncle Mick's art forger friends had made a pretty penny off his work in recent years.

It occurred to me that any thief worth his salt would have recognized the value of these pieces. They weren't particularly large, and why not take them if they would take a vase?

"Will you tell me about what happened here on the day in question?" Major Ramsey asked, taking control of the conversation.

Mr. Lazaro looked at him and sighed, expelling a cloud of thick smoke. "It's all so tedious. I don't hold out much hope that the police will be able to do anything."

"Nevertheless, we're interested in your story." The patience in his tone sounded a bit more fragile than what he'd had with Madame Arnaud. I had the impression that Mr. Lazaro would not be treated with the same kid gloves.

"I had seven others here for dinner." He rattled off their names, his emphasis on them indicating they were important people, and I dutifully noted them down. My shorthand was a bit rusty, but I remembered it well enough. And, anyway, I didn't think we would need the notes.

"We were having boeuf bourguignon. I was able to acquire enough for a dinner party, though I don't like to advertise the fact that our menu was a bit extravagant, if you catch my drift."

Black-market goods, he meant. There was a thriving black market now that food and other rationed items were scarce. Those who were able to get supplies sold them at greatly increased prices, and, as a lot of people were more than willing to pay, they were making a great deal of money. We knew a few people who were benefiting from such a scheme.

Nacy disapproved of taking more than our fair share of the available commodities, however, so we had thus far made do with our ration coupons. Of course, we hadn't had the Earl and Countess of Whatsit for dinner.

"I do hope you won't report that bit," he said with a smile that told us it wouldn't matter if we did.

"I'm not interested in what you had for dinner." It seemed the major's patience was slipping.

"It was very good boeuf bourguignon."

I could sense Major Ramsey mustering his tolerance, probably because he'd done the same thing with me on multiple occasions. "Did you notice anything in particular about their appearance?" he asked.

"I've told all of this to the police," Lazaro said.

"Of course, but you'll recall that I'm not with the police," Major Ramsey replied.

Lazaro smiled. "No, of course. I sometimes forget that I can share more with someone in your position. I've become accustomed to saying as little as possible except to my closest confidants."

There was a slightly sly gleam in his eyes as he said the words, but I couldn't quite determine if he meant something by them or if that was just how he naturally looked.

"You can rest assured that anything you tell me will be kept in confidence as far as matters go," the major said in a tight voice. He had given up on trying to hide his annoyance.

"There were three men. They wore masks. They were all of average height and build, nothing special worth marking. Though, I'll admit, I had other things on my mind at the moment." His eyes slid to me. "I wanted to keep my female guests safe. They were, I'm sure you can imagine, rather terrified."

I gave him a bland smile.

"As I've just mentioned to you, I had some very important guests. It would never do for something to happen to them in my home. Needless to say, there was quite the variety of responses to an armed robbery at one of my dinner parties."

He was talking a great deal without saying much, and I had the distinct impression he was hiding something.

I found my mind wandering, even as I jotted down notes about his guests' reactions to the robbery. They were all fair maidens in need of a man to save them, and Mr. Lazaro had cast himself in the role of knight in shining armor, though it didn't seem to me he had done much in the way of bravery.

"Did they speak with any discernible accents?" Major Ramsey cut in at last.

Mr. Lazaro took another drag of his cigarette as he considered. "I assumed they were English. The accents were not foreign enough to draw notice. But, now that you mention it, there was a hint of some other accent, I believe. Not enough that I could tell you what it was."

This was not surprising. Especially not if they had been German agents masquerading as English robbers.

"You were in Lisbon recently, I believe," Major Ramsey said.

It seemed to me that Mr. Lazaro's gaze sharpened ever so slightly, but he took a careless drag of his cigarette. "Yes. I had some diplomatic business there. Rather a lot of excitement in Lisbon these days."

"So I've heard," Major Ramsey said. "I will not, of course, ask you to reveal the nature of your diplomatic work, but was there anything else of interest that happened while you were there?"

"Not worth noting," Lazaro said with a smile.

"And you brought nothing back with you that may have . . . attracted interest?"

Lazaro shrugged. "Nothing of a sensitive nature. I bought some art. I always buy art when I'm in Lisbon. There is a great deal of it to be had as of late. Families that have left their countries behind and hope to be rid of unwieldy items before relocating to America or other far-flung places. The market for art is rather good."

He was taking advantage of the desperation of others for his own gain, was what he meant.

I realized suddenly that, as I had robbed the safes of people who had fled London for the safety of the country, I couldn't exactly judge him. I was surprised at the guilt that assailed me at the thought. Had I come so far from my prior life? I didn't know how to feel about the vast distance between then and now.

"And were any of those items stolen during the robbery?" Major Ramsey asked this so casually that it seemed as if he wasn't the least bit interested. I was watching Lazaro carefully but could see no hint of anything telling in his features as he answered. In fact, I found myself skeptical of his careless manner.

"No, those pieces weren't here at the time. I hadn't had them picked up yet. In fact, the crate arrived only a little before you did.

I haven't even sorted through everything yet." He smiled. "I find I don't often get much work done before late afternoon."

I coughed suddenly. The men both turned to look at me. Mr. Lazaro looked solicitous, Major Ramsey coldly suspicious.

"I'm sorry," I said, still coughing. "I seem . . . to . . ." Cough. ". . . have something . . ." Cough. ". . . in my throat. Will you excuse me to find a drink of water?"

"I'll ring for Cheevers to bring it," Mr. Lazaro said.

"Oh, no. Please don't trouble him," I said, rising. I could feel Major Ramsey's gaze on me and refused to meet it. "I'll just find a glass of water myself."

"Miss Donaldson—" Major Ramsey began.

I threw in another few coughs to drown him out. "Excuse me."

With an apologetic smile amidst the coughs, and ignoring the daggers the major's eyes were no doubt shooting at me, I hurried from the room.

CHAPTER NINE

Out of the sitting room, I moved in the direction of the dark hallway that led farther into the flat, remembering to cough occasionally in case they could still hear me.

I pulled the pick from my pocket as I slipped into the shadows. It was Uncle Mick who had trained me to always carry my tools with me. *You never know when you might need them, Ellie girl.* It had proved useful on more than one occasion.

I probably didn't have long. Mr. Lazaro struck me as sharper than he gave the appearance of being. He was louche and cavalier, but that sort of persona made an effective diplomat. After all, when one isn't taken seriously, one is much more likely to learn things.

There was also the danger of running into staff. Thus far I hadn't seen anyone other than the disapproving butler, Cheevers, but I suspected there were more employees about somewhere. At least a maid or two for Lazaro to harass.

I didn't hear anyone as I slipped down the hall, trying doors as I went. There was nothing much interesting in the first two. They were both bedrooms, unused ones by the look of it. There were blackout curtains on the windows, so they were dark, but everything seemed untouched. If I were a thief—well, technically I was, but if I were a thief robbing this house—I'd pass these rooms by.

There was a bathroom, all marble and brass. I turned on the tap to give the illusion of getting myself a glass of water to calm my cough.

Then I slipped back into the hall. Another bedroom. This one seemed to be Lazaro's, from the overwhelming smell of cigarette smoke and aftershave hanging in the air. It would be the best place to find out more about our host, and I debated a quick look around, but that wasn't the focus of my search, and time was of the essence.

I encountered a locked door at the end of the hall, which I hoped was the right one. Inserting the pick into the lock, I was in within a few seconds. I slipped inside and closed the door behind me before switching on a light.

It was indeed an office of sorts. There was a large desk scattered with papers, shelves stacked with books, and not one but two telephones on the desk. It struck me that I had been correct about Mr. Lazaro. I suspected he cultivated his disreputable appearance. Not that I'd trust him to keep his hands to himself in a dark room.

The crate he had spoken of was sitting on the floor on one side of the desk. The cover had been prized off but was still resting atop the box at an angle.

I moved quickly to the crate and shifted the heavy lid slightly to the side. It was, I realized to my dismay, filled with large, wrapped items. There could be any number of things in here that might be the object the thieves were looking for, and I didn't know where to start.

There certainly wasn't time to go through them all now.

I wondered if now might be the time to level with Lazaro, but that would be up to the major. He would know better than I did whether we could trust the man enough to take him into our confidence. Somehow, I had the impression that the answer would be no.

If so, I would need much more time to break in and get a good look at the contents of the crate. Taking just a moment, I shifted some of the cloth as best as I could without disturbing it too much.

There were at least three paintings as well as what seemed to be some kind of bust. Likely of a buxom woman, knowing Mr. Lazaro.

I didn't think the Germans would be interested in any of this art, not to the extent that they'd stage a burglary to steal it. Could the item, whatever it was, conceivably be hidden inside something else? It was a possibility to consider.

I left the crate as I had found it. Cracking open the door to be certain the coast was clear, I slipped out of the office, locking the door behind me, and made my way back toward the sitting room.

I could hear Lazaro still talking as I approached. Major Ramsey was answering in monosyllables.

I came back into the room with another apologetic smile. "I'm so sorry," I said. "I don't know what came over me. The cold weather has left my throat in such a state."

The major's flinty eyes narrowed. I was in for a scolding, but it wouldn't be the first time.

"I think we've taken up enough of your time," said the major, turning back to Mr. Lazaro. "Thank you for seeing us."

He rose and Mr. Lazaro rose with him, stubbing out his cigarette. His eyes flickered to me. "It was my pleasure to see you."

I cast my eyes down like a proper little secretary and prepared to follow the major from the room.

Mr. Lazaro's voice stopped me, however. "Miss Donaldson."

I turned.

"I'd love to see you again," he said. "You have rather exquisite proportions, if you don't mind my saying so."

"Lazaro . . ." Major Ramsey began.

Mr. Lazaro held up a hand. "Yes, yes, I know. One must observe the proprieties . . . especially with secretaries." His eyes met mine. "But you are not *my* secretary, Miss Donaldson."

Under other circumstances, I would have told him what I really thought of his tactless overtures. Instead, however, I offered a semi-encouraging smile. We wanted to keep him on our side, after all.

"I'm having a party on Saturday night at nine o'clock. Can't let the blighters win, after all. I'd love it if you could come."

"Come along, Miss Donaldson," the major said, taking my arm. He was doing a good job feigning just the right amount of jealousy. It would work with Lazaro, I realized. He enjoyed annoying people, and so the major had not bothered to hide his annoyance. Major Ramsey really was frightfully good at this sort of thing.

Mr. Lazaro chuckled like a practiced lothario and called out, "Pencil me in to your calendar."

I glanced over my shoulder at him, then made a show of flipping open my notebook and writing it down. Lazaro grinned at me.

Major Ramsey's grip on my arm tightened and he led me from the room.

Major Ramsey said nothing as we left the flat and took the lift back down to the gleaming lobby. I could, however, feel the irritation wafting off him like steam from a teacup. Whether it was directed at Mr. Lazaro or at me, I wasn't sure, though I suspected it might be a bit of both.

As we stepped outside, I got my share of it.

"I distinctly told you before we came into this building . . ." he began.

"I know," I told him. "But I couldn't resist the opportunity. It was clear he wasn't going to care about my absence, so I thought I should make a go of it."

"I don't know how many times I need to tell you to follow orders."

"Oh, don't be cross with me," I said, feeling conciliatory rather than provoking for once.

He looked over at me, and I could see the sternness of his face softening ever so slightly. He was used to my fighting him; I had caught him off guard with my change of tactics. I would have to remember this strategy in the future.

"Did you find something?" he asked.

I smiled. "There was an open crate in his office with several art pieces inside. But there were too many things for me to look at any of them thoroughly. I was concerned about being caught."

"Oh, were you? I was under the impression you thought you can do whatever you please with no consequence."

I frowned at him.

We reached the car, and he pulled the door open for me.

"Don't you think we could ask him to look at the objects?" I asked, when he had gone around to his side and slid in beside me.

"I had considered it," Major Ramsey said. "But I'm not entirely sure we can trust him."

"He's a lecher, of course," I said. "But you don't suppose he's spying for the Germans? After all, if he had whatever object they wanted, he could just hand it over to them."

"Perhaps. But I still don't know that we should lay our cards on the table. His mother was Italian. There's been some talk that he may have sympathies that lean that way. One thing about Lazaro, he's smarter than he looks."

"I don't doubt it."

"He does an excellent job of appearing useless, but he has a reputation within diplomatic circles of a man who gets things done. And in the business world, he's somewhat cutthroat. His nightclub is perhaps the most successful in the city after the De Lora clubs."

I knew he meant Leon De Lora, the American gangster. He'd opened a series of London nightclubs over the past decade, all of them a roaring success.

My family had never had much to do with members of the organized crime rackets, but Uncle Mick had played cards with some of De Lora's men over the years and said they were good enough fellows for rough American hoodlums. I felt an odd bit of pride by association that Lazaro's nightclub was not quite as popular.

Another thought occurred to me. "Do you think Lazaro is

using his position as both a diplomat and nightclub owner to engage in espionage?" I asked. "The nightclub would be an excellent place to exchange information."

"I wouldn't put it past him, but only if the profit was substantial," the major said. "Nico Lazaro is not the sort of man to do anything that requires much effort."

"You disapprove of people who have too much fun, I think," I said. "You must remember that not everyone is as seriously minded as you."

"I don't expect people to think as I do," he said. "But clearly you can see that he's . . . not a man of high moral character."

I bit back a laugh and pretended to consider. "Yes. Although, one would think a man who claims to be so successful with women would not need quite so many naked images of them scattered about his house."

Major Ramsey shot a disapproving look at me, but I was certain there was a gleam of amusement in his eyes. He was not quite as prim and proper as he pretended to be.

"Well, perhaps his scandalous reputation will prove useful, too. He's taken a liking to me, it seems," I said. "That party would be an excellent opportunity to look around a bit more."

Major Ramsey turned to me, his features set. "That may well be, but you're not going to attend it. You will not interact with him on your own."

"Is that an order, Major Ramsey?"

"If it needs to be," he answered tersely.

He was not in the mood to be teased, it seemed. Well, we would argue about my attendance at the party if the need arose.

"Did you learn anything of value from him while I was out of the room?" I asked.

"He didn't confide in me his reason for being in Lisbon, but I have the feeling it was not related to the robbery. However, I'm certain he's hiding something."

"I had the same impression," I said. "Do you suppose he knows what they're looking for?"

"It wouldn't surprise me. He overdid his bafflement as to why they would choose to rob him a bit. As if a flat of priceless objects and a room full of people wearing valuable jewelry wasn't enough to commit a robbery."

"So, what now?" I asked.

He appeared to consider. "I'm going to speak with Colonel Radburn in the morning. I'll contact you when I've determined next steps."

It was unlike him to be working so closely with his superiors. He had always seemed to have been kept on a very loose lead in our other operations. Were they watching over him more carefully now that he had been injured? I knew he would chafe if wrapped too tightly in cotton wool. I had already seen how much he resented his sister's fussing.

"Is there anything I can do in the meantime?" I asked.

"You can consider if there are any of your connections who might have heard something about this. Perhaps your uncle can find out something."

I nodded. The thought had already occurred to me, and I had an idea of where I might go for information.

CHAPTER TEN

Pony Peavey was a local gambling den owner and a fellow of what one might call all-around ill repute. He had a rough reputation, and he'd never been amongst the circle of acquaintances that Uncle Mick considered friends. But we operated in the same general area, and our paths had crossed, professionally speaking, on a few occasions.

It seemed to me that Pony was the ideal person to ask about the men we were looking for. He had runners in every area of the city, and he dealt in information as much as he did in the illegal drugs he sold to the gamblers in his club. If one wanted to know what was going on in some area of the criminal underworld in London, one usually had to go only as far as Pony's Place in Harrow.

I did not, of course, relate this idea to Major Ramsey. I knew Pony well enough to know he wouldn't take kindly to my bringing a government man along to his establishment. And, despite his telling me I should speak to my contacts, I knew Major Ramsey well enough to know that he would not want me going around alone asking questions at a place like Pony's.

And so it was best that I kept the whole business to myself for the time being.

Major Ramsey left me with few parting words, as he was wont

to do when he was in a bad humor. He hadn't enjoyed dealing with Nico Lazaro; I, on the other hand, was secretly pleased that he had been annoyed at Mr. Lazaro's flirting with me.

I went home, but Nacy was at the shops and Uncle Mick was out on a job, so I scribbled a note that I would be home for dinner and left it on the kitchen table. I didn't tell them where I was off to. With any luck, I would be home before them and able to retrieve the note before they even saw it.

Uncle Mick might have been the most logical choice to go and visit Pony Peavey, but I thought I might have more luck finding out what I wanted to know. Pony would be wary of Uncle Mick, but he had known me since I was young and was the sort of bloke who wouldn't expect a young woman to have ulterior motives. There was a chance I could charm him into telling me something.

I held no illusions he'd be interested in helping for the sake of pure altruism, whether we were fighting a war or not. Pony was not the sentimental type, and the sort of business he ran could function just as well in wartime as in any other time. Better, perhaps. I had no doubt wartime produced a thriving market for drugs.

These unsavory thoughts aside, Pony was the best person I could think of to help me locate the men we were looking for. I had to hope that he would be in an obliging sort of mood.

I bundled back up and went out again into the frigid afternoon air.

I took the Tube, glad to be out of the cold wind for a short while. I will not say that, as the train trundled toward Harrow, I didn't have a few qualms about the errand I was on. Pony was a rough customer, and the type of men who hung about his establishment were nothing to write home about either. But if I could get answers, it would be worth the small risk. Besides, Uncle Mick's own reputation as a man not to be crossed would provide me with an added bit of protection.

It was approaching sunset as I came out from the Underground

tunnel and began walking in the direction of Pony's. Looking up at
the orange-and-pink-streaked sky, I hoped the Germans avoided
London again tonight. I didn't wish the bombs on anyone else, but
I was also immeasurably glad that the bombs had ceased to fall every
night. It was difficult to state the impact being bombed for nearly
two months straight had on morale. In one sense, we had rallied tre-
mendously and withstood everything that they threw at us. We were
strong, and they hadn't been able to break us. But even unbroken
objects could wear down under constant strain.

Pony's establishment wasn't so much a pub as it was an underground gambling den. It could have existed a hundred years ago,
the dissolute sons of wealthy families looking to spend an evening
and a few pounds of their inherited money slumming it amongst
the lower orders.

There was still something of the same atmosphere now, though
it was mostly the lower orders that had won out. You didn't see too
many swells at Pony's Place.

It was, as it had been for years, in the cellar of an old haberdasher's shop that had gone out of business. The building had a
deserted, derelict look about it, which suited its purposes fine. As
Pony was running an illegal gambling establishment, along with assorted other criminal dealings, it was just as well that the building
called no attention to its occupants or their movements.

It had occurred to me on the Tube that there was the possibility
the building had been lost in the bombings. If that was the case, I'd
have to ask around to try to locate Pony.

As I rounded the corner of the street, however, I saw the place
was still standing, though there were two other buildings on the
street that had been reduced to rubble. The thought crossed my
mind—uncharitably, perhaps—that if anyone's building deserved
to be razed to the ground, it was probably Pony's. But fate didn't
play favorites, and neither did Luftwaffe bombs.

I gave four sharp raps, the standard signal if I remembered

correctly, on the tarnished brass knocker on the front door of the haberdasher's shop. It was opened a moment later by a redheaded woman I didn't recognize. She nodded an indifferent greeting and moved back to the chair where she had been sitting, a glass of amber liquid and a game of solitaire laid out on a battered wooden table.

Those in the know required no directions, and it seemed I had passed the first test.

I moved through the shop, past the shelves that still held out-of-fashion hats, now bedecked with dust and cobwebs, toward the door in the back that had once led to a stockroom. There were shelves in that room, too, piled with moldering hatboxes. Another shelf held hatless wooden mannequin heads with peeling painted faces, looking out on the proceedings with weary disapproval. The stories those ladies could tell would fill a book, I was sure.

To one side of the stockroom was a heavy wooden door, behind which was the rickety staircase that led down to the cellar where Pony Peavey held court.

Evening was coming on, and I knew there would be a decent crowd in the place. Nightlife may have gone dim in London, but that didn't mean it had died out. Even Felix and I had been to a nightclub on a couple of occasions, dancing and enjoying the music, despite the ever-present threat of enemy bombs.

So much had changed that I didn't blame anyone for trying to go on as normally as possible.

I pulled open the door and descended into the thick atmosphere of cigar smoke and liquor fumes. Pony was here, then. He had smoked those foul-smelling cigars for as long as I had known him. Not that I minded the smell of a good cigar, but these were clearly cheap. The odor reminded me of burning rubbish, and they were strong enough to override the dozens of cigarettes being smoked in the same vicinity.

The cellar was bigger than one might have imagined, given

the size of the building above, stretching back into shadowy corners where barrels and crates were stacked. There had been no concessions made to décor. The walls were grime-streaked brick, and several tables were scattered about with unmatched chairs. A long, well-stocked bar stood against one wall, the wide array of gleaming bottles being the only hint of the sort of good money Pony pulled in.

In one corner, at a lopsided old piano, an elderly gentleman was playing an indifferent jazz tune.

It wasn't yet time for the night crowd, but there were, as I had expected, several people already here playing cards, and no one paid me much mind as I reached the bottom of the steps.

I knew Pony and his closest associates always sat at a table in the corner, and I made my way in that direction. Sure enough, he was seated there with two other men, cards spread on the table before them, pint glasses of ale already drained to bubbles despite the fact it was too early for dinner.

Pony Peavey was a big man, tall and broad, with a wide face from which flashed watchful dark eyes. The ever-present cigar was clamped between yellowed teeth. He noticed me before I reached the table.

"Ellie McDonnell," he said with a crooked grin. "What brings you to my fine establishment?"

"How are you, Pony?" I said. "I've come for a favor."

He chuckled, expelling a cloud of smoke. "I like a girl who's straight to the point."

"I thought you might." I moved to the table, pulled out a chair for myself from a nearby table, and took a seat, as it was clear none of the men intended to offer me one. "I need to know if you've heard anything about the burglary at that swell's flat in Mayfair. Nico Lazaro's his name."

He eyed me shrewdly, and I knew he was inwardly assessing the reason for my interest. I let him ponder. I wasn't going to volunteer any more information than necessary.

"I heard about it," he said at last.

"Do you have any idea who might have done it?"

"I've been wondering about that myself," he said. There was little expression in his tone, but I understood from the words that he wasn't happy about it. Pony was a man who liked to be in the know, and, if he was in the dark about it, it was another hint that we might be dealing with out-of-towners.

"I heard they busted in during his dinner party, bold as brass," I said, hoping to get him talking. "They must've planned it that way so they could steal from all the guests."

"Didn't take much in the way of valuables." The rough, low voice came unexpectedly from the man beside me. I looked over at him, but his eyes were on his cards. One side of his face was badly scarred by what looked like the remnants of a broken bottle in some long-ago bar fight. "And none of the uncles I know have seen any of the goods."

Uncle was an old slang term for a pawnbroker. If the thieves weren't attempting to off-load the valuables they'd stolen, it was yet another sign that the robbery was meant to hide other motivations.

I glanced at Pony, wondering if he would be displeased that his associates were talking to me, but he was motioning to a buxom barmaid in a low-cut dress to come and refill his glass.

"Not even Sooty?" I asked the scarred man beside me, referring to Sooty Smythe, a local pawnbroker who was well known as the person to see about fencing stolen goods.

"No, and he's the first bloke they'd go to, if they was local."

"Word is they were using Lugers," the man across the table said as he fished a pack of cigarettes from his pocket.

"German guns?" I asked casually.

"Not impossible to come by, of course. But an interesting choice." Just before the cigarette reached his lips, he remembered his manners and offered it to me. I didn't relish it given the state of his fingernails, but, in the spirit of things, I accepted it. The fellow beside me struck a match and lit it for me. His knuckles were more scarred than his face.

"Interesting indeed," I said, inhaling deeply before blowing out a stream of smoke. It was a cheap brand, but at least it didn't taste like Pony's cigars smelled.

"What would a group of stickup men with German guns be looking for at some toff's dinner party?" I mused.

Pony had taken a deep drink of his ale, but as he set the mug back down on the table his dark eyes came back up to me. "What's all this to you, Ellie?"

"I came here to get information, Pony, not give it." I flashed a smile at him to soften the words, but I didn't intend to give him any more information than that.

He chuckled. "You're your uncle's girl, all right. Never met a fellow could keep his lips tighter than Mick McDonnell."

I nodded, still smiling, then examined the tip of my cigarette as I asked casually, "Do you suppose, if you do learn something, you can let me know?"

Pony didn't say anything for a long moment. Then he motioned, and a man stepped out of the shadows and came toward him. It occurred to me that a lot of Pony's associates had a similar look: like you might not want to run across them in a dark alley.

"There's a card game over at Red's tonight," he said to the man. "I want you to go. Ask around. See what else you can find out about the stickup at Nico Lazaro's in Mayfair last week."

Red's, I knew from vague talk I had heard, was a pub that even I wouldn't have dared to venture to, where the worst sorts in London congregated. I was gratified that the information wheel was already beginning to turn on my behalf.

The man nodded and left without comment.

I smiled at Pony. "Thank you."

He smiled back. "You know I don't give anything away free, Ellie. I don't suppose you'll mind owing me a favor now."

It wasn't unexpected, but I didn't like the idea of owing Pony Peavey anything. Still, what else could I do?

I nodded. "Fair enough."

The week was putting me rather in debt as far as favors went.

I stubbed out my cigarette in the overflowing ashtray at the center of the table and rose from my seat. I nodded at the men before turning back to Pony. "I look forward to hearing from you."

He raised his glass in salute. "Always a pleasure, love."

CHAPTER ELEVEN

I made it home before dark, but not in time to prevent Nacy from seeing the note I'd left. Luckily, she was too preoccupied with cooking dinner to ask many questions.

She did wrinkle her nose as I peeked over her shoulder to see the contents of the pot. "Where have you been, dear? You smell like burnt rubbish."

"Hard to escape smoke these days, Nacy," I said lightly. "I'll just go take a bath before dinner."

"Yes, you've plenty of time," she said, sifting through the spices in her cupboard. "This will be another three-quarters of an hour at least." Nacy had taken rationing as her own personal battlefront, and thus far she had marshaled her troops into winning every engagement.

I went off to my flat and bathed away the smoke. Unfortunately, this meant washing my hair, and my hair freshly washed was about as manageable as wild horses.

I was sitting before my mirror in my robe, ruthlessly brushing out the last of the tangles, when there was a familiar rap at the front door.

I knew at once who it must be. Even if I hadn't recognized the pattern of the knock, there were few people who would be at my door at this hour.

I tossed the brush onto the dressing table and hurried across the flat.

"Who is it?" I called through the door, as a precaution.

"A tall, dark, and handsome stranger," came the reply.

As I suspected.

I unlocked the door and pulled it open. Felix stood on the doorstep, his outline silhouetted by the last pale blue hues of twilight.

"Hello, my lovely," he said. He came inside and pushed the door closed with his foot as he took me into his arms. He was cold, all of him. His coat, his face, his lips against mine.

"You're freezing," I said as I finally pulled back. "Let me make you some tea."

"That sounds wonderful."

I went into my little kitchen and put the kettle on the hob as Felix discarded his coat and muffler and moved to take his usual seat on my sofa.

"Just let me go and make myself decent," I said as I came out of the kitchen, remembering I was still in my robe. "And then you can tell me about your trip."

His eyes ran over me, and I saw the glint in them right before he grinned at me. "Don't put on clothes on my account."

I shot him a look and turned toward the bedroom. "I won't be a moment."

"Do you need any assistance?"

"I can manage, thank you."

I left the bedroom door open a crack so I could talk to him as I pulled on a green double-knit dress and a heavy jumper. "Nacy has dinner nearly ready. She and Uncle Mick will be glad to see you."

"I was hoping there would be a dinner invitation. I'm half-starved, in addition to being frozen clean through."

"It's so much worse when the sun sets, even as little sun as there's been. You could have come to see me in the morning."

"I didn't want to wait. Besides, the weather here is practically balmy compared to what it was in Scotland," he said. "I thought I might have to shovel a tunnel to get to the train station."

"When did you get back?"

"Just this afternoon," he said. "I had a few things I had to tend to, and then I came right to you."

"I'm glad," I said, coming back into the living room. "I've missed you."

"I've missed you, too."

He smiled up at me, and I realized again how handsome Felix was. He was tall and suave and elegant, with his slick dark hair and thin mustache in the style of Douglas Fairbanks, Jr., or Laurence Olivier. His brown eyes were always warm when they looked at me, but there were also the flashes of mischief that lurked just below the surface, ready to spring out at a moment's notice as they had when he'd suggested he help me dress.

I took a seat on the sofa, and he reached out and took my hand in his, giving me a gentle tug. "You're much too far away."

I moved closer, leaning into his side, and he slipped an arm around me. It felt comfortable to be close to him. Safe. When I wasn't with Felix, I sometimes had doubts about the depth of my feelings for him, but when we were together, everything felt so very easy.

Oh, I know girls generally like the thrill of romance, the heart-racing uncertainties that come with new relationships, but I think we sometimes underestimate the appeal of being so completely secure with someone. Felix and I were the same in so many ways; we understood each other. There was attraction there, too, of course, but it often felt more relaxed than urgent. And in this moment, when I was tired from a long day, I relished the cozy security of his arm around me.

I leaned my head against his shoulder with a little sigh, and he turned to kiss my forehead. "Everything all right?"

"Yes," I said. "I'm just glad you're back."

"Me, too. I should be home for at least a fortnight this time," he said.

I knew I needed to press him about what was going on in Scotland, but I couldn't bring myself to do it, not now. After the uncertainty of the past few days, I only wanted to enjoy being near him.

So we just sat close together on the sofa, talking about superficial things, until the kettle began to whistle.

I went to the kitchen to get the tea-things and returned with a little tray with cups for both of us.

"Rather nice that Jerry gave us a break over the holiday, wasn't it?" he said. "I'm sure you were glad not to have to descend to the cellars every night at dusk."

"Do you think they'll start up again as bad as before?" I asked. I knew on a practical level that it was likely but I'd been trying not to think too much about it.

"Perhaps not," Felix said, lying gallantly for my sake. "Perhaps they've realized it's not going to do them any good and will only make half-hearted efforts from here on out."

I smiled at his assurances. "Let's pretend so. At least for tonight."

We settled back onto the sofa with our tea, and I told him about the recent job Uncle Mick and I had done at the shop and some of the news from the neighborhood.

I didn't tell him about the job I was working on with Major Ramsey. Official Secrets Act aside, Felix didn't like the major, and there was no sense in spoiling his mood.

"Have you given any thought to that other matter?" he asked as he took a sip of the steaming tea.

I knew exactly what "other matter" he meant. He was talking about my father's involvement in espionage.

I appreciated his careful way of inquiring, giving me the opportunity to push the topic away if I didn't feel up to discussing it. But I needed to talk about it with someone, and I had been feeling his absence as my closest confidant keenly.

"I may have discovered something," I told him. I related the discovery I'd made in the trunk in the cellar and the step I'd taken in asking Mr. Frank Doyle to see if he could decipher the code.

"I'm half afraid he won't be able to crack it and half afraid he will," I said. "I don't know what I want."

Felix squeezed my hand. "You know I'm with you, sweet. Whatever way the wind blows."

"I know," I said, looking into his warm, dark eyes. "Thank you, Felix. I suppose it's just that, in some ways, it would be easier if I never have to know."

"There's a reason they say ignorance is bliss."

I nodded. "I never really appreciated the truth of that until now. But it's also occurred to me that, if my father *was* involved in some sort of espionage, whoever killed him might still be working for Germany now. Perhaps living and spying in this country."

"It's been almost a quarter of a century," he pointed out.

"Yes. You're probably right. All the same, everything is complicated by the fact that we're at war with Germany again. If I go digging too far, I might end up in over my head."

He set his teacup down, his eyes on it rather than on me. "Have you considered talking to Ramsey about it?"

He asked this casually, but there was a note in his voice I could not quite interpret. He and the major had never got on, and, at least on Felix's side, that was mostly to do with me. Felix was exceptionally perceptive, even when it came to strangers, so it was not at all surprising he had sensed the undertow of attraction that existed in my relationship with Major Ramsey. He'd recognized it even before I'd been willing to admit it to myself.

Which made his suggesting that I confide in Major Ramsey seem a very sweet gesture. But I didn't want Ramsey to know about this. I didn't want to give him any excuse for getting rid of me—and my being the daughter of a possible German spy was a particularly good excuse.

"No," I said. "I don't want him to know about this."

"Why not?" he asked, turning to look at me.

"I . . . it's . . . I don't . . ." I faltered, trying to put it into words without confessing to Felix exactly how complicated my feelings for the major had become.

"He could probably find out for you," Felix was saying. "I'm sure there would be files somewhere that he has access to, if your father really was spying for Germany."

"Perhaps," I agreed. "I just don't think I want to share it with him right now."

"It's your decision, of course," he said, reaching into his pocket for his cigarette case. He put a cigarette in his mouth and flicked on his lighter. The tip of the cigarette flared to life and Felix took a deep drag. "I think it's a waste of a good resource."

"I'll think about it," I said, rising from the sofa. "In the meantime, we'd better go to the house. Nacy will be cross if she has to come out in the cold to fetch us."

It was still dark when I was roused from slumber by a tap on my bedroom door.

"Ellie?" It was Uncle Mick's voice.

I sat up, instantly awake. He wouldn't be at my door in the middle of the night if it wasn't important. There hadn't been any sirens, so it must be something else. Was it Nacy?

These thoughts crossed my mind in the space of an instant as I tumbled out of bed, grabbed my robe, and hurried into the sitting room.

"What's wrong?" I asked, sweeping my hair out of my face.

"It's all right, love," he said gently. "I'm sorry to wake you up, but there's a bloke at the house looking for you."

"What?" I asked, still trying to get my head on straight. If I hadn't been half-asleep, I might have noticed Uncle Mick's searching gaze before he spoke his next words.

"There's a fellow come to the door saying Pony Peavey sent him." His tone was mild, but his expression told me that I was going to owe him an explanation.

"Oh," I said, rubbing a hand across my eyes. My brain was finally beginning to catch up with my body, and I realized that Pony must have already discovered something about the robbery at Nico Lazaro's flat. That had been quick work.

"What's this all about, Ellie?" Uncle Mick asked.

"It's to do with my new job with the major," I said, hoping that explanation would suffice for now. Grown woman or not, I didn't relish being in my uncle's bad graces.

"And I suppose that's all you'll be telling me for the time being."

I gave him an apologetic look. "You know how it is, Uncle Mick."

"Aye, love. I know." He smiled. "Well, then. You'd better not keep the fellow waiting."

"I won't be a minute." I hurried back to my bedroom and changed into a pair of black trousers with a blouse and thick gray jumper. I didn't bother trying to manage my hair but put on a blue wool beret over it. It was freezing outside, so I might as well kill two birds with one stone.

I grabbed my coat and pulled it on as Uncle Mick and I stepped out into the frigid air. The light had the dark blue quality of early morning, and I guessed it would be perhaps an hour until dawn.

My breath came out in a cloud of white steam as I followed Uncle Mick out across the frozen garden, snow and frost crunching beneath our feet, to the front of the house.

It didn't take me long to recognize the fellow I had seen in the shadows of Pony's cellar. He stood in the shadows now, too. He was wearing a hat low on his forehead, but the slouch of his shoulders beneath his coat was identifiable.

The hat turned in my direction as we approached across the garden. He wasted neither time nor words.

"Pony says you might want to come. We've got one of the blokes you were looking for."

CHAPTER TWELVE

"You've . . . got one of the thieves?" I said, bewildered. To begin with, I hadn't even really known who we were looking for. I also didn't know how they had managed it so quickly. It had been less than twelve hours since I'd visited Pony's Place.

"He didn't come easy, but we've quieted him down. We're holding him so you can talk to him."

They'd taken the man captive, then. The idea was a bit alarming, but it was also very convenient. "All right," I said. "Thank you. I'll be there soon."

The man gave a short nod and departed, quickly disappearing into the early morning gloom.

I turned to Uncle Mick, who regarded me with a raised brow.

"I need to tell the major," I said, deciding against trying to make explanations at present. "He'll want to come with me and question the man."

"I don't know what this is all about, but Pony's boys are rough. You're likely to find your man in bad shape. I don't suppose Major Ramsey will be pleased about that."

"No," I said, taking my gloves from the pockets of my coat and pulling them on. "I don't suppose he will."

"Do you want me to go and fetch him?"

I considered it. It was tempting to send Uncle Mick on this errand, but I thought I should probably break the news to the major that Pony's men had abducted someone myself.

"Maybe you should go to Pony's and be sure they don't let the man get away . . . or worse," I said. It sounded as though they had crossed a bit of a line already.

"You're sure you'll be all right going to the major's alone?"

"Yes. I'll be fine."

"I'll go to Pony's directly, then."

I squeezed his arm. "Thank you. I'm sorry to get you involved in this, but it always makes me feel better to know you're with me."

"I'm always with you, Ellie girl."

We parted ways. I was going to have to make my way across London in the dark, but at least there hadn't been an air raid tonight. That was something.

I briefly considered telephoning the major, but I thought this would best be explained in person. And then we could make our way directly to Pony's.

The sun was edging over the horizon as I reached the major's street, and I felt like a block of solid ice.

I hadn't given it much thought before now, but I did hope he wasn't still abed. I didn't like the idea of waking him up. Given what I knew of Major Ramsey, however, he was probably up before the sun every day.

There were people moving about already, some of them on their way home from overnight jobs and some on their way to work after evenings likely spent tossing and turning, ears tuned for the air-raid sirens.

I was a few doors away, on the opposite side of the street, when movement caught my attention. I stopped, concealing myself in the shadows of a doorway, from habit more than anything else.

There was a woman leaving the major's town house. She was familiar, though I hadn't yet got a good look at her. Was it his sister? If so, she was certainly up and about early.

These thoughts passed through my mind in the space of an instant, and that was when I realized that it was not Noelle Edgemont.

It was Jocelyn Abbot, the major's former fiancée.

I watched as she got into a car, and I was certain I was not mistaken. I had met her more than once during our earlier operations.

She was leaving the major's flat, and she was wearing an evening gown beneath a long fur coat. A clear implication occurred to me: she had spent the night.

I drew in a sharp breath of cold air. I was surprised by the little jolt of dismay in my chest, the sense of loss that hit me unexpectedly like a punch to the gut.

But this was silly. I was jumping to conclusions. And, anyway, he was not mine to lose. He'd made that very clear, and our recent collaboration changed nothing.

Besides, a part of me had long suspected that he was still a little bit in love with her. He had, after all, kept her letters and the engagement ring he had intended to give her. And there had been a certain sort of strain in his eyes when he spoke of her, despite his insistence that things had ended between them long ago.

Now it looked like I might have been correct. It seemed they were involved romantically once again; what other interpretation was there for her coming out of his town house in last night's clothes?

I swallowed the lump that had formed in my throat. This was not the time for contemplation of their relationship, or my own unresolved feelings about the major. There were much more important things to think about at the moment.

Still, I hesitated. I didn't want to arrive at his door too soon and let him know that I had seen her departing.

Then I chided myself for my hesitation. Time was of the essence.

I hurried up the steps to the front door and rang the bell.

It was only a moment before the major opened the door. He'd probably assumed it was Miss Abbot, returning for something she'd forgotten, but his customary sangfroid did not desert him, even at finding me on his doorstep in disarray instead.

"Miss McDonnell. Good morning." If he was thinking what a close call it had been to my crossing paths with Miss Abbot, there was no sign of it. Then again, why should he care?

"Good morning," I said, a bit breathlessly. "I think I may have found one of the thieves."

"Come in out of the cold." He took me by the elbow and guided me into the foyer, closing the door behind us. Then he turned to face me. He was wearing his uniform shirt and trousers, but he didn't have a jacket on. It was, all things considered, one of the more informal ensembles I'd seen him in. But it was barely dawn. And it seemed he'd had company until very recently.

"Now," he said. "What do you mean you've found one of the thieves? Have you done something you oughtn't?"

I opened my mouth, but he didn't give me time to formulate a denial.

"Never mind. I'm sure you have. Just tell me what."

"I talked to a contact yesterday, like you said I should," I said, just a bit defensively. "Pony Peavey. One of his men just came to the house and said they've got one of the thieves in . . . uh, custody."

I expected questions and, likely, irritation, though he could not exactly be angry with me when I had presumably captured a vital source of information. But he only said, "Let me get my jacket."

I nodded.

I waited in the foyer, enjoying the warmth of the house after my cold walk.

I didn't think I was imagining the faint hint of perfume that hung in the air. I wondered what time Constance normally arrived. I wondered if she knew about Jocelyn Abbot.

Stop it, Ellie. It's none of your business.

He soon came walking back into the foyer with his tie on, buttoning up his uniform jacket. Then he reached around me to get his coat off the rack.

"Let's go."

I led the major back to Pony's establishment. There was a man at the front door this time, but he let us pass with only a short nod in my direction. I was expected, after all.

We went inside, through to the storeroom, and down the creaking staircase without comment from Ramsey. I had no doubt that he was taking in all the details and would have more than a few questions for me later.

The place was deserted this morning. I supposed everyone had wandered off to find a bed after a long night of cards, drinks, and . . . kidnapping, apparently.

There was a man tied to a chair in the middle of the room. Either he had put up quite a fight or Pony's men had taken liberties in their treatment of him, for his face was already bruised and there was crusted blood on his nose and lips.

I fought down my sympathy. If we were right, this man had been part of the group that had battered Anna Gillard to death in her hotel room. A bit of a beating at the hands of Pony's men was less than he deserved.

And, if he was a spy, he would face worse than this. He would eventually be tried and executed. I tried not to grimace at the thought. I knew the man was our enemy, that he had been actively working to destroy us. Nevertheless, it was hard to think about the things I was doing that were contributing to the deaths of other people.

Every action has a consequence, Uncle Mick had always told

me. And, despite what I was doing to save lives, I'd had my part in costing them, too.

It was difficult sometimes, this job. It's easy to think of the enemy as a shadowy figure until he's a man bleeding on a cellar floor.

I saw him glance at us through swollen eyes as we arrived, but he was careful to betray no particular interest. He would, I assumed, continue to pretend that he did not know what we were talking about. Pony's men would be ruthless enough to get the truth out of him, but I wasn't sure how much more effort I wanted them to put into the task.

Then again, my authority here was limited. Pony had captured this man at my request, but we were in Pony's domain, and we'd have to play by his rules.

The major glanced once at me, and then turned his attention back to Pony. He had gathered, then, who was in charge here. Now he was determining how best to move forward, what tactics would best work in our current situation. Major Ramsey, for all his posh and proper upbringing, knew how to adapt to situations as well as any criminal I'd ever known.

While the major was taking stock of Pony, Pony was taking stock of him.

"Who's your fellow, Ellie?" Pony asked me at last.

"He's . . . a colleague," I said, remembering how the major had described me to his sister.

Pony eyed the major, the gleaming buttons of his uniform. "He's not one of us."

"No," I admitted. "But that's not got anything to do with what we're doing here."

Pony didn't look convinced. He was even less inclined to like outsiders than most of our associates, and he certainly wasn't prepared to like a man in an officer's uniform.

"I'll vouch for the major. That should be good enough for you,

Pony." The voice was Uncle Mick's. I hadn't seen him where he stood, off to the side of the room.

I glanced over at him, and he gave me the slightest nod.

"Besides, we had an agreement," I said, turning back to Pony.

Pony shrugged. "Your business is your own." He made a gesture of exaggerated courtesy. "Be my guest."

I looked over at the major, ready for him to take the lead. It was not lost on me that he'd remained silent so far, letting me deal with Pony, an acknowledgment that we were not in his world but mine.

"Before we begin," he said, addressing himself to Pony. "What is this man's connection to the robbery?"

"My boys caught him at Red's, bragging about what happened at Lazaro's," Pony said. "Flashing this around."

He pulled something out of his pocket and tossed it to the major. Ramsey caught it deftly and examined it. I could see it was a gold cigarette lighter. No doubt the one with Lazaro's initials emblazoned on it.

Major Ramsey put the lighter in his pocket and stepped forward. "We need to know who you're working for."

The man glared straight ahead, said nothing.

"How many of you are there?"

The man spit blood on the floor, still refusing to meet the major's gaze.

In response, Ramsey drew up a chair before him and sat with a glance at his watch. "We have all day, of course. It makes little difference to me, all things considered, how long it takes you to talk. It may, however, make a considerable difference to you."

I looked at Major Ramsey. I had seen him in action, seen that mask of steel drop over his features, his eyes cold and hard, but it was still a bit chilling when it happened. It was a reminder that he was not afraid to do what needed to be done, and the man before us recognized that as well as I did.

He held the stubborn set to his jaw, but there was a new wariness on his features.

"Why did you kill the woman at the hotel?"

I saw a flash of what looked like genuine surprise on the man's features. "I've never killed no woman," he said.

"But you were there when it happened."

The man shook his head. "I don't know nothing about a dead woman."

"You expect me to believe that?" Major Ramsey asked mildly.

"I don't care what you believe."

"You should."

The man glowered, but I could tell he was thinking. He'd stood up well enough to the fists of Pony's boys, but it was clear that Major Ramsey was a different kind of threat.

As an intimidating interrogator, Ramsey was terribly effective, I had to admit. In addition to his imposing size, there was something very intense in his manner and the quiet voice in which he spoke.

Even knowing him as I did, I was not entirely certain he was above violence if the man didn't tell him what he wanted to know. I had to imagine that the man was much more uneasy than I was under the cold scrutiny of the major's steely gaze.

"I didn't pull the job at Lazaro's," the man said at last.

The major said nothing, nor did his expression change.

The man spit again. Pony was going to have some cleaning up to do before the place opened this evening. Then again, his clientele weren't the sort to quibble about a bit of blood on the floors.

"There was a fellow come into Red's a few nights ago, said he'd pulled a few jobs but hadn't been successful in getting what he wanted, so he was looking to hire someone local. I told them I could find someone, and they gave me the lighter, said there'd be more money when I'd come through on my end. I'm supposed to meet them Tuesday night."

Tuesday. The day after tomorrow.

Major Ramsey's brows rose expectantly as he looked at the man.

"They were looking for a yeggman."

I felt a jolt of surprise.

They wanted a safecracker.

CHAPTER THIRTEEN

Major Ramsey didn't get much more out of the man, and I suspected it was because the prisoner honestly didn't know any more than he had told us. He hadn't been a member of the original robbery gang but had been commissioned by them to locate a safecracker.

We'd got his name—Dugan—out of him, but other than that he'd insisted he had nothing else to tell. He was to bring the safecracker in question to Red's in two days' time, Tuesday evening, to meet with the group of thieves. That was a lead, though we were not as close to catching the thieves as I had hoped we might be.

It was perhaps an hour later when Ramsey, Uncle Mick, and I had made our way out of the cellar and into the chilly morning light.

"Pony continues to be as charming as ever," Uncle Mick said, breaking the silence.

"Whatever else might be said about him, he gets quick results," I replied.

"When did you come to see him?" Uncle Mick asked casually.

"Only yesterday evening."

Major Ramsey turned to me. "You came here to talk to him alone after you'd left me?"

I shrugged. "He's harmless enough."

Ramsey uttered a curse.

"I don't like it any better than you do, Major, but our Ellie's apt to do as she pleases," Uncle Mick said.

The major scowled at him. "How much has she told you?"

"Nothing. I just happened to answer the door when Pony's messenger came to the house this morning."

Ramsey nodded. "It looks as though we're going to need to bring you in on this, McDonnell."

"I take it I'm to be the yeggman."

Major Ramsey nodded. "If we can have you go with Dugan to Red's and make contact with the thieves. It would be ideal to have you in place there. Your reputation amongst this set of people will be invaluable."

"It's too dangerous," I said.

Both men turned to look at me. I realized the irony of my saying the words, but that didn't change them.

"It's not the first dangerous work I've done, lass." Uncle Mick's tone was gentle, but I caught the faint reprimand in the words.

Still, I couldn't help myself. I was afraid for him. "This isn't like one of our usual jobs, Uncle Mick. These men are spies . . . They're killers."

"I can handle myself, Ellie."

It was then Ramsey decided to make things worse. "Mr. Mc-Donnell, why don't you see your niece home and then come to my office. We'll discuss things there."

I whirled to face him, my voice rising along with my temper. "Don't you dare be high-handed with me. I will *not* be put out of the way."

There was a moment of silence, both Uncle Mick and the major trying to decide how to deal with me, no doubt.

"Miss McDonnell . . ." Ramsey began. I wanted to scream in

frustration. He always said "Miss McDonnell" in that odious way when he planned on reasoning with me.

"Ellie . . ." Uncle Mick said.

I was fairly steaming with anger by this point, but not so much that I didn't notice the major shoot Uncle Mick a speaking look.

"There's a tobacconist across the road there," Uncle Mick said suddenly. "I'll just go get a bit to fill my pipe. Won't be a moment."

And then he strode away across the road, leaving me alone with the major. I watched Uncle Mick's retreating form, my arms crossed, my teeth clenched in anger. Once again, I was being nicely pushed aside so the men could do the dangerous work.

"You know as well as I do that your uncle is the right man for this job," Major Ramsey said, as if in answer to my thoughts.

I didn't reply.

He took my arm and gently turned me to face him. "I am not putting you out of the way. But now is not the time for your interference."

My chin tipped up defiantly, and I glared up at him. "I should be in on the planning."

"And you will be. But at this stage, it's better if it's just your uncle and me. I'm asking you to trust us."

I let out an irritated breath. "It's not fair of you to put it that way."

"It's what it comes down to. Let us do what we need to do. And stay out of the way so we can do it."

I realized his hand was still on my arm, and somehow, despite my anger, I had shifted closer to him.

He realized it at the same moment I did. Our eyes caught. And then he dropped his hand.

"Tobacconist is closed. Have we decided on a plan?" Uncle Mick asked. I hadn't heard him walking up, but, admittedly, I'd been a bit distracted.

"You're going to see Miss McDonnell home and then meet me back at my office," Major Ramsey said.

"I can see myself home," I said shortly.

Perhaps it made sense for the two of them to plan without my worries distracting Uncle Mick, but I didn't like it, and I couldn't take my defeat graciously. Not yet.

Uncle Mick didn't argue. "Tell Nacy I may not be home for dinner."

I nodded. Then I turned and left them to concoct their schemes in peace.

I was still brooding that afternoon.

If I examined things dispassionately, I could understand where Ramsey was coming from. My protests and concerns for Uncle Mick's safety would not be useful to either of them. All the same, I didn't like to be left out. Especially when I was the one who had called this operation to the major's attention in the first place.

For Ramsey's part, maybe he wanted me out of it because he wanted to put distance between us. If things were growing serious again with Jocelyn Abbot, that made sense.

My thoughts were interrupted by a knock at the door. I wished it was Felix, who would quickly cheer me up, but I was accustomed to his knock, and this one had a different quality to it.

I pulled open the door and was surprised to see my friend Julia Logan standing there. I hadn't seen Julia in . . . well, I couldn't remember when I'd seen her last, but it had been months.

"Julia!" I said. "How nice to see you."

"Hello, Ellie. It's been an age, hasn't it?" she said, a bit breathless, her dark brown eyes meeting mine for a moment before darting away. "I'm sorry to drop in on you like this, but I wondered if you had a moment to talk."

"Of course," I said, opening the door to invite her in.

Julia had grown up in the neighborhood with the boys and me, but she was more than a childhood friend. Until the war had started, we had spent rather a lot of time together. As it had done so many things, the war had changed our friendship. We had drifted apart, both of us consumed by our own worries and cares, though we still spoke warmly whenever we encountered each other.

Julia was a tall girl with glossy chestnut-colored hair and big brown eyes. She had a smattering of freckles across her nose, and there was usually a smile on her lips. Today, however, she looked tense.

"Shall I put the kettle on?" I asked as she took a seat at the end of the sofa.

"Oh, no. That's not necessary. I . . . I only wanted to speak to you for a few moments."

I wondered why she was so nervous. My instincts told me there was more to this visit than a chance to catch up.

I took a seat and waited for her to tell me why she had come.

"I . . . I was seeing a fellow for a while . . ."

"Brian," I said, remembering the young man she had gone with since we were teenagers. The two of them had always been inseparable. He had enlisted as soon as the war had started, and I had the uneasy feeling she was about to tell me he had died.

A flush creeped up her face, and she wouldn't look at me. I knew then that what she was going to say was not what I had first suspected.

"No. I . . . I was seeing someone else. Brian is still on the Continent."

"I see," I said. So she'd been two-timing Brian, had she? I didn't approve of such things, but I also wasn't one to judge. I'd found that few things in life were black or white. I'd had my own bit of trouble ironing out my feelings for two men, hadn't I?

"He told me that I was free to do as I pleased, that he wouldn't hold me to our relationship," she said in a rush. "I . . . went with another fellow for a while because I was so very lonely. You know how it is."

She looked at me pleadingly, and I gave her a nod, more to urge her to continue than to agree, though I could relate to the feeling of loneliness. I missed Felix a great deal when he was away.

"So I saw this other fellow for a bit," she went on. "But then I realized how much Brian means to me. How much I love him. We . . . well, I hope we're going to be married next time he comes home."

"I'm sure you'll be very happy," I said, still not sure why she had come to see me. We had shared personal confidences over the years, but I had the impression there was more to this visit than the need to relieve her conscience.

"That's just it," she said. "I'm afraid we won't be. I realized almost at once that I had made a terrible mistake with this other fellow. He didn't mean anything to me, and it didn't last very long. But I . . ." Her voice trailed off and the color crept up her face. "I wrote him some letters while we were seeing each other."

There was a moment of silence as I digested this information. I realized, of course, what she wasn't saying: there had been something compromising in those letters.

"When I broke it off with him, he was terribly angry," she went on. "He swore that he'd get even with me. I'm afraid he's going to show the letters to Brian."

I considered this for a moment. "Can't you make a clean breast of it to Brian?" I asked at last. "Explain what happened but that you truly love him and not this other man."

It was always easier to give advice from outside a situation, of course. My own life was much more complicated than it needed to be because of secrets I was keeping, because of truths that I was too afraid to speak out loud.

But I remembered Brian as a sweet boy who adored Julia. I was certain he would forgive her.

She shook her head. "No. I can't tell him. I just can't. He would forgive me, but it would break his heart. And I can't bear the thought of doing that. Not when he'll be going back to war with those memories. Those worries." Her eyes filled with tears, and I sympathized with her. It was a tricky situation she'd put herself in.

"What other option is there?" I asked, still a bit unsure of how I could help.

Then she looked up at me and made the matter clear. "I thought perhaps you could get the letters back," she said.

While my family had always kept most of our illegal activities a secret from those who weren't our associates, there was a faction of the community who knew what we were involved in. Julia's own family had often walked the line between the illegal and the legal. Her brothers had committed a few petty crimes with my cousins in their younger days.

So it wasn't really a surprise that she had come to me. She wouldn't have felt comfortable asking Uncle Mick, of course, but we had always been friends, and she knew I would want to help if I could.

"I didn't want to ask you," she said. "It's so embarrassing. I've been so stupid. But I have to do something. I don't want to hurt Brian." Her voice broke and her eyes filled with tears, but she managed to keep her composure.

I considered her problem. While I still thought honesty might be the best course of action, I could understand her wanting to keep this from her fiancé. If they were to be married before he went back to the war, it would only plague them both for him to know the truth. Julia had realized the error of her ways, so what was the use in making more trouble of what had happened?

Besides, I hated that this other man was threatening her just because she had decided that she no longer wanted to see him. What a cruel thing to do.

"Who is this man?" I asked.

She drew in a slow breath, as though steeling herself to speak about him. "His name is Peter Varney. He's a minor government official, a bit older than me."

"Do you know where he's keeping the letters?" I asked. After all, if I was going to retrieve them, it was first important to establish their location.

"I think they're probably in his flat," she said. She gave me an address in Knightsbridge.

"Are you sure he means to use them?" I asked. "Perhaps they are only empty threats."

She shook her head. "He means it. I can tell. He's not a nice sort of person. Only I didn't realize it until it was too late."

I felt sorry for her, but I was still hesitant to involve myself in her troubles. After all, she had made the choice to see the other man, to write him things that would have been better not put on paper.

"Julia," I began, "I'm not sure . . ."

"Uncle Frank said I should give you this," she said, fumbling in her handbag.

I froze. "Uncle Frank?" I repeated slowly, realization dawning.

She pulled out the book I had left with Frank Doyle. I hadn't known he was her uncle. In all the years we'd known each other, she'd never mentioned the reclusive mathematician. But I supposed we all held on to our secrets.

I took the book from her outstretched hand, though I didn't open it. Whatever he had discovered, I would look at it when I was alone.

"He said . . . he said that if I gave you that, you would be willing to help me."

I had made a bargain with him, after all. It was only fair for me to pay up.

Major Ramsey had forbidden us from participating in any illegal activities while we were working for him, but, then again, what Julia was asking me to do was not technically a crime. After all, the letters rightfully belonged to her; I would just be retrieving them.

She was looking at me with such desperation that I didn't have the heart to refuse her. She had been indiscreet, but that did not mean that her life should be ruined. If I could help her, I felt bound to do so. And then I would be able to scratch out my debt to Frank Doyle.

"All right," I said. "Yes. I'll do it if I can."

"Oh, Ellie! Thank you!" She embraced me, and I pushed aside my doubts. Julia might have made a poor choice in seeing someone else while Brian was off fighting, but that didn't give this Mr. Varney the right to threaten her and try to ruin her life. It was ungentlemanly, and he should be stopped.

She left shortly afterward, and I went to put the kettle on, wondering if I'd just made a sound decision or a big mistake.

My cup of tea prepared, I took a seat on the sofa and picked up the book Julia had brought with her. I could see the folded piece of paper with the message on it sticking slightly out of the top of the book.

Mr. Doyle had certainly made quick work of solving the puzzle. I was half afraid to open it, and I found myself wishing that Felix were here.

But there was no waiting, of course. I needed to know what it said.

I had been able to make no sense of the letters written on the page, but Mr. Doyle had neatly decoded the message. The words were written in surprisingly tidy letters, and I read them over three times before I allowed myself to try to interpret what they meant:

Be careful. I believe that you may have been discovered. This could mean danger to you and to your family. I suggest you take cover at once. Hand off your information to Chambers. The flowers are dying.

CHAPTER FOURTEEN

The flowers are dying.

I didn't know what that cryptic bit of information meant. It seemed to be a code within a code. What was more, I didn't know who or what this Chambers was, but this seemed to prove that my father had, indeed, been involved in some sort of dangerous scheme that had cost him his life.

The question became: What did I want to do now?

I kept turning all the possibilities round and round in my head until I was nearly dizzy, but I didn't know what I should do.

I supposed it all came down to the same thing it had before: Did I want to know the truth?

It was an automatic impulse to insist that I did, but then I hesitated. I had been determined to learn the truth about my mother at all costs, and now it turned out that the cost had been rather more than I'd expected. What other unpleasant secrets might I uncover if I continued to pursue this?

As it turned out, I didn't have much time to contemplate the matter that evening because the Germans returned. Uncle Mick had been home for only a short time, the entirety of the day having been spent plotting with Major Ramsey, when the air-raid sirens sounded.

When this war was over, I would never be able to listen to the sound of a plane the same. For the rest of my life, I would remember that slow, creeping dread as I heard the low, almost indistinguishable buzz of the engine coming closer and closer.

There was a strange sort of feeling it created in the pit of your stomach, the dull ache of uncertainty. The body tensed with waiting, knowing what was coming and being completely powerless to stop it.

You knew that if it didn't hit your house, it was likely going to hit someone else's. Even if no one died—and no doubt many people would die—there would still be untold damage by morning.

I tried not to resent the time spent in the cellar. There were people who had no shelter available to them and some who were choosing not to go into one. I was glad, at least, that my family had a cellar and that they were persuaded to use it.

Uncle Mick might have been mistaken for a man with the sort of bravado that would keep him from retreating to the cellar. Thankfully, he was also a man with a good helping of common sense.

"No sense in being blown to bits if it can be helped," he said cheerily as we gathered up an armload of blankets and made for the stairs.

There was a certain sort of hominess down there in the cellar. I didn't know if I should be sad or glad that we had become accustomed to spending nights in our shelter.

During the worst of it, there had come to be a terrible sort of routine. Before sunset, Nacy would fill the thermos with hot tea and put whatever baked goods she made that day or the day before into a paper sack. And when the siren sounded, we'd descend and settle in for the evening, Nacy with her knitting, me with a book, and Uncle Mick with his pipe.

We had tea, we had biscuits, we had one another.

Tonight, Uncle Mick smoked his pipe placidly and said little about his meeting with Major Ramsey. I didn't want to ask, not after I had been purposefully excluded.

He noticed my avoidance of the topic, as I should have known he would. Uncle Mick knew me better than probably anyone else in the world, and he was never one to let me stew. He'd rather things be out in the open and dealt with.

"You'll be wanting to know what Ramsey and I discussed," he said.

"Didn't he forbid you to tell me?" I asked lightly, though I couldn't quite keep the edge from my tone.

Uncle Mick smiled. "He said you'd still be angry with him. He knows you well, it seems."

"I'm not that difficult to figure out," I said, dismissing the little hint of satisfaction I felt that Ramsey had been thinking of me.

Nacy looked up from her knitting. "You can deny it all you like, Ellie, but the major understands you. That's not something to be taken lightly."

I could think of nothing to say to this, so I didn't respond. Thankfully, Uncle Mick picked up the conversation.

"He caught me up on what happened, showed me the list of stolen items. It's a bit odd, all right. That was quick thinking, Ellie girl. If you hadn't called it to the major's attention, it might have slipped through the cracks unnoticed."

"We might not even have connected them ourselves, except for the fact of Lisbon. The major is the one who put that together."

He nodded. "If I had paid attention as you had, I might have noticed that these fellows seem to be from somewhere else. It's odd that we haven't heard even a whisper about these robberies within our own circles. Granted, I'm not in the thick of things like I used to be, but something of this scale usually makes the rounds."

"And so you're to meet these men the day after tomorrow," I said, unable to keep from asking.

"So it seems. That fellow Kimble brought Dugan back to the major's, once he'd cleaned him up a bit."

"Was he badly hurt?" I asked, still unable to keep from feeling sympathy for the man.

"Pony's boys had roughed him up good, but nothing that won't heal. And I think he'll be pleased to help us for the chance to keep himself from being charged as a spy."

"But can you trust him?" I asked.

Uncle Mick took a thoughtful puff of his pipe. "That's always the question when dealing with criminals, isn't it, love? But I suppose Dugan would rather see this through than meet the hangman."

I sincerely hoped so.

"He's going to introduce me to the men at Red's on Tuesday. With any luck, they'll give me the lowdown on the job and we can move from there."

I still didn't like the idea of Uncle Mick walking into the lion's den, but if anyone could pull it off, I knew he could.

As I always did when the worries seemed to be piling up around me, I forced myself to focus on the moment. In this moment, we were safe, and we were together.

And so I settled under my blanket on my little cot in the corner, and I fell asleep to the sound of distant explosions and the rumbling of the earth around me.

I went to case Varney's flat Tuesday morning. Julia had given me the address, and I needed to case the place before I did the job, to get some idea of his routine and the routines of the others who lived there.

I hadn't done a great deal of this sort of thing. For the most part, Uncle Mick and my cousins had done the reconnaissance in our past jobs, and I was included in the planning and the execution

of the burglaries we had committed. Nevertheless, I was confident
I could do this on my own.

I had, of course, thought about asking Uncle Mick for help, but
Julia had been adamant she didn't want anyone else to know. She
was terribly embarrassed about all of it, so I could understand her
reluctance. Besides, Uncle Mick had enough to worry about at the
moment. He didn't need the distraction.

Well, no matter. I felt perfectly capable of doing this simple
job alone.

I knew I needed to look around a bit before I actually decided
to break in, but the longer I spent in the vicinity, the more I risked
the possibility that someone might remember me and point me out
if the police or anyone else came around asking questions.

Not that I thought he would be likely to call the police, not when
I would be stealing only the letters he was using to blackmail Julia.

All things considered, I decided my best course of action would
be to get to know as much as I could from the outside and only
venture into the building when it was time to do the job.

Mr. Varney lived in a nice building of flats in Knightsbridge. It
seemed he did fairly well for himself. Not nice enough for a doorman, though, which worked in my favor.

Julia had mentioned that he worked long hours during the day,
so I assumed it would be safe to enter his house in the daytime. I
had only to make sure there weren't a good deal of people about at
this particular time of day.

I watched for about an hour and saw only two people leave
the building. One of them was an elderly man with a cane, who
took a slow walk around the block before returning inside. I assumed he would be the sort of man who kept to this daily routine, so I marked the time and decided I would avoid him if at all
possible.

The other person to leave the flat was a younger woman who

I assumed to be on her way to work, from her clothing. She had a rushed, distracted air about her, and I didn't think that she would pose much of a problem.

All things considered, I thought it would be a fairly easy thing to get in and out of the building without notice. I had no worries about getting into Mr. Varney's flat. There were few doors in London that posed me much of a problem.

I would wait to see how things went with Uncle Mick's mission this evening, and then I would decide on a day to proceed with my plan. Hopefully, I would be able to retrieve the letters easily and have the job completed and checked off my growing list of things that were weighing on my mind.

I went home on a different route from the one on which I had come. Uncle Mick had taught me that, as well.

Not that I expected many people to be monitoring my progress today. People were concerned with cleaning up the damage from last night's air raid.

It occurred to me how strange it was that all of this had become normal: the sight of people picking through the rubble, of children in dirty clothes sitting on the curb while their mothers tried to salvage things from the ruins of their houses. A few months ago, I could not have imagined such a scene. Now it attracted only a sympathetic glance as I continued on my way.

We helped as much as we could, but there was no way to help everyone. I had learned it was impossible to try, that I could not let myself become invested in the plight of everyone I encountered. It was too much of a burden to bear, an impossibility in a city that faced death and destruction on a massive scale.

But that in itself was another of the horrors of war: the way what would have once seemed unfathomable became ordinary, the way we had to allow ourselves to become callous sometimes so that we wouldn't crumble from the weight of it all.

I was walking down a narrow street of mostly destroyed buildings when a noise caught my attention. It sounded like it was coming from inside the pile of debris.

I stepped closer to the ruined structure. It looked as though it had been a business of some sort, but whatever it had been, it was now completely obliterated.

The sound came again from beneath the pile of rubble at the edge of the street. I moved toward it, hoping I wouldn't find someone trapped beneath the wreckage. I could tell from the look of things that these buildings had not been demolished last night. The damage here was from an earlier bombing, so surely no one would be left inside. But I couldn't move on without investigating. There was no one else around, and if someone needed help, I might be the only one able to give it.

"Hello?" I called.

The sound repeated itself, and then I saw a pair of glowing eyes before a tiny bundle of fur moved out into my path.

"It's a kitten," I said to no one in particular.

I wasn't sure how the little thing had survived, but he was clearly not very old. He was a tiny, scrawny calico with unusual markings. He had black paws and a black face. A pair of pale green eyes blinked up at me.

"You poor little thing," I said, scooping him up. "Have you been lost?"

There was no one around, and it would be impossible to find the kitten's owner. If he had one. Besides, there hadn't been a house here. I assumed he'd wandered away from his litter and was trying to survive on his own. Which he certainly wouldn't be able to do for long all alone.

Without thinking much about it, I put him inside my jumper, and I felt him immediately settle against me. A moment later, he was purring contentedly.

I knew I was going to have to keep him. Nacy would grumble

about us having to share our milk ration, and then she'd end up giving him extra.

It had been a long time since I'd had a kitten. The boys and I had had a lot of pets growing up. Colm and Toby were always bringing home stray dogs they found, and Nacy would feed them until they wandered off again.

We'd gone through a lot of cats that way, too, strays who were happy to have a short-term home before they went in search of other pastures. There were two cats who had lived long and happy lives with us, but we'd seen the last of them years ago.

Somehow, I felt an immediate connection to the little creature. Perhaps we were both in need of a friend at the moment.

I looked at the little black mask across his calico face.

"Burglar," I said. "I'm going to call you Burglar."

He gave a little meow of approval.

CHAPTER FIFTEEN

It was going to be a long day waiting for Uncle Mick's impending job this evening. I was still angry that I had been excluded from the planning, but I managed to keep from going to the major's house to pester him for details.

He'd wanted me out of the way, and I was determined to show him that I wouldn't butt in where I wasn't wanted.

I hoped he would miss my interference just a little.

In the meantime, I returned to my flat and looked again at the decoded message that had been in the book of Greek myths.

Hand off your information to Chambers. The flowers are dying.

What on earth did it mean? Even assuming it was a real name and not an alias, I didn't know anyone named Chambers, and I couldn't recall our family ever having dealings, personally or professionally, with someone of that name. Of course, if they had been involved with my father's espionage, and possibly his murder, I doubted they would have kept up communication with the family.

For lack of a better place to start, I took the City Directory from my shelf and flipped to the Cs. I scanned the list. As I had suspected, Chambers was not an uncommon surname. There was no way to know which of them might be the Chambers in question.

On a whim, I went through the list again, looking for floral first names. There was a Violet Chambers as well as a Rose Chambers. I contemplated ringing them up, but what would I say? Besides, if the flowers had been dying, it was not likely they would be in the telephone directory twenty-five years later.

An idea struck me suddenly, and I turned from the list of personal telephone numbers to the trade directory. It was just possible . . .

A moment later, I was looking down at it: Chambers Flower Shop.

What were the odds of that, I wondered.

"What do you think?" I asked Burglar. He had been in my flat for only a few hours, and I was already glad of the company. It was nice having someone to talk to, a companion who would listen without judgment.

He tilted his head at me and blinked.

"That's what I think, too," I said with a nod. "There's only one way to find out."

I found the little shop in Finchley. It was a small building wedged between a tea shop and a greengrocer in a row of tidy Victorian-era buildings.

I stood on the other side of the street and studied it. There was certainly nothing sinister looking about it. Then again, if it had been designed to conceal the activities of spies, it would be best if it fit in.

Not that I suspected I had really hit upon a clue this easily.

I decided it wouldn't hurt for me to go inside and look around. After all, any association it had had with my father had been decades ago. What were the chances there was still some connection to be discovered?

And so I crossed the street and went inside.

I expected to be hit with the scent of a perfusion of flowers as I entered, but, in truth, the shop was somewhat bare. I knew, of course, that the flower trade was dwindling during the war. There were a lot more important crops to be grown now that many of the former trade routes were effectively cut off.

Of course, people still needed flowers. There were a lot more funerals now than before.

There were shelves and small, high tables around the room with flowers on them. One corner still held wreaths and evergreen and holly arrangements leftover from the holidays. In the center of the room were two tables with large, bare tree branches that stretched artfully toward the sky. It was a clever way to fill up space and, I had to imagine, cost-effective. Still, there was something elegant about it.

In addition to the bouquets of fresh flowers, I noticed that there were arrangements of silk flowers. It was a smart idea. No doubt this shop's adaptability was what had kept it in business through two world wars—perhaps that and its sideline of espionage?

Looking around, I found it hard to believe that this place had anything to do with that sort of thing. It merely seemed like a little shop doing its best to carry on.

A woman approached me as I entered. She was perhaps sixty, her gray hair swept up stylishly, her dark green dress fashionable. "Hello, miss," she said. "May I help you?"

"I'm looking for a bouquet of flowers," I said. "I'm not awfully particular about what. I just want something pretty."

"We have several already arranged. Would you like to take one with you?"

"That would be lovely."

She walked me around the shop to show me what was available. I looked the bouquets over, trying to determine which of them would be cheapest. I didn't have a lot of spare money to spend on flowers, but I was certainly willing to spend whatever I could afford if it led to information about my father.

I decided to try out the phrase that had been written in the coded message.

"It must be hard to keep bouquets in stock during winter," I said. "The flowers are dying."

Was it my imagination or did she give a slight pause at the words? "We have a good partnership with a local greenhouse," she said. "They keep us in stock all winter."

"Oh, that's wonderful. Well, I'll take this bouquet," I said, indicating one of roses, ferns, and baby's breath, and some kind of dark berries I didn't recognize.

"Do you want the vase?"

I imagined that would cost extra. "That's not necessary. I have one at home." Or, at least, an old jar I could put them in.

"Very good. I'll wrap them up for you."

She took the vase to the counter.

My visit was drawing to a close. I tried to think of some way to introduce my name, to see her reaction to it.

"I think I may have had a bouquet of flowers delivered to me from this shop before," I said. "Though I can't be sure. I don't suppose you'd remember if you've ever delivered a bouquet to Electra McDonnell?"

If I was looking for a reaction, I wasn't disappointed.

She dropped the vase, and it shattered on the floor.

"Oh, how clumsy of me!" she said. "Please watch out for the glass. I'll have someone come and clean this up."

"Is there anything I can do to help?" I asked.

"No, no. I'll get the shopgirl to bring out the broom." She picked up the bouquet from among the glass and shook it to dislodge any shards.

"Would you like a different bouquet?" she asked.

"No, that one's fine. I don't imagine the glass harmed it."

She nodded and began wrapping the stems of the flowers in a large sheet of tissue paper.

"As to your question, I'm fairly certain we haven't delivered flowers to you before. Your name isn't familiar."

"Electra is an unusual name," I said. "I suppose you'd have remembered."

"Yes," she said, though she didn't meet my gaze. I felt certain I was onto something, but I didn't know what to do next. Should I press her for answers?

"My middle name is unusual, too, for a girl. It's Niall, after my father."

She looked up at me, and this time, there was something sharp in her gaze. I kept my expression blank.

The note had spoken of Chambers as an ally, a person to hand the information to. But in that case, it meant these people were likely German spies. I would have to tread carefully and weigh my options.

"That's a pretty name," she said, after a long pause. Then she gave me the price for the flowers.

I paid her and picked up the bouquet. "These are lovely," I said. "I'm sure I'll be back soon."

Her eyes met mine, and she nodded. If she knew something, she wasn't going to tell me, not now.

But I had made it plain who I was. I would give her time to think things over and then I would come back.

I said goodbye and left the shop, the bouquet tucked in the crook of my arm. Between the lovely flowers and my new flatmate, Burglar, things were going to be quite cheery at home.

Uncle Mick left after dinner for his rendezvous with the criminals. We hadn't told Nacy much about the nature of what he would be doing, so she wasn't as anxious as I was. Besides, she'd had many more years than I had to learn to be sanguine about Uncle Mick's criminal forays.

I spent the evening with her in the parlor, Burglar curled up on my lap. As I had known she would, Nacy had muttered about the kitten being another mouth to feed and then commenced serving him prime scraps of meat from yesterday's stew, minced into kitten-sized mouthfuls.

At last, she went off to bed. I remained in the parlor near the fireplace, waiting. The minutes ticked slowly by, an hour, then two. I had hoped the thieves didn't intend to do any sort of job this evening, just to meet and discuss whatever they were plotting. It was a lucky thing for us that they'd needed a safecracker, but I did wonder what safes they intended to break into. The note we'd found in the ashtray in Anna Gillard's hotel room had pointed us to Nico Lazaro, but the thieves hadn't seen that note. So where did they intend to strike?

At last, the door opened, and Uncle Mick came in along with a burst of cold air.

"Ah, Ellie girl," he said, pulling off his coat and gloves. "You haven't been waiting for me, have you?"

I had been worried about Uncle Mick's safety, but I had to have known that he would simply find the whole thing an enjoyable lark. His eyes were bright with amusement, and there was an energy about him that I hadn't seen since the last time we'd been about to pull a job.

"It all went well, I take it?" I said.

"Right as rain, Ellie girl," he said with a grin. "Those fellas took to me like a duck to water. I've been initiated into their gang of thieves, and we're ready to pull a job."

I knew I shouldn't ask any questions, especially since Major Ramsey didn't seem to want me included in this part of the mission. All the same, I was curious about the gang of killer thieves, and what they were after.

"Did they say what they're looking for?" I asked, unable to help myself.

"I went to see Ramsey on my way home tonight," he said. "He told me to send you his way tomorrow afternoon, and he'll tell you everything you need to know. Now I'm off to bed. All that plotting makes a man bone weary."

CHAPTER SIXTEEN

I didn't go to see the major too early the next afternoon. I didn't want to appear overeager after all the time he had made me wait. I took my time eating lunch, and then I decided to walk most of the distance to his house, rather than taking the Tube. Perhaps it was childish of me, but I was annoyed with him, and I didn't think there was any reason I should have to jump to attention just because he'd finally decided I could be of some use.

Of course, it ended up hurting me more than it did him. The long walk was frigid, and I was frozen nearly clear through by the time I arrived. Not only that, but I had come at a bad time.

"Good afternoon, Miss McDonnell," Constance said as she answered the bell. "I know Major Ramsey was expecting you, but I'm afraid he's in a meeting at the moment. If you'd like to sit in the parlor and wait, I'll let him know you're here as soon as he's free."

"All right. Thank you, Constance."

"Oh, Miss McDonnell," a voice said. "How nice to see you again."

I looked up to see Noelle Edgemont, the major's sister, standing on the stairs.

"Hello, Mrs. Edgemont."

"Call me Noelle, please. I couldn't help but hear you're waiting to see Gabriel. I came down to talk to him as well, but since he is occupied, you must come up and have tea with me. We'll wait together."

I hesitated. This was rather an awkward position to be put in. After all, I wasn't here as a guest. My eyes flickered to Constance to see if I could gauge her thoughts on the matter, but she was carefully avoiding my gaze, arranging papers on her desk.

"I think perhaps I'd better just wait here."

"Nonsense," she said with a wave of her hand. "It's cold, and there's no fire in the front parlor. Come along."

She turned and began going back up the stairs. She had something of her brother's commanding manner, and it felt both difficult and rude to refuse.

"You'll . . . let him know where I've gone?" I said as I passed Constance's desk.

"Yes, of course."

I had never been upstairs in the major's house. He used the ground floor as an office, and most of the furniture had been disarranged to accommodate his professional pursuits. The parlor now served as a waiting room of sorts, and Constance's desk had been placed off to the side of the foyer.

I knew from experience there was also an empty room with only a table and two chairs down the hall of the ground floor, which could be used as a holding cell or interrogation room.

But I assumed the first floor was still used as his living quarters, and it felt rather personal to be invited into them. Of course, he was not the one doing the inviting.

Upstairs was tastefully decorated. The walls of the hallway were papered in dark green, and there was good art on the walls. Nothing flashy by French masters or anything of that sort. I wouldn't have expected Major Ramsey to be a collector of ostentatious paintings. He was about as different from someone like Nico Lazaro as it was possible to be.

It occurred to me what a surprise it would have been to find a large statue of a naked woman at the head of the stairs, and I pressed my lips together to suppress a smile.

Noelle led me into a little parlor where she'd apparently pushed back the blackout curtains to let in the afternoon sun. The floor was a gleaming golden parquet beneath a very nice rug, and the furniture was sturdy, comfortable, and high-quality. A fire crackled cheerily in the marble fireplace.

I knew Major Ramsey was from a wealthy family, but I'd never thought of him as wealthy, per se; he was always the military man to me. But standing in the upper rooms of his house reminded me that he came from money. His uncle, the Earl of Overbrook, would have been very comfortable in this house.

Noelle led the way to a little table that had been set with tea-things and motioned for me to have a seat.

She poured from a silver tea service as I settled into the chair. "Sugar, wasn't it?" she asked and then scooped in a generous amount without waiting for my answer.

"Thank you," I said as she handed me the cup and saucer.

I took a sip. It was hot, strong, and very sweet. Perfection.

"How long will you be in London?" I asked as we settled into conversation over our cups.

"Not much longer. I went to our country home in Hampshire to check on things and came back yesterday." That would explain why Jocelyn Abbot had been able to make her overnight visit, my mind put in unhelpfully.

"I suppose I'll take the train up to Cumberland in the next day or two to reunite with my family," she said. "I'd stay longer, but I miss my children. The little brutes."

"How many do you have?"

"Two boys. Twins, actually. They're eight, absolute terrors, and I adore them to pieces."

I smiled. "I grew up with two boys. My cousins. So I understand perfectly."

"Do they ever become less . . . exuberant?"

"Not much, I'm afraid."

She sighed. "I thought as much. Gabriel has given me a false sense of what little boys grow into. He's so very steady."

I felt as though this might be her way of drawing me out on the subject of her brother, but I didn't intend to wade into that if I could avoid it. "I imagine responsibility has a sobering effect."

She nodded. "He was a lively enough child, but there's always been something of a serious side to him. Have some sandwiches," she said, handing me the plate of them. "Cheese and chutney, I think. What are your cousins like?"

And so we ate sandwiches and biscuits, I told her stories of Colm and Toby's childhood hijinks, and she related stories about her sons that proved that boys had changed very little in the past two decades.

I liked Noelle Edgemont very much. We were from entirely different worlds, but in some ways we were very much alike. It was surprising to me, as she reminded me a lot of her brother. I would never have guessed I'd one day be drinking tea and eating biscuits with an earl's niece, but here we were.

"Am I interrupting?"

I had not even heard Major Ramsey come into the room.

I turned to look at him. It was hard to tell what he thought of my being chummy with his sister. Did he disapprove of our spending time together? Or was he indifferent?

I had to assume it was the former. He wouldn't like the mixing of personal and professional lives. He wasn't frowning, though. That was something.

"Come and have some tea with us, Gibby," Noelle said.

If he was annoyed by his sister using a childhood nickname in front of me, which I assumed he was, he gave no sign of it.

Instead, he came to the table and pulled out a chair. He was moving a bit stiffly today, I noticed. Noelle poured tea into a cup and set it in front of him.

He picked it up and took a long, appreciative sip.

I passed him the plate of sandwiches, and he took one without comment.

I didn't miss the little glance Noelle darted between her brother and me as he ate the sandwich.

For a few moments, we sipped our tea and chatted about generalities. It wasn't uncomfortable, but it was strange, the three of us sitting here. Almost as though we were friends.

For just the briefest moment, I allowed my mind to wander to what it might be like if we were friends. If, perhaps, the major and I were more than friends, spending an afternoon with his sister.

I quickly pushed the thought away.

"You're hurting, aren't you," Noelle said suddenly. "You ought to take your medicine."

"I'm fine."

Noelle looked at me with a roll of her eyes. "One would think he enjoys suffering. He positively excels at depriving himself of things. Especially things he really wants."

I didn't dare look at the major, but I could feel the heat creeping up my neck.

He set his cup down in the saucer on the table. "Would you like to come back down to my office, Miss McDonnell? We have some matters to discuss."

"Yes, of course."

Midnight must always strike for Cinderella, I supposed.

He rose and helped pull back my chair like he would have done for a lady at a fancy restaurant.

"Thank you so much for the tea, Mrs. Edgemont," I said. I felt a pang of regret that our lovely teatime had come to an end.

"Noelle," she reminded me. "And it was lovely chatting with you, Ellie. I hope we can do it again sometime."

I smiled, knowing the possibility was slim to none.

"Take your tea with you," she said, motioning to the cup. "No use letting it go to waste just because my brother has no patience."

She had just refilled my cup, and as I hated to waste the sugar, I picked up the saucer and carried it with me. Then I preceded the major out of the room and down the stairs into his office.

He closed the door behind us, and I took the seat that I had begun to think of as mine.

He went around his desk to sit down.

"What has Noelle been talking to you about?" he asked. I couldn't tell from his tone whether it was a casual question or a weighted one.

"Oh, we discussed the hazards of young boys," I said with a smile.

He nodded. "My nephews are . . . rather a handful."

"I told her about Colm and Toby. I didn't, of course, tell her the story of my background—the sort of work I do for you. If you'd like to do so, I don't mind."

"I haven't said anything to her about that. She knows that I'm not free to discuss my work with her."

I nodded.

"Did you speak with your uncle?" he asked.

"He told me that he managed to arrange things with the thieves. But he said you wanted to discuss it with me."

He shifted ever so slightly in his chair. "He spoke with a man at Red's who seems to be a part of the group of thieves from Lisbon. They've narrowed their focus, and they need a man with the talent to get what they want. That's where your uncle comes in."

"Have they said what they're looking for?"

"They were cagey about that with your uncle, but as far as he could glean from the things they said, they seem to be looking for a map."

"All of this for a map?" I asked. "A map of what?"

"That's the question. One of my Lisbon contacts is arriving this afternoon, and I assume he will have more information about the situation in Lisbon than I've been able to ascertain. I'm going to meet him this evening."

I waited.

"Would you like to accompany me?" Was this his way of making it up to me that he'd excluded me before?

"Are you sure I won't be in the way?" I asked tartly, before I could think better of it.

A muscle in his jaw tightened. "You needn't come if you don't care to."

I didn't want to quarrel with him, but I couldn't seem to get my mouth in check. "It's just difficult to know when I'll be interfering."

I expected—and perhaps deserved—a sharp retort, but instead he sighed.

"Must you turn everything into a battle of wills, Electra?" he asked wearily.

I was startled, both by the words and by his use of my given name. He almost never called me Electra; he certainly hadn't since Sunderland.

And, despite the justified reprimand, I felt warmed by the intimacy of the question, in the personal history it held. Our eyes met across the desk, and I felt the prickle of awareness at the base of my neck. I could lose myself in that violet-blue gaze if I wasn't careful.

"I'd very much like to come with you," I said. I could think of nothing else to say.

He nodded.

I felt thrown off-balance by what had passed between us, and so I returned to the firm footing of the mission. "Did they tell Uncle Mick where they think they'll find this map? What's the plan?"

After all, I wasn't sure where the new information had left us. We still didn't know who had the map and where the thieves intended to strike next.

He gave a rare grimace, whether from the pain he was in or from what he was about to say, I didn't know. Perhaps it was both.

"They're going to attempt a job tomorrow night, though they didn't yet give him the location."

I felt a shiver of fear. "Then we won't be able to stop them. Uncle Mick will just be walking in blind."

"Not if we discover something in the next twenty-four hours."

As far as I could tell, the odds didn't seem good.

CHAPTER SEVENTEEN

I returned home and sought out Uncle Mick in his workshop.

He was sitting at the worktable tinkering with a walnut-and-brass lockbox, but he looked up when I came in. "Ah, there you are. I've been expecting you."

"Then you already know what I'm going to say," I said, pulling up a stool at the table.

Uncle Mick's workshop was probably my favorite place in the entire world. It was filled with all the wonders associated with the trade. As a child I had marveled at the tools and gadgets and devices that covered every surface, at the wall of assorted keys that tinkled with music when I ran my fingers across them. Even as an adult, I still felt some of that same awe when I entered Uncle Mick's inner sanctum.

The very air in the place smelled like metal and mystery. That's the thing about locks: they hold both riddles and the solving of them; all one needs is a key.

"The major told me about the job. I'm worried for you," I told him, absently toying with a padlock sitting on my side of the table. "You're in with these people, but you don't know what the job is or where it is, so how can Major Ramsey help you?"

"You act like I haven't been part of this world since before you were born," he said. "These aren't the first cutthroats I've dealt with."

"I know," I said, feeling for the second time this afternoon that I was receiving a setdown I deserved.

"Don't look so glum, Ellie girl," he said. "Your old Uncle Mick will come through."

I nodded, my throat tight with the effort of holding back tears.

"Now, hand me that file, will you? We can get this finished up before Nacy calls us in to eat."

A chill twilight descended over the city as we made our way to meet the major's contact. He had picked me up after dinner and told me we would be meeting the man at a pub. It was less conspicuous than the contact coming directly to his office upon arriving in London.

The car pulled in front of the house, and the major got out to open the door for me as I approached.

I settled into the seat, glad we didn't have to walk in the cold, and we set off. We undertook the drive in silence. The major was clearly not feeling communicative, but I was lost in my own thoughts at the moment and wasn't particularly concerned about his. Although I did notice he was holding himself stiffly, as though the pain his sister and I had noticed in him this afternoon still had him in its grip.

The pub, the Pale Lantern, was located in Kensington. It wasn't one I recognized, but I knew the type well enough. It would be warm and cozy inside, and the food would be good. The thought was comforting.

Jakub parked the car down the street, and we walked to it through the whipping wind. I determined not to complain about the heat of summer when it came—if it came.

The major opened the door for me, and we went into the pub together through the narrow entrance hall. It was warm and slightly smoky from the fireplace. It was wonderful to be out of the wind.

We took a narrow, creaky flight of stairs to the main sitting area. I was glad to see a fire was cracking merrily in the fireplace because my coat was once again proving insufficient for the bitter weather we were having.

The major led me to a table in the corner, and I glanced around, noting with approval the cozy ambience of the place. The tables were dark wood, the walls were papered in a dark floral, and the windows were pretty stained glass. I looked closer and found the designs were of various types of flowers.

I found myself hoping that the windows would make it through the war. I felt a sudden pang of sadness at all the stained glass the city had already lost, all the beauty that had been destroyed. It was a trivial thing, perhaps, but that's how grief is, isn't it? It sneaks up on you in small ways when you least expect it.

"May I take your coat?" the major asked, pulling me from my glum thoughts.

"No, I'll keep it for now, thank you." We were near enough to the fireplace for me to feel the heat, but I wasn't ready to shed the extra layer of warmth just yet. As I pulled off my worn blue wool gloves, I noticed there was a small hole in the index finger of the right-hand one.

"You need a new pair," the major said, looking down at my hands.

"Yes, I keep meaning to get around to buying some," I said, slightly embarrassed he had noticed the state of them. I shoved them into my coat pockets.

He removed his own greatcoat and took a seat across from me.

A moment later, the barmaid came to our table. "What'll you have?"

"A pot of tea, please," I said. The thought of something a bit stronger was tempting after the day we'd had, but I was cold, and nothing sounded better than tea at the moment. Tea always had a way of soothing me.

"Scotch," the major said. I looked at him, surprised. I'd never seen him have a drink before. And then I noticed the tightness of his jaw and the ashen complexion of his skin. He was hurting badly.

"Are you all right?" I asked when the barmaid had gone.

"Fine," he said. He didn't look at me as he said the word but instead reached into his pocket to remove a piece of paper, which he set on the table.

I hesitated for just a moment. The line between professional and personal was so hazy, especially now that Jocelyn Abbot was in the picture.

I wasn't sure how far I should press the issue. But we were at least friends, weren't we? Or something like it. And so I went ahead and said it. "You've been pushing yourself too hard, and you're not fully healed. You need to be resting."

"I'm fine," he said again.

"Major . . ."

He looked up then, his eyes meeting mine. They were dark tonight, a dusky gray-blue. "I appreciate your concern, Miss McDonnell, but you know as well as I do that the sort of work we're doing isn't going to wait for me to rest."

He was right, of course. Time was of the essence in nearly every aspect of this war, and we were on a deadline for this job.

All the same, he'd almost been killed three months ago, shot full of holes that still made me shudder when I thought too long about them. After something like that, a person needs time to heal. I was concerned that this new mission was going to harm him. That he was driving himself too hard.

"Is there anything . . ."

I paused as the major's gaze went toward the movement at the staircase, and I turned to see a young man walking toward us. He was dressed in an army uniform, his cap tucked under his arm.

He was tall and thin and surprisingly young. I had expected someone closer to the major's age. This man looked younger than me. He had an open, friendly countenance that felt at odds with this sort of work. Perhaps it was an asset. I had learned over the past few months never to underestimate anyone.

"Hello," he said cheerily as he reached us. "Dreadful night, isn't it?"

"Miss McDonnell, this is Captain Archibald Blandings," Major Ramsey said. "Blandings, Miss Electra McDonnell."

"How do you do, Miss McDonnell." He took my hand in his, and it was warm, despite the weather.

"Captain Blandings."

"Archie, please," he said, taking his seat.

"Then you must call me Ellie."

He smiled. "All right."

The barmaid returned then with a tray holding my tea-things and the major's scotch. She set our drinks down before us and looked at Captain Blandings.

He ran a hand through strawberry-blond hair that managed to be slightly untidy despite its shortness. "A pint of bitter, I think. It's hard to come by in Lisbon."

I stirred the sugar into my tea, but I noticed the quick way the major downed his drink, the empty glass clinking on the table as he set it back down. I hoped it would help, but I knew a long night's sleep would be more beneficial. Unfortunately, I doubted he would get it.

"What's the lay of the land, sir?" Archie asked.

"I've told Miss McDonnell that you've been in Lisbon. She is apprised of the relevant information. You may speak freely in front of her."

"Yes, sir," Archie said. His light brown eyes, the color of caramel, came back to me, and I saw him reassessing me, taking note of the major's trust in me. He was a clever young man; that much was clear. I liked him very much already. Perhaps he would be able to shoulder some of the weight currently on the major's shoulders.

The barmaid returned with his pint, and he took a long, appreciative drink. I sipped my tea, the warmth of it seeping into me. I slipped out of my coat, letting it rest on the chair behind me.

"I was working at the consulate there when the war broke out," Archie said as he set the glass back down. "I've been in Portugal for the last three years."

"Do you like it there?" I asked.

"Yes," he said. "The weather suits me much more than these bitter climes. I guarantee you it's much nicer in Lisbon at the moment."

As if to prove his point, the wind whistled outside the window, rattling the pane near our table. Archie smiled at me.

"Captain Blandings has been instrumental in building up a network of informants in Lisbon," Major Ramsey said, bringing an end to the small talk. "Locals who have an ear to the ground and can collect information unobtrusively."

"Spies," I said.

He nodded. "It's useful to make friends with the locals, as I don't exactly blend in myself," he said with a lopsided smile. "But I have managed to make myself comfortable there, and, as I give off rather a harmless air most of the time, people don't seem to regard me as much of a threat."

I wondered if it was my turn to reassess him. Something in the light way he spoke the words made me think he was more dangerous than he seemed on the surface.

"And so I've made a good many friends in the country. It's useful to have prewar friendships once a war starts. You can't trust everyone, of course, but I've rather a good instinct for that kind of thing."

Major Ramsey quickly related what we had learned so far about the thieves in London and their apparent search for an object brought back from Lisbon. "They've indicated it may be a map that was in a stolen attaché case. Have you heard anything about that?"

"Yes, there's been some chatter about a missing map," he said. "As far as I can ascertain, it has something to do with an undiscovered tungsten mine. The Germans are importing a lot of their tungsten from Portugal. They use it for armaments among other things. There are deals in place with the Portuguese government to provide them with a certain amount of tungsten, but the Germans are nothing if not opportunistic. If they knew the existence of a tungsten mine that they could access without having to go through the usual channels, it would be worth a great deal to them."

"A good enough deal to go to all this trouble?" I asked.

"Oh, yes," Archie said. "The Germans are eager to acquire as much as they can. And they've been known to kill for less."

I felt a little wave of queasiness at the words, remembering what I had seen in that room at the Valencia.

These people were certainly willing to kill. They had killed at least once in pursuit of whatever they were looking for, and they were growing increasingly desperate.

"I had a man in Lisbon who was feeding us a good deal of information," Archie went on. "He went by the name of Santos. He told me there were rumors about a hidden tungsten deposit the Germans were trying to get their hands on. There was a detailed map of the area where it was located, but it was being kept under wraps. He was going to find out more. The next thing I knew, I heard about the theft of the attaché case. My immediate suspicion was that Santos was the one who stole it, but I've lost contact with him. It's possible he handed it off to someone and has gone to ground. Lisbon is rather dangerous for informants now, and he may have found it expedient to go into hiding. Especially if there is something big happening."

"Or he's dead," Major Ramsey said.

Archie nodded. "I've never known him to be out of contact this long. It's possible the Germans found out Santos took the map and killed him and are now searching for the person to whom he handed it off. Obviously, he didn't tell them who it was, even under torture, as they're still searching."

"The Gestapo have been known to be overly enthusiastic with their interrogations," the major said. "If they caught and tortured him, they may have killed him inadvertently before he told them what they wanted to know."

I felt a chill at the casual way these men discussed death and torture. I knew, of course, that such things were done by the Germans, but it was a stark reminder that the sort of work we were doing was dangerous—that it had been deadly more than once.

"This is the list of everyone who left Lisbon on that flight," Major Ramsey said, handing Archie the folded sheet of paper he had taken from his pocket.

Archie unfolded the paper and ran his eyes over the list.

"Do you recognize anyone?" Major Ramsey asked.

"A few of them," Archie said. "Nico Lazaro, of course."

"Who is the map going to?" I asked, the thought occurring to me suddenly. "They must be delivering it to someone. Can't we go directly to the proper authorities and see if it's been delivered?"

Archie looked at the major and then back at me with a chagrined expression. "That's a bit of a problem as well. You see, if Santos took it he likely did not do so on the grounds of patriotic fervor. He would have done so to make a profit. I believe the map was probably stolen to be sold to the highest bidder. Someone hopes to profit from this, and I doubt they will be eager to admit the map is in their possession until they have secured a buyer."

"So," I said, "to put it in a nutshell: the Germans want it, but we don't want them to have it. Whoever does have it may be inclined to give it to someone else we don't want to have it. So the best thing we can do is get it for ourselves."

"That sums it up rather nicely," Archie said. "Of course, if I could get it back and bring it with me to Lisbon, it would go a long way toward securing many of my connections there."

"Germaine Arnaud said she thought that Anna Gillard was the one in possession of it," I said. "But she's dead. Major Ramsey found a burnt piece of paper in the ashtray that mentioned Lazaro. Is it him? And, if so, where did Anna Gillard fit into all of this?"

Major Ramsey looked at Archie Blandings. "Who do you suppose is most likely in possession of the map?"

To my surprise, Archie grinned. "Lazaro is a good possibility. It's the sort of thing he'd enjoy doing. The money would be good. He has a lot of connections in Lisbon. Santos even mentioned him once or twice. It's possible he induced Santos to hand the map off to him."

"I spoke to him about the robbery," the major said. "He was evasive, as one might expect."

"Perhaps we could just ask him about it," I said, knowing even as I said the words it was unlikely. "Can we trust him?"

"Not a bit," Archie answered cheerfully.

Then it was as we had assumed. We would not be able to take him into our confidence where the map was concerned.

"He does seem a bit of a slippery fellow," I said.

He looked at me. "You've met him?"

I nodded. "Briefly."

"And? Did he invite you to one of his parties?"

I was surprised. "Why, yes. He did, as a matter of fact."

Archie shook his head. "I'd advise you to go on your guard. His parties have been known to get rather . . . exuberant."

"She won't be going to his party," the major said.

Archie drained the remainder of his glass. "If that's everything, sir, I'd best be on my way. I have another contact to meet before I can retire for the evening."

Major Ramsey nodded. "Thank you. I'll be in touch, Blandings."

"May I keep this list?" he asked.

"Yes. It's a copy."

Archie slipped it into his pocket, stood up, and pulled on his coat. "I'll make a few inquiries. I'll ring you up tomorrow."

"Good."

Archie turned to me. "It was a pleasure to meet you, Ellie."

I watched him leave. He had impressed me very favorably. I hadn't been sure what to expect, but it hadn't been someone with such an innocent, affable face.

"He's very young," I said to the major when Archie had gone.

"He looks younger than he is, but he is young," Major Ramsey said. "Most of the people fighting this war are."

I nodded, thinking of my cousin Toby. I tried not to think too often of what it must have been like for him out on the battlefield. I had seen Toby under pressure. I knew that he never lost his good nature and sense of humor. But to think of him with shells raining down around him always gave me a sick feeling in the pit of my stomach. I felt the same way when I thought of him being in a German prison camp, perhaps starving. I didn't know what outcome to hope for where Toby was concerned. Since I couldn't bear to think of it, I pushed the thoughts aside.

"Do you want another drink?" the major asked.

I shook my head. I had finished my little pot of tea and enjoyed it immensely.

"All right, come along. I'll take you home."

"You don't need to. I can walk." The sooner he got home and rested, the better.

"You're not walking in this cold," he said, rising. I stood, too, and he picked up my discarded coat from the chair and held it up for me to put on.

I didn't feel like arguing with him. I was tired, and I didn't relish the idea of walking home in the blowing snow.

He didn't put on his greatcoat as we prepared to leave, just draped it over his arm. He must have been hurting too bad to pull it back on. I was worried about him. He was going to make himself dangerously ill if he wasn't careful, but he was too stubborn to admit it. I sighed and added it to my list of worries.

We went back down the stairs and out into the chill night air. It felt as though the temperature had dropped several degrees since we had come inside.

I shivered, pulled my gloves out of my pockets, and put them on.

"You need to wear a warmer coat," he said as we walked down the street toward the car.

"Yes," I agreed. I didn't feel like admitting that I didn't have another coat. I would get one when I had the time, along with new gloves. It was not high on my list of priorities just now.

We were passing an alleyway between two buildings when a dark figure slipped out and into our path. In the moonlight, I could see the glint of the knife in his hand.

CHAPTER EIGHTEEN

Before I could even be sure of what I was seeing, Major Ramsey was moving. He pushed me behind him as the man rushed us. The pavement was icy, and the sudden movement made me slip. I struggled to keep my footing even as I caught the flash of the blade again. It was a big knife by the looks of it, and my heart leapt to my throat.

It turned out to be beneficial that Ramsey had not put on his greatcoat, for it gave him easy maneuverability when he dropped it. He went on the offensive, stepping into the man's path with that agile grace that was always surprising in a man his size. He moved so quickly I couldn't have recounted later exactly how he did it, but he grasped the man's arm and a moment later I heard the clatter of the knife against the pavement. The assailant threw a punch, which Ramsey dodged, before turning to look for his discarded knife.

It had fallen near my foot, and I reached down to grab it. He certainly wasn't going to get his hands on it if I could help it. His eyes trained on me, and I gripped the knife's handle, determined to protect myself if need be.

But before he could start toward me, Ramsey had grabbed him. There was a brief scuffle, and then the major had the upper hand. He held the assailant with his arm around his neck, locked against him. I felt a moment of relief. I would call a policeman and this whole thing would be over without much harm done.

And then the man brought back his elbow in a series of vicious blows to the major's ribs. I flinched at the sickening thuds and heard Ramsey grunt. He must have loosened his grip then because the man slipped free of his grasp.

"Mind your own business," the assailant hissed. "Keep asking questions, and you'll be sorry."

And then he was gone, the sound of his footsteps fading in the darkness.

I was afraid Ramsey would go after him, but he was bent over slightly, holding his side. He had already been in pain; those blows to the site of one of his bullet injuries were the last thing he needed.

I hurried to him, the knife still in my hand.

"Are you all right?" he asked me, through gritted teeth.

"Yes, don't worry about me. Did he hurt you badly?"

"I'll be fine in a minute." His voice was so tight and breathless that I felt a stab of alarm.

The car pulled up beside the curb, and Jakub quickly got out. "I saw something happening and a man running," he said. "Is everything all right?"

"We need to get the major to the hospital," I said.

"No. No need for that," he said, straightening. "Take me home."

I hesitated. I couldn't force him to go to the hospital, but I was worried the blows to his side might have reinjured him internally.

"We'll drop you home first," Ramsey said, though his face was colorless with pain.

"You absolutely will not," I said, taking his arm. "Jakub, will you help me get him to the car?"

"I'm fine," Ramsey said, in what had become a habitual lie.

He didn't shake off my hand on his arm as I escorted him to the car and into the backseat. I went back to collect his coat. I reached into the pocket and, just as I knew I would, discovered a handkerchief. I wrapped the knife in it so anyone handling it wouldn't leave fingerprints. Then I went to the car and got in, and Jakub hurried to get us back on the road.

I looked over at Ramsey, who, if not exactly slumped against the seat, was sitting in a much less formal posture than I was used to. "I still think you should go to the hospital."

He shook his head. "He caught me in the place where a bullet broke some ribs. It's sore, but no real harm done."

I wasn't convinced. "He might have broken them again. Will you at least see a doctor?"

"If the need arises."

I let out a frustrated breath. "Whoever is trying to kill you needn't bother because you're doing a jolly good job of it yourself."

He didn't answer.

I looked over at him. "By the by, who *is* trying to kill you?"

"You think he was after us specifically?" Something in his tone led me to believe this was his assumption, too, but he wanted my opinion without influencing me.

"That wasn't a street known for muggings. Someone was trying to get to you. He said, 'Mind your own business,' as he ran away. It was clearly a warning."

"I wish I'd been able to go after him."

I held up the handkerchief-wrapped object in my hand. "He left the knife. Perhaps you can get fingerprints from it."

He nodded. "Good work."

When we arrived back at his house, he got out of the car before I could come around to help him and started up the front steps. "Jakub, take Miss McDonnell home, please," he called without looking back.

"Just a minute, Jakub," I said. "I want to see the major inside."

He nodded, the concern in his expression telling me I was not the only one who was worried about the major's condition.

I followed Ramsey up the steps to the door. "Is your sister here?"

"Yes, but I'd rather not alarm her."

"Then let me help you get settled in your office, at least."

He didn't argue with me. I took it as a bad sign.

We went inside, and he led the way to his office, switching on the lights and moving to a little wooden cabinet along the wall. He took a bottle and glass from inside and poured himself a drink. He downed it in one swallow before turning back to me.

His jaw was still clenched, and his color was off. His skin had taken on a whitish-gray hue that reminded me forcibly of when he had been lying shot only a few months ago. I felt a wave of alarm.

"You look terrible," I said. "You'd better sit down."

"I'm fine."

"Major . . ."

His jaw clenched again.

"Major, sit down." I said this in my most Nacy-like tone, and I was gratified that it worked. He moved and sat carefully on the edge of his desk, too polite to fully seat himself while I stood.

"There's nothing to be alarmed about," he told me. "I still have some occasional pain, and the elbow to the ribs happened to exacerbate it."

"Of course, it did," I said. "You had four bullets in you not three months ago. Your insides are probably still healing."

"Don't fuss, Electra," he said.

There it was again, that feeling of intimacy, as though we were two people who truly knew each other. In moments like these, I felt a little tug of affection for him, something deeper than the spark of attraction. It was disconcerting in a way I couldn't quite name.

"It's nothing a little rest won't cure," he said.

"Noelle says you're not getting enough rest."

He swore. "I don't need the two of you discussing me."

"What can I get you?" I asked. "Are there some tablets you can take?"

"There are, but I'm not going to take them. I have work to do, and I need to concentrate."

"You can't concentrate when you're in pain."

His eyes met mine. "I certainly can. I do it every day."

I sighed. "It's taking its toll. Your health is of vital importance, you know. Not just for you. You're not going to be able to keep working at this pace. It won't do anyone any good if you work yourself to death."

"All right, all right," he said irritably. "I'll rest. I'll go to bed now."

"Take the tablets first."

He sighed. "Fine."

I raised a brow expectantly.

He glared at me for a moment and then went around his desk and pulled open a drawer. He removed a bottle of tablets, shook two from it. My teacup from this afternoon had not yet been cleared away. He picked it up from the corner of the desk and swallowed the tablets with a sip of cold tea.

"Satisfied?" he asked.

"You'll feel much better now," I said.

"I'll be useless for hours."

"I think the country will carry on long enough for you to get a bit of sleep," I said, my tone gentle.

He looked up at me and sighed. "I suppose they'll have to."

"Now, will you go lie down, or do I need to put you to bed as well?"

His eyes caught mine, and I flushed to the roots of my hair. It had been the sort of thing I would have said to my cousins, but I realized it could have a different interpretation given what had happened between us.

His lips parted then closed as he seemed to think better of what he was about to say. But then he went ahead and said it anyway. "As tempting as the idea is, I think you'd better go home now."

"Yes," I whispered. "I suppose I'd better."

"I'll see you out," he said.

We walked down the hallway and into the foyer. "Thank you for your assistance," he said. "I'll ring you up tomorrow when we learn something."

I nodded.

We stood there, looking at each other, and then I nodded toward the stairs. "Why don't you go up. Just so I can be sure you made it all right."

"I can manage the stairs," he said with poorly disguised impatience.

"Humor me."

He sighed again. "Good night, Electra."

"Good night. Sleep well."

He shot me a look and then turned to the stairs. I watched him as he made his way up, his posture as perfect as ever.

Major Ramsey had, upon our first acquaintance, seemed more machine than man to me. It was only gradually that he had begun to seem more human. He was not a man who easily revealed his vulnerabilities, and though I hated to see him in pain, I liked him better knowing that he wasn't invulnerable.

I left then, making my way down the front stairs and toward the car on the curb.

Before I reached it, however, the front door opened, and Noelle Edgemont stepped out onto the porch.

"Ellie," she called with a wave of her hand. "Wait a moment, will you?"

I turned back to her, worried something had happened to the major.

"What did you say to him?" Noelle asked when I reached her.

"What do you mean?"

"How did you get him to take his medicine and go to bed?"

I gave a little laugh. "Oh, I don't know. I just told him that he needed to do it."

Her brows rose. "I don't suppose you realize what you've accomplished. I've been arguing with him for a fortnight."

"He wasn't happy about it," I admitted. "But I think he's been hurting more than he likes to let on."

I didn't, of course, tell her he had been given several good blows to the ribs. That was his information to share, if he chose to.

She was watching me with an expression I couldn't interpret. It wasn't speculative, exactly, but there was something assessing in it.

"Will you come have tea with me again on Saturday?" she asked. "Since our lovely chat was interrupted today?"

I hesitated. I knew Major Ramsey didn't particularly approve of my growing friendship with his sister, but, after all, what would it hurt?

"I'd like that," I said.

CHAPTER NINETEEN

I was up bright and early the next morning. Today was the day I retrieved Julia's letters from Mr. Varney's flat.

Uncle Mick's job with the thieves was this evening, and I thought my own job would be a good way to distract myself from my worries. It would also keep me out of Uncle Mick's way as he prepared himself. After all, it had been a while since he had done a safe job.

Uncle Mick could, of course, open a safe in his sleep, but I didn't want to be the least bit of a distraction to him.

I was preparing to leave the house when I caught sight of the bouquet of flowers I had purchased at Chambers Flower Shop. If that had been a dead end, I needed to determine soon what my next course of action would be. I had yet to read the love letters between my mother and father. Perhaps there would be something in them that would give me an idea of where to proceed next.

But first things first. I had a robbery to commit.

I made my way back to Knightsbridge on the Tube and then walked the rest of the way to Mr. Varney's building. I had few worries about this job. Mr. Varney would be at work, and I had seen for myself that the flats had little daytime traffic. It should be an easy in and out.

Across the street, I stood shivering in a doorway, pretending to be waiting for someone with frequent impatient glances at my wristwatch. I had been at it for perhaps half an hour before the man in question emerged, attaché case in hand. Julia had shown me a photograph of him. He started down the street without even a glance in my direction.

I waited another ten minutes to be sure he was well and truly gone and then I walked confidently across the street and into the building.

I encountered no one and moved to the little metal postboxes in the lobby. It was easy enough to find the one with the name VAR-NEY on it. Flat 3B.

I took the lift up to the third floor. It opened onto an empty corridor, and I made my way to the door of 3B. So far, so good.

I gave the door a good rap. I was confident that Mr. Varney would be away for hours, but it was always best to make sure there wasn't anyone hanging about before one began to break in. It was entirely possible he had a new mistress lounging in his bed, and there were several good reasons I wouldn't want to walk in on her.

I waited a moment and, when there was no answer, knocked again. Nothing.

It appeared the coast was clear.

With a glance up and down the corridor, I removed my lock-picking kit from my pocket. It was a small leather pouch with hoops inside to hold all of my picks and other small tools. I removed a pick and slid it into the lock. These old flat door locks never posed much of a problem. They weren't really made to keep people out, not in any real sense. A child could have picked them. Or, at least, a child raised by Uncle Mick.

The lock gave, and, with one more look up and down the hall, I pushed the door open and stepped quickly inside, closing it behind me.

Inside the flat, I stood still for a moment and listened, taking in my surroundings. It was dark inside, since the blackout curtains were drawn, and the air was heavy with stale cigarette smoke and the underlying odor of general uncleanliness. My nose wrinkled. I felt for the nearest light switch and, ready to chance that I was alone, flipped it on.

The place looked as though it had already been robbed, though I suspected it was just Mr. Varney's lack of housekeeping skills. The table before the sofa was littered with bottles and empty glasses, and an overflowing ashtray rested precariously near the edge.

Items of clothing were strewn about, jackets and neckties resting on the furniture as though he flung them off every day as soon as he entered. Untidy heaps of magazines and letters rested on the side table. I went there first, flipping through them to see if there was anything of interest, but they were mostly bills. Mr. Varney had expensive tastes for a man of his position in life.

I did a quick going-over of the living area, searching all the usual places and some unusual ones for any sign of Julia's letters. I didn't think Varney would be the type of man to overthink about his hiding place. He would likely believe he had the upper hand and wouldn't be concerned that Julia might try to find the letters. He certainly wouldn't have anticipated her sending a professional thief.

All the same, I looked under sofa cushions, behind paintings for a hidden safe, and in a vase filled with artificial flowers. There was nothing to be found but dust and, in the case of the couch cushions, matchbooks, coins, and assorted crumbs.

I did a quick sweep of the kitchen. I had been avoiding it, as I knew it was likely to be the dirtiest place in the house. There were dirty dishes piled about and empty tins sitting feet from the bin. I wondered if Mr. Varney hired a maid. If so, I hoped he paid her well.

I went to the bedroom next. I looked for hidden recesses in his bureau drawers—most of which were hanging open and overflowing with clothes—and beneath the mattress. There was nothing hidden in the shelves of his wardrobe or in the cupboard behind his bathroom mirror.

I had saved the desk in the corner for last, and I went over to it now.

I opened one drawer, rifling through the papers in it. There were several folders of various documents that were of no interest to me. But tucked at the back of the drawer was a stack of letters, tied loosely with a hair ribbon. I pulled them out and glanced through them. They were Julia's letters, all right.

I smiled to myself. In a robbery, there was nothing as euphoric as the feeling of getting your mitts on what you were after.

On the way back through the sitting room, I stopped at the liquor cabinet. There was nothing hidden there, but I checked the bottles and found a vintage whiskey I knew Uncle Mick would like. I slipped the bottle into my pocket.

I was preparing to leave the flat, but something stopped me. It wasn't so much a sound as the sense of movement outside the door. Was someone in the hallway? I stilled, hoping whoever it was would continue on their way.

A moment later, there was the rattle of a key in the lock.

I froze, looking quickly around and trying to decide where the best place to hide would be. I didn't want to get cornered in the bedroom, so I hurried over to the windows and concealed myself behind the blackout curtain. I hoped there was no one on the street below who would happen to notice my odd position, pressed up against the window. At least I was on the third floor.

I pushed the stack of letters into my pocket and waited.

The door opened a moment later, and I heard an exclamation and then a resigned sigh as the person in question began to mutter to herself. Then there was the clinking of glasses. It seemed Mr. Varney did have a maid, after all.

There was the sound of retreating footsteps, so I ventured a glance around the curtain. I could see the maid's back as she made her way into the kitchen. I hoped that she would stay there until I could make my way out of the apartment.

I heard a sound of dismay, followed by a good deal of tutting and mumbling under her breath. I didn't blame her. I certainly didn't envy her the job of cleaning up this mess.

I thought about making a break for the door. At that moment, however, she came out of the kitchen and began cleaning up in the sitting room. I felt a wave of dismay. How long would I have to hide behind this curtain? What if she spotted me here?

This was as close as I had been to being caught in a robbery, aside from the time Major Ramsey had set us up in order to convince us to work for him.

Thinking of Major Ramsey, I knew how bad it would look if I was caught here, in this particular man's flat. It would look as though I were doing some freelance thievery. It would be even worse because Varney was, after all, a government official. I needed to get out of here without being caught, that was all there was to it.

Providentially, the telephone began ringing just then, and the woman went to answer it.

Moving quickly, I slipped out from behind the curtain and hurried to the front door. I opened it soundlessly and escaped into the hallway, breathing a sigh of relief.

I walked home at a leisurely pace, Julia's letters tucked safely in my pocket. Knowing the job was done was at least a bit of weight off my shoulders.

It was not until I reached home and pulled the letters from my pocket that I realized one of my blue gloves was missing. I patted down my pockets looking for it, but there was only one of them, the left hand.

I was not sad about the loss of the glove itself. After all, I'd been needing a new pair for some time. But I sincerely hoped I hadn't dropped it in Mr. Varney's flat. I remembered how I had shoved the letters into my pocket. It was possible the glove had been dislodged then and fallen behind the curtain.

If I had committed the most amateurish of housebreakers' sins—leaving a clue behind at the scene—I had been out of the game for far too long.

Of course, even if Mr. Varney did discover it, he had no way of knowing where it had come from. Unless he frequently looked in the hiding spot in the drawer, it might be some time before he even realized that Julia's letters were missing. By that time, he would have no way of tracing the robbery back to me.

As far as the glove, it was clear he often entertained. Any woman who entered his flat might have left it. He might even assume it belonged to the cleaning woman.

Besides, it was possible the glove had fallen out at any point between Knightsbridge and here.

I tried to push that worry aside as I went to telephone Julia that she might come and pick up her letters.

She was at my door within fifteen minutes. I opened it to her urgent tap, and then she was inside and embracing me. "Oh, Ellie, I don't know how to thank you!"

"I'm glad I could help, Julia," I said, giving her a squeeze before ushering her into the room and motioning to the coffee table, where I had set the stack of letters.

She quickly took a seat on the sofa and picked up the stack, sifting through them.

"Are they all there?" I asked.

"Yes, I think so," Julia said. "I don't remember the exact number, but this seems to be all of them."

"I doubt he would have separated them," I said.

She looked up at me, tears glistening in her eyes. "I don't know what I would've done without you, Ellie."

"It's a lucky thing he kept them where I could get to them," I said. I didn't want to scold the girl, but I hoped my meaning was clear. She should take more care with the men to whom she wrote letters in the future.

She looked down at the letters in her hands. "I've been thinking about it, and I feel a bit guilty I used the favor you owed Uncle Frank to convince you to get them back. It wasn't, perhaps, a nice thing to do to a friend."

"I owed your uncle the favor anyway," I said lightly. "It's just as well you could make use of it." I realized, however, that, while I didn't blame her, I did feel slightly differently about our friendship now. I hadn't particularly wanted to do the job, and I might have refused had I not been required to balance my account with Frank Doyle. Julia had forced my hand.

Looking at her shining eyes and the relief on her face, though I knew I wouldn't hold it against her. Perhaps she had done the wrong thing, but it had been for the right reason. And, after all, a debt was a debt.

"I hope you and Brian will be very happy," I said.

"I know we will. Thanks to you. I'm going to burn these letters and never think about Peter again. Brian is the only man for me."

She left a few moments later, and I closed the door behind her with a sigh. That was one favor repaid. Now I owed only Pony Peavey.

CHAPTER TWENTY

I accompanied Uncle Mick to the major's office that evening.

Uncle Mick was going to meet up with the thieves at Red's, and from there he planned to accompany them on their job at the undisclosed location. Major Ramsey would send someone along to follow the thieves, and then, if they retrieved the map from the safe as planned, Uncle Mick would signal to their tail that he should move in and make the arrest.

It was a dangerous plan that put Uncle Mick in a difficult situation, but it had been the best they had been able to devise without knowing where the thieves planned to strike.

In the meantime, the major and I would confer with Archie Blandings to see if he had learned anything about the map or what might have happened to his contact, Santos, in Lisbon.

Uncle Mick and I reached the major's office, and Constance greeted us with a smile.

"Good evening. He's expecting you," she said. Her tone today led me to believe he was in a better mood than usual. Perhaps the rest had done him good.

Uncle Mick and I went down the hallway and found the door to his office open.

"Hello," he said, standing up from where he sat behind his desk. "Come in and close the door, please."

I did as he bid me, looking him over in the process. He definitely looked better than he had last night. His color was much improved, and, though his movements were still a bit stiff, it seemed the assailant had done no lasting damage.

His eyes caught mine, and something passed between us. He gave me only the barest of nods, and, somehow, I knew just what he was telling me. He felt better after a good night's sleep and the relief of the pain medication, but he didn't particularly wish to discuss it.

I gave him a faint smile, and then he turned his attention to Uncle Mick.

"Are you prepared for this evening?" he asked. I knew the major was frustrated with the lack of intelligence. He didn't like Uncle Mick going into this blind any more than I did. But we needed to get the map. If the Germans were able to get their hands on that tungsten, it would only aid them in their weapons production. It might seem minor, but every German tank we could take off the battlefield felt like a victory.

My uncle nodded as he took a seat. "As prepared as I'll ever be. I don't imagine the job itself will pose much trouble. So long as your man stays with us, I don't foresee any problems."

"I'll have Kimble on it. He'll stay with you."

I knew Kimble from previous jobs with the major. He was a former Scotland Yard man who was as cool and composed as he was competent. I felt better just knowing he would be the one helping Uncle Mick.

There was a tap at the door, and, at the major's call to enter, Constance brought in a tea tray and set it on the corner of the desk.

"Thank you," Major Ramsey said.

"Yes, sir. Would you like me to pour?"

"That won't be necessary. Thank you, Miss Brown."

"Mr. Kimble has just arrived. Shall I send him in?"

"Yes, please."

Constance went out, closing the door behind her, and Major Ramsey rose from his seat. He moved to the tray and poured tea for the three of us.

A moment later, Kimble came in. He was the very definition of a nondescript man, of average height, build, and unremarkable coloring. His eyes, however, were a cold, placid gray.

"Hello, Kimble," I said brightly.

He was the most expressionless, unexcitable man one could imagine. Naturally, he displayed no enthusiasm at seeing us again. He merely nodded his head in our direction.

"Have a seat, Kimble," the major said.

Kimble drew up a chair from the corner and sat.

"We're just going over the plans for this evening. Mr. McDonnell is to meet them at Red's. You went there today, I think?"

Kimble nodded. "Got a good look at the place. It's not likely they'll be driving to their destination. Won't want to call attention to themselves. So we'll follow them on foot. I've got several of our best men set along different possible routes. All McDonnell has to do is give the signal, and we'll move in."

Kimble was a man of few words, but he was certainly saying the right ones to make me feel better about what Uncle Mick was walking into.

At last, Uncle Mick stood. "I guess it's time to be on my way."

I rose, too, and reached to give him a hug. "I know you're tired of my saying it," I said into his ear, "but please be careful."

He patted my cheek. "I will, Ellie girl. Don't you worry about your old Uncle Mick."

With a nod at the major, he went out of the room, and Kimble followed wordlessly behind him.

I took my seat again, saying a silent prayer for Uncle Mick's safety.

"Your uncle is wilier than most of military intelligence. I wouldn't worry too much," Major Ramsey said.

I looked up at him, realizing I had been biting my lip as I fretted. "It feels different than our old work somehow."

"It is," he said. "But he's no less capable of it."

He was right, of course. Uncle Mick knew what he was doing, and I had to trust that everything would go according to plan.

I picked up my teacup from the desk and raised it in salute. "To a successful evening."

He raised his own cup. "I'll drink to that."

Another concern occurred to me then. "Do you suppose the thieves are onto us, and that's why the man with the knife came to warn us off?"

"I have someone looking into that," the major said. "I doubt it was the thieves who sent him, as they would have been more likely to confront your uncle directly. It's possible it has something to do with our connection to Blandings and his work in Lisbon. He may have been followed when he arrived in London."

It was then, talk of the devil, that Archie Blandings arrived.

He took the seat beside me, rumpling his hair with his hand as he removed his hat just as he had at the pub. It was an endearing gesture that added to the impression of youth about him.

"Things have got rather interesting," he said without preamble.

Major Ramsey waited. It seemed he was not going to mention the assailant. Or perhaps he and Archie had already discussed it.

"To begin with," Archie said, "I may have found your Anna Gillard."

I frowned. The last we had seen of Anna Gillard was her bloody body in that hotel room. "What do you mean?"

"She's holed up in a hotel in Aylesbury."

I tried to make sense of what he was saying, and it seemed there was only one possible option.

"Do you mean to say that the dead body in the hotel wasn't Anna Gillard?" I asked.

"It seems that way," Blandings said. "The body doesn't match the description that I received from an acquaintance of Anna Gillard's in Lisbon. Furthermore, I had someone look into matters at the hotel, and it seems that one of the staff has gone missing. I can only assume it was she who walked into the room and encountered the burglars and was killed because of it."

This was a startling revelation.

"Do you want me to pick Miss Gillard up?" Blandings asked Major Ramsey.

"Tomorrow."

They finalized the details, and Blandings took his leave. My thoughts were still whirling. If Anna Gillard had survived, why hadn't she sought out help? Had she gone to see Nico Lazaro, or had she simply gone into hiding?

I realized suddenly that the major and I were alone and sitting in silence. It was, surprisingly enough, not uncomfortable. I was glad things were feeling less awkward between us, even if that persistent pull of attraction had begun to make itself known to me again.

Ramsey moved to stoke the fire, and I sipped my now cool cup of tea.

When the clock struck midnight, I was surprised. I had not realized it was growing so late. Perhaps the job would last longer than we had thought. Perhaps I should return home and wait for Uncle Mick there.

I found, however, that I was loath to leave the cozy warmth of the room, with the crackling fire and the yellow glow of the lamps. It felt easy, comfortable. And it was a long way back home in the cold alone.

Major Ramsey came and sat, too.

It was then I looked down and noticed something gold on the floor. It was a tube of lipstick. I reached down to pick it up before I could think better of it.

I glanced at it before setting it on the edge of the major's desk without comment.

His eyes flickered to it before coming back to me. He would claim it was his sister's.

"Jocelyn Abbot was here," he said at last. "She must have dropped it."

I wondered what he was trying to tell me. If he was merely speaking the truth, or if he was letting me know that his romantic interests lay elsewhere. Why was talking to a man sometimes very like trying to decipher a code?

I decided to be honest as well, and equally vague in my feelings.

"Yes," I said casually, though my throat felt tight. "I saw her leaving the morning I came to bring you to Pony Peavey's."

His eyes met mine, and I felt myself flush. I hated that I couldn't keep myself from blushing when I could otherwise do a credible job of appearing nonchalant in an awkward moment.

He was silent for a long minute, and I sensed he was trying to decide what to tell me. Trying to decide how personal he should make his reply.

"As you know, Jocelyn has been gathering information for me since the conclusion of that first time you and I worked together."

"You don't have to . . ." I started, but he held up a hand.

"She has been gathering intelligence from several of her highly placed friends. She was at a party all night and stopped to relate something to me very early that morning."

"It's none of my business," I said.

"She didn't spend the night here."

I forced myself to look up at him. His eyes met mine, his gaze intent. "I told you once before: things were over between Jocelyn and me a long time ago. That hasn't changed."

I nodded, unsure of how to respond.

I didn't know why I felt so relieved to hear that he had not resumed his romance with Jocelyn Abbot. It wasn't as though he had admitted some sort of feelings for me. But there was some acknowledgment there of something between us, wasn't there? Some reason he had felt the need to explain.

Why must things be so complicated?

There was a well-timed sound outside the door, and a moment later Uncle Mick came in. I was surprised to see that Kimble was right behind him. I had assumed he would be overseeing the arrest of the culprits.

Unless something had gone wrong. Uncle Mick sat down, his expression cheerful but not as elated as one might have expected after a successful job.

"Well, we have good news, and bad news," he said.

"Yes?" Major Ramsey demanded. He really was not at all patient in situations like this, and Uncle Mick's indefatigable cheeriness would always be a trial to him. Despite the difference in their methods, however, they worked well together.

"It seems tonight was just a bit of a test run," my uncle said. "They took me to a vacant house and had me break into a safe there. We didn't get away with much, but I'll happily turn over my share of the loot, so as not to be breaking the terms of my employment." Uncle Mick looked over at me and winked.

A trial run. The thieves had been testing his sincerity and his abilities. It wasn't ideal, but it meant we were still in the game. We could still get the map back.

"So you didn't arrest them?" Ramsey asked Kimble.

"McDonnell never gave us a signal, so we never made the move," Kimble said.

Ramsey nodded. His expression had grown distant as he appeared to be considering the next course of action. "It seems we're back where we started," he said at last.

"Well, as to that, not entirely," said Uncle Mick. "Now that the boys had reason to trust me, and a new appreciation of my skills, they were a bit more forthcoming."

The major and I both turned to look at Uncle Mick expectantly.

"They told me the location of the spot they mean to strike next, and a little bit of the plan," Uncle Mick said as he removed his pipe from his jacket pocket and put it to his lips. "It seems they plan to rob a fellow called Nico Lazaro."

CHAPTER TWENTY-ONE

I stared at him in surprise. "But they've already robbed Nico Lazaro," I said at last, when the silence stretched.

Uncle Mick turned to look at me as he filled his pipe with tobacco. "They told me a bit about that, too," he said. "Seems whatever they were looking for was not there at the time that they previously robbed him. Now they've received word it's in a safe, and they want to give it another go. This time, a bit more in the shadows, so to speak."

"Did they say who gave them this information?" Ramsey asked.

"As to that, they were fairly vague," Uncle Mick said. "Seems they were making their way through a list of people who might have had the object in their possession. They took what they found along the way to disguise it as common thievery rather than call attention to their true motivations."

"If we know where they're going, then we can get it before them, and perhaps even replace it with a useless map." We had pulled such a job early in our acquaintance with the major, substituting false documents for the ones the Germans were looking for. Would it work again with this lot?

Major Ramsey swore and took a seat behind his desk, rubbing a hand across his jaw. "This complicates things. But the idea of replacing it and causing the Germans even more trouble has its merits."

"I don't know much about cartography," Uncle Mick said. "But I'm willing to bet Felix could help you create a false map. If it was something you were interested in doing."

The only hint that the major didn't particularly like the suggestion was the way his face showed no expression whatsoever at the mention of Felix's name. All the same, I knew Ramsey was fair enough and smart enough to let Felix in on the job if he thought it would work.

"And I have the perfect opportunity to replace it," I said suddenly.

Major Ramsey looked up at me. "You are not going to that party."

My chin went up. "The opportunity has fallen right in our laps. I think it would be a mistake to ignore it simply because you don't like the man."

He looked over at me, seemed to consider his words carefully. "Lazaro is . . . not a good man. I'd rather not put you in that position," he said at last.

"I can do it," I said.

"I know you can," he replied. "That's not the issue."

"Then it's settled."

Major Ramsey's face said he did not at all approve, but he didn't argue this time.

Uncle Mick smiled. "Well, Ellie girl, it sounds like you've got a party to go to."

I rang up Felix the next day, and he agreed to accompany me to Major Ramsey's so we could all discuss the plan. Felix was also to work with Archie Blandings on creating a believable map of Portugal we could use to send the Germans mining in the wrong place.

Uncle Mick had gone to Red's to see if he could learn anything else. In that easy way he had of putting people off their guard, he was ideally placed for the task.

"Once again, you're putting yourself in harm's way," Felix said as we walked from the Tube station toward the major's house. "You're not happy unless you're throwing yourself into the lion's den."

"Yes, well. It came out all right for Daniel, didn't it?" I said. "Besides, I'm the only one of us with an invitation to the party."

"And why, I wonder, would Nico Lazaro, noted lecher, be wanting you to attend his party?" Felix said.

"You let me worry about Nico Lazaro," I replied.

Felix seemed to sense that I was growing frustrated because he dropped his teasing tone. "I can't help worrying about you, sweet."

"I know, Felix," I said, squeezing his arm.

"After all, the chivalry in me makes me want to rise to your defense."

"Oh, is that what it is?" I asked.

He shrugged. "Well, that and I'm afraid you'll fall in love with Lazaro and move to Lisbon with him to lounge about eating arroz doce in a lace negligee."

Bending down, I picked up a handful of snow, packing it into a little ball as best I could, and hurled it at Felix. It hit him squarely in the chest.

He grinned, his eyes flashing. "Oh, that's how it's going to be, is it?"

"Chivalry!" I reminded him, backing away.

"In the name of chivalry, I shall give you three seconds' head start."

"Felix!" I shrieked, laughing, even as I turned and began running as best as I could on the slippery ground to dodge the snowball he was making.

It hit me on the bottom. I whirled, still laughing, and it was too quick a move on the icy ground. My feet slipped out from under me, and I tumbled into the snowbank that edged the pavement.

He made his way to me, laughing. "I'm sorry, sweet."

"You wretch! You aren't the least bit sorry!"

He was still laughing as he reached out his hands to help me up. I sometimes forgot that his artificial leg was not as steady as his other one, and it failed him now. His foot slipped out from under him, and a moment later he had tumbled forward, knocking me back into the snow.

He rolled off me, and we lay side by side in the snow, laughing as we had done as children.

That was when the front door opened, and Major Ramsey stood looking down at us.

"Oh," I said, sitting up. "Hello."

"Hello," he said, his eyes moving from me to Felix. "Hello, Lacey."

"Ramsey," Felix said, getting nimbly to his feet and reaching to help me up.

"We were just having a minor disagreement," I said lightly, dusting myself off. "Where has my hat gone?"

I looked back to see it had fallen off down the pavement.

"I'll get it," Felix said.

He began walking back to retrieve it as I made my way up the front steps of Major Ramsey's house.

And then I stooped, scooped up one more handful of snow, packed it tightly, and threw a parting snowball that hit Felix squarely in the middle of the back.

Then I darted inside of the house. Major Ramsey followed.

"You must forgive me, but I had to win," I said as I turned to him, my eyes still gleaming with the triumph of that last well-aimed snowball. I knew I must look a fright, dusted with snow, my hair windblown and my cheeks pink with laughter and cold.

So I was startled by the heat in his gaze as his eyes met mine. There was no mistaking it. Not angry heat. The other kind.

Then Constance was there, taking my coat and muffler, and helping me brush the snow from my hair.

"No gloves?" the major asked as I rubbed my hands together briskly to warm them.

"Only one. I dropped the other somewhere else. I seem to be dropping things all over London."

Felix came in with my hat. "We still have the walk home, you know," he said with a good-natured smile.

"Yes, so you had better watch out."

By the time we reached his office, the major had reached his usual appearance of complete indifference to me. Sometimes I wondered if I imagined those moments between us. But then I remembered that explosive kiss—the few moments of electric connection we had shared—and I knew that it was still there somewhere. I couldn't help but feel a bit pleased at the way he had looked at me.

It was very bad of me, I knew, to want him to want me. But I couldn't seem to help hoping that it was difficult for him to cast me aside after one kiss. I simply couldn't get that kiss out of my mind.

I sighed. It was all so ridiculous. I was not some schoolgirl to lose my head over a handsome boy who had kissed me.

What unsettled me was that, deep down, I was beginning to realize it was more than that. And, of course, where did that leave Felix?

But now was not the time to consider all of this.

"So what's the plan?" Felix asked when we were settled. "Ellie tells me she's been invited to a party at Nico Lazaro's and intends to get into the safe. I foresee only one problem."

"And what's that?" Ramsey asked.

"Lazaro letting her out of his sight long enough to get the job done."

"Oh, stop it, Felix," I said. He was doing it on purpose, flirting with me in front of Major Ramsey.

But Ramsey, it seemed, had his own cards to play. "She won't be going in alone."

I looked up at him. This was not something we had discussed.

"You'll be accompanying her?" Felix asked.

"I'm not invited to Lazaro's parties," Ramsey said. "But I have an associate who is. He'll be arriving shortly to make introductions. We'll go over the details of the plan while you and Blandings work together on the map. You've brought everything you need?"

Felix nodded to the little leather bag he'd brought with him. "All the tools of the trade in one tidy package."

"Good. Blandings will be able to give you up-to-date specifics on what should be included in the false map. I'll show you where you can set up. If you'll excuse me for a moment, Miss McDonnell."

The men left the room, and a few minutes later, Major Ramsey was back.

"You didn't tell me I was to have a date to the party," I said.

"I think it best, all things considered. Backup is always preferable in any situation."

I didn't argue with him. "And who is my date to be?"

"His name is Aristide Dupéré. He is, obviously, a Frenchman. He's been working with intelligence here, while assisting with the resistance movement in France. He also happens to be someone comfortable in Lazaro's set. There are a few things you should know about him in advance."

Now I was intrigued.

Before the major could continue, however, there was a tap at the door.

"Come," he said.

The door opened and Constance looked in. "Monsieur Dupéré is here, Major Ramsey." I was surprised to notice that her normally placid face was a bit pink. I wondered if she was feverish. I'd never seen Constance's color that high.

There was a slight pause before the major answered. "Show him in, Miss Brown," he said in a tone that sounded almost resigned.

"Very good, sir." Constance retreated, and shortly afterward there was the sound of footsteps down the hallway.

A moment later, the door was flung open and a man swept in, talking loudly enough that his voice would surely carry back to Constance. "Ah, *Majeur,* mademoiselle is far too *jolie* to be a secretary. I am trying to convince her to run away with me. She says no, but I am nothing if not *persistant.*"

I turned to look at the man who had just entered. I could see at once why Constance had been flustered. In addition to his clear amorousness, he was extraordinarily handsome. He was tall and dark, with flashing black eyes that matched the gleam of his pomaded hair. There was something of a Rudolph Valentino air about him that was immediately noticeable.

His eyes lit on me, and I at once saw a focused intensity in them that might have been alarming if I was at all the sort of woman to be swept off my feet by French *charisme.*

Then he shot a look at the major, one eyebrow raised. "Do you keep all of the loveliest women in London here in your *maison?*"

Major Ramsey sighed audibly. "Miss McDonnell, allow me to present Monsieur Aristide Dupéré. Dupéré, this is Miss Electra McDonnell."

He came to me and took my hand, bowing so low over it that his warm lips brushed my skin. "*Enchanté,* mademoiselle."

"Pleased to meet you, Monsieur Dupéré."

"You must call me Aristide."

"I'm called Ellie."

He still held my hand as his dark eyes studied my face. "But you are the lady with whom I am to work? So young and beautiful . . . and you are brave, too? *Magnifique.*"

Major Ramsey cleared his throat. "That will be sufficient, I think, Dupéré. I was just discussing the matter with Miss McDonnell."

"Then I have come at a good time."

He took the seat beside me, crossing one leg over the other.

"The party, as you know, is tomorrow night. You and Miss McDonnell will attend together. At some point in the evening, she will enter Lazaro's study and replace the map with the one we are currently drawing up."

Monsieur Dupéré waved a hand. "*Facile.*"

"Simple, it may be," Major Ramsey said. "But there are any number of things that could go wrong."

"We'll pull it off all right," I said.

"*Oui.* Ellie and I are going to be *bons amis*, are we not?" he said, flashing his very white teeth.

"Dupéré . . ." Major Ramsey said.

But Dupéré had leaned closer and taken one of my hands in his, studying it. "Such soft, delicate hands to do such important work."

Major Ramsey said something sharply in French, to which Dupéré responded with a grin.

There was then an exchange in rapid-fire French, of which I could understand perhaps one word in ten. I presumed that was the reason Major Ramsey had chosen to use it.

Aristide waved a languid hand, his words flowing in an amused tone.

Major Ramsey answered with evident fluency and what sounded like a perfect accent, but without any of the accompanying gestures. It was remarkable, I realized suddenly, how Major Ramsey managed to sound stern even in French.

"I'd rather you not discuss me as if I weren't here," I said at last.

Both men turned to look at me.

"Ah, but pardon, *chérie*. It is unforgivably *impoli* of us."

Major Ramsey was less apologetic. "I think that's everything for the time being. You can go, Dupéré. Miss McDonnell, be here tomorrow evening at nineteen hundred hours."

"Actually, I'll be here tomorrow afternoon," I said. "Your sister invited me for tea."

Major Ramsey's face went impassive again, as it did when he didn't want me to know what he was thinking. Then he gave a short nod. "Very well. You can get ready here afterward, and Dupéré can pick you up."

Dupéré smiled. "I shall be looking forward to it."

He rose and took my hand in his. "*Au revoir,* Ellie. Until tomorrow night."

With a nod at the major, he left, and a moment later I heard him bidding Constance farewell with similarly flowery language.

I turned to look back at Major Ramsey, my brows raised in amusement. "Rather throwing me to the wolves between him and Lazaro, aren't you?"

"I don't suppose I need to tell you that Dupéré . . . has a reputation," Major Ramsey said. "I wouldn't give him too much encouragement."

"Do you suppose I just go about throwing myself at attractive men who happen to cross my path?" I asked it pleasantly enough, but I didn't suppose Major Ramsey missed the edge to the words.

If it came down to it, I would remind him that it was he who had kissed me and not the other way around.

His eyes flashed, and he looked as if he was about to reply and then thought better of it. He paused for just a moment, and when he did speak, his voice was neutral. "Of course not, Miss McDonnell."

CHAPTER TWENTY-TWO

"He'll try to seduce you," Felix said merrily as I related the details of my meeting with Aristide Dupéré on the way back to my flat.

"You're not the least bit jealous," I said indignantly.

"No, because if you'd wanted a charming ne'er-do-well, you'd be head over ears in love with me by now."

I looked up at him, wondering if there was more to the words than his cheery tone implied.

"Felix . . ."

He smiled. "It's true, of course, that I'm not French. But it's not the Frenchman I'm worried about."

I didn't say anything. I knew what he meant. And I also knew that I couldn't deny it. But now was not the time for this conversation.

There was, however, another conversation I needed to have with him.

We returned to my flat and took a seat on the sofa. Burglar jumped into my lap with a little meow. He had taken to living with me with great readiness. I was already accustomed to the little presence in my flat, keeping me company.

"When did you get a cat?" Felix asked, reaching out to stroke his head.

"I found him in the rubble of a bombed-out house," I said. "I couldn't leave him there. He's called Burglar."

Felix smiled. "A suitable name."

"Yes." I petted the kitten, the purr surprisingly soothing as I mustered my courage for the coming conversation. At last, I came out with it. "Felix, I need to talk to you about something."

He looked at me. "This sounds serious, sweet."

"It is. At least, it's important to me."

"What is it?"

I drew in a deep breath. "I need you to tell me what you've been doing in Scotland."

I expected a light reply, Felix's customary humor putting off the question, but, instead, his expression grew serious. His eyes met mine. "I can't tell you, love."

"Why not?" I whispered.

"There are . . . reasons. It brings me no enjoyment to keep things from you."

I should have let it drop, but for some reason I felt unable to. There was so much uncertainty in my life, and I needed answers. "You can trust me, Felix. You know you can."

He sighed. "It isn't that, Ellie. You know it isn't. But there are some things that it's better for you not to know."

I started shaking my head even before he finished speaking. "I don't want things to be that way between us. We're friends, aren't we?"

"You know you don't ever need to ask that, Ellie," he said, grasping my hands in his. "You know how I feel about you, don't you?"

I looked into his eyes. They were so warm and familiar. I always felt comforted when I looked at Felix somehow. It was as if I knew that I was safe.

"If it's a job, I swear I won't tell anyone. Not even Uncle Mick."

He hesitated.

"Or is it the major you're worried about me telling?"

His eyes didn't quite meet mine, and I felt my heart sink.

"That's it, isn't it?" I whispered. "You think I'd betray you to Major Ramsey."

The feeling that he didn't trust me was like a punch to the gut, and I felt tears spring to my eyes. I set Burglar down on the sofa and stood, walking a few steps away so I could collect myself without Felix's eyes on me.

"No. No, Ellie." He came up behind me and turned me to face him, slid his hands up my arms. He was looking down into my face, but I couldn't read his eyes. "I trust you with my life. You know that."

"I wouldn't tell him," I said. "I wouldn't betray you."

"I know, love. I know." He leaned down to kiss me, but it wasn't a passionate kiss. It was to reassure me, to reestablish the connection between us.

"Come back and sit down," he said after a moment, taking my hand and leading me back to the sofa.

I did as he asked. "I'm not trying to make things difficult for you," I said. "I just worry about you."

"I know." He reached into his pocket for his cigarette case. He put one in his mouth then flicked on his lighter. "The truth of the matter is, I've been doing a little work of my own for the government."

I stared at him. This was the last thing I had expected him to say.

"What sort of work?"

"I can't tell you that, Ellie. I've already said too much."

"You mean you're not . . . you haven't been doing illegal work in Scotland?"

He blew out a stream of smoke and smiled. "I know you haven't exactly taken me for the hero sort. But I figured, one-legged or no, I can still do my bit. Chivalry, remember?"

I gave a little laugh. "Are you . . . forging?"

"Something like that."

I realized he wasn't going to give me any more details, and that was fine. There was just one more thing I wanted to know.

"Is it dangerous?"

He shrugged. "No more dangerous than anything else I've done."

I knew very well what that meant.

I didn't know if I felt better or worse knowing what Felix had been up to. On the one hand, some part of me was surprisingly relieved that he had not been committing crimes. I didn't know when, exactly, I'd become such a law-abiding citizen, but I couldn't deny the feeling.

"Thank you for telling me, Felix."

His eyes came up to mine, warm and full of affection. "You know I can't resist you, Ellie. Never could."

I wasn't exactly surprised when one of Pony's men came to fetch me that evening. Pony had said he wouldn't do the work for free, and he wasn't a man who said things for the fun of it.

There was a sharp rap on my door as I sat reading a book, Burglar on my lap.

I opened the door to see a grim-faced man I didn't recognize. "Pony wants ye" was all he said.

"Now?"

He gave a nod.

"Let me get my coat."

A moment later, we set off.

Pony had a job for me, then.

Well, it was best that I do it and get it done with. At least I could put it behind me and no longer dread the day when he might turn up asking for a favor.

The hulking bloke he sent to collect me said nothing as we made our way back to Pony's. It occurred to me that it must be something pretty urgent if I hadn't even been given the liberty of coming in my own good time.

I felt a bit uneasy about it all, truth be told, but I'd learned a long time ago to hide any such feelings, especially from men like these.

We reached Pony's quickly and found the basement mostly empty except for a table of men with loosened ties and sweaty shirts, indicating they'd been playing all day and showed no signs of slowing down.

Pony wasn't at the table, though. Instead, the man led me wordlessly through the room to a door on the other side.

I expected some sort of office, but it was more of a storeroom. What use would Pony have, after all, for a desk? There was a table there, though, where he sat with a plate of dinner before him, a great pile of eggs and what looked to be thick steak and warm buttered rolls. It seemed that Pony had connections on the black market.

"Have a seat, Ellie," he said, motioning to the place across from him.

There was no chair there, but at his words the man who had brought me from my house slung one over from a wall. The chair's feet skidded across the concrete floor but came to a stop directly across from Pony.

I moved forward and took a seat.

I didn't like anything about this situation, but I also knew I couldn't do much to change it. Nor did I feel as though I was currently in danger. If I did as Pony asked, all would be well. After all, he wasn't likely to harm me when he had use for me.

All the same, I would be glad to be out of this basement and back in the winter darkness.

He took a long swig of tea from a chipped cup before he turned his attention back to me.

"I've got a bit of a problem that I think you can help me with."

"Oh?"

He took a large bite of eggs and then glanced down at the plate. "Would you like some dinner?"

"No, thank you."

He took another bite. He was enjoying himself, clearly. Pony was the kind of man who liked people to be afraid of him, to worry about what he might say or do. I didn't intend to give him the satisfaction.

"I do hate to rush you, Pony, but I've an appointment this evening," I said. I didn't, but I didn't intend to sit here all night waiting for him to make his reveal.

He looked up at me and grinned. "Few people rush me these days, Ellie McDonnell. I like your mettle."

"After all, I'm doing a favor for you."

"Right you are," he said. "Right you are."

He motioned to the man, and he moved to a stack of crates that stood in the corner. He picked up something from the top crate and brought it over to Pony.

Pony set it on the table between us and then pushed it toward me. It was a photograph.

I looked at the man in the photo. He was distinguished looking, with dark hair and eyes and a trim mustache.

"Do you know him?"

I looked from the photograph to Pony. He was watching me, and I wondered if he expected me to recognize the man.

Just to be sure, I glanced at the photo again. Then I set it back down on the table and shook my head. "I've never seen him before."

"Good," Pony said. "I need you to take care of a little matter for me, and it's better if you don't know the man."

"I hope you don't expect me to kill him," I said. I was making light of things, but I wouldn't entirely put it past Pony.

He laughed boisterously. "No, nothing like that. If I wanted him dead, I'd send Jonsey here," he said, jerking his head toward his employee who still stood motionless in the shadows.

That wasn't exactly comforting, but at least I knew he didn't expect me to play the assassin.

"This fellow is in possession of something I want. I need you to get it for me."

That seemed simple enough.

"What is it?" I asked.

"That's for me to know, love."

"You'll have to tell me something if you want me to do the job."

"It's not exactly an object, so to speak. It's information."

I narrowed my eyes. "How can I get that?" I hadn't been about to kill a man for Pony, and I wasn't going to seduce one for him either, if that's what he had in mind.

"You will need to get into his office without leaving a trace. I've got a little device I want installed. It'll allow me to listen in on his conversations."

So he wanted to wiretap the man. I'd heard of such things, though no one I knew dabbled in that sort of work.

This was better, I supposed, than some of the other job options Pony might have given me. And I knew the sort of people Pony dealt with. If this mystery man was an associate of his, it was likely he was up to no good. Their business was none of my concern. I would do the job and be well rid of Pony.

I couldn't help but feel a bit like the fly who'd walked right into the spider's web.

Well, this was my own doing, and there was no undoing it now. I didn't allow myself to think of what Uncle Mick might have to say about the matter, and I certainly didn't give myself time to think about what Major Ramsey would do if he found out.

I'd made a deal with the devil, and now it was time to pay up.

"All right," I said. "I can do that."

"I know you can. You'll do it tomorrow."

I thought of all that was already happening tomorrow and shook my head. "I'm busy tomorrow. I'll do it the day after."

He gave a little nod, spearing his steak with his knife. "Don't make me wait too long."

CHAPTER TWENTY-THREE

I tried to put my encounter with Pony out of my head the next day. One job at a time. That was what Uncle Mick always said.

Felix was absent today, putting the finishing touches on the map he was crafting.

He had, unsurprisingly, got on very well with Archie Blandings. There was an easy sort of boyish charm about both of them that put them at ease with each other.

Felix gave me few details about what the map would entail, but I had every confidence it would be enough to fool both the thieves and the Germans.

The thought of Germans wasting both time and resources trying to find a nonexistent deposit of a valuable mineral was extremely satisfying, and I hoped we would be able to pull it off.

And, with that goal in mind, I made my way to the major's residence that afternoon. I had brought along the dress I'd worn to a fancy affair with the major the previous year as well as everything else I would need to make myself presentable.

But first there would be tea with Noelle. I was looking forward to chatting with her. I only hoped I would be good company when my mind was preoccupied with the evening's job.

I could have canceled my meeting with her, of course. But she was going back to her children soon, and I thought it would be nice to wish her well on her way. We might never have the chance for tea again. I didn't know when she would next be back in London, and my work for the major was of a transitory nature.

Constance opened the door for me, and I entered along with a gust of cold wind.

"Hello, Constance," I said, pulling off my hat and gloves. I'd found an old pair of Toby's to replace mine for the time being.

"Hello, Ellie. Freezing out there, isn't it? I'm afraid the major isn't here at the moment, but I'm sure he won't be long if you'd like to wait."

"Oh, actually . . . I'm here to see Mrs. Edgemont."

"Oh, I see," she said. Whatever she thought of this, it was impossible to tell. I had the impression that Constance didn't nec-essarily approve of my crossing the personal/professional boundary, but perhaps I was just putting my own misgivings onto her.

As if on cue, Noelle arrived at the top of the stairs. "Do come up, Ellie."

I went up the stairs again and we entered the same little sitting room where we'd shared tea before.

"The weather continues to be dreadful," she said as we set-tled into our seats with our tea. "I'm not looking forward to going north."

"Have you decided when you're leaving?" I asked, picking up my cup.

"Tomorrow, I think. I've been away from the children too long as it is. It's just that . . . well, I've felt that Gabriel has needed some looking after. I feel better about leaving now, though."

"Yes, he seems to be healing," I said.

"That's not what I meant," she replied, her eyes meeting mine over her teacup. "I meant you."

I set my teacup carefully back on the saucer. "Me?"

She gave me a half smile that reminded me very much of her

brother. "I haven't known you long, of course, but I know my brother. You're obviously special to him."

I flushed. "We . . . work together," I said.

"We both know it isn't just that. He works with Constance, and he doesn't look at her the way he looks at you."

I sighed, feeling deeply uncomfortable. I debated on my answer but decided the truth would probably be best. Noelle Edgemont was obviously fond of plain speaking. "There is, perhaps, a bit of . . . attraction between us," I said. "It doesn't mean anything."

"It always means something," she said, setting down her teacup.

"When two people are pushed into close contact frequently, it isn't unusual for . . ."

She shook her head, silently cutting me off. "It isn't like that with Gabriel. He doesn't fall into casual romances."

"There isn't a romance," I said.

She raised a brow. "No?"

She wasn't going to let the topic die, so it seemed I would have to tell her what she wanted to know. Apparently, persistence was a trait that ran in the Ramsey family.

"We did kiss once," I admitted. "But we agreed that it shouldn't happen again. I . . . come from a very different world than he does. I don't think we would suit."

She surprised me by letting out a derisive scoff. "Oh, tosh. This is 1941, not the Victorian era. That sort of thing doesn't matter, especially not in the middle of a war."

"But it might matter when the war is over," I said.

She gave me a hard look. "Did Gabriel say this to you?"

"He . . . he didn't have to," I said. I didn't want to tell her that it was more than social status. It was the fact that I was the child of a convicted murderess, that I had grown up to be a thief. That we had met because I'd been caught breaking into a house.

"Then he likely doesn't feel that way."

"He has said it would be inappropriate for us to have any sort of relationship," I replied. That was true enough. It was the reason he had given me after our kiss, that such a thing could not be repeated.

She sighed. "That does sound very much like Gabriel."

"We work well together," I said, trying to draw the conversation to a close. "It's a comfortable partnership, and I think we're both satisfied."

"I very much doubt it," she answered dryly.

As much as I wanted to change the subject, there was something I wanted desperately to know, and this might be my only opportunity to find out. Granted, it was none of my business, but I couldn't stop myself from asking.

"What happened between him and Jocelyn Abbot?"

She looked up at me. "You know about Jocelyn, do you?"

"I've met her," I said. "There seemed to be some . . . unresolved feelings between them."

She lit a cigarette as she considered what she was going to say. It reminded me of her brother, the careful way she thought about things before she spoke. Perhaps it, too, was a family habit.

"He met Jocelyn about five years ago. They met and suddenly they were inseparable. It was all rather whirlwind, I think. Unlike Gabriel. He's had romances before, of course, but nothing too serious. His first love has always been his career."

"But he fell in love with Jocelyn," I said.

"He is not the type to declare his feelings far and wide, but yes. I think he was very much in love with her. It was commonly assumed they would be married, but then the war started and Gabriel was called to North Africa. I don't think he ever officially proposed."

But he'd bought the ring. I knew that much.

"And then what happened?" I asked.

"She realized that he was not going to be what she wanted."

"What do you mean?" I found it difficult to believe that Major Ramsey was not what most women wanted.

"Jocelyn will always be a woman who thrives in society. She didn't want to be an army officer's wife. She wanted to be the wife of an earl's nephew."

"Oh," I said. We were talking of a world that was entirely foreign to me, and so the possibility had never really occurred to me. "I see."

"Since childhood Gabriel has been committed to a career in the military. He never wanted anything else. He was a soldier before the war, and he will be one after."

"Yes," I said. He had told me as much in an unguarded moment in Sunderland. Told me about his father's service and injury in the last war, about his desire to serve his country.

"I don't think either of them wanted to admit that they knew it wouldn't work long-term," she said. "And so they both went on ignoring the fact for years when they should've put an end to things. They finally broke it off while he was in North Africa. I knew it must have been very difficult for him, so far from home. But, of course, Gabriel was not going to mope about it."

"And he doesn't talk about her?" I realized that my interest in the topic of Major Ramsey's love life must be very transparent, but this might be my only chance to learn something about that part of him.

"I mentioned her to him a time or two, but he's always brushed the matter aside. He said that he knew it was over long before they ended it."

"All the same," I said. "I think he felt it very deeply."

"Perhaps. As I'm sure you can imagine, Gabriel has always been a bit reserved. We shared a womb; I imagine I know him better than anyone else in the world. But sometimes I can't figure out what's going on in that head of his." Her gaze met mine. "But it's been easy enough for me to see how he feels about you."

I took a sip of tea so I wouldn't have to respond.

I considered what she had told me. Just because he had known things wouldn't work with Jocelyn didn't mean he didn't still feel the loss of that love. I had never been entirely certain that, despite his insistence that things were done between them, there weren't some lingering feelings.

Another thought occurred to me: Was his hesitance to get involved with me because of what had happened with Jocelyn? Did he worry about the instability of wartime romance? I had to admit, it made sense.

Thankfully, Noelle changed the subject then. We talked easily for some time of trivial things and also of her boys and my cousins. She had me laughing over the antics of her young sons. I told her about Toby, and she said she would pray for his safe return.

At last, I realized it was time I start getting ready for the party. Her company had proven an excellent distraction, but now it was time to get down to business.

"I have a party to attend tonight, something to do with my work with your brother. Might you direct me to a place where I could dress?" I asked.

"Oh, a party," she said. "I'm so envious. I haven't been to a party in ages. Will you let me help you get ready?"

I hesitated, but she looked so delighted at the prospect that I couldn't very well say no.

"If you really want to," I said.

"We will make you the belle of the ball," she said, standing and moving to take my arm. "Come along. I'll make you irresistible, just leave it to me."

I had never particularly enjoyed dressing up. It wasn't something I'd had much occasion to do over the years, and, being the only girl in the family, not much emphasis had been placed on it.

Noelle Edgemont's enthusiasm was contagious, however, and it was rather fun allowing her to fuss over me.

Not only that, but she'd given me the loan of a brand-new dress.

I'd tried on the burgundy velvet for her, and she'd shaken her head. "It's too big. You'd need it altered."

I had lost a bit more weight than I'd realized over the past few months. I didn't think the dress was too big to wear, but if Noelle with her superior knowledge of fashion noticed it, it would probably draw the attention of others as well.

"I don't have another dress that will do," I told her honestly.

Her eyes had lit up. "I have just the thing. I bought it just before I left London, and I never had a chance to wear it. I think it will fit you perfectly."

"Oh, I couldn't—"

"You most certainly can," she said adamantly. "There's no use in a good dress going to waste. By the time I have a chance to wear it, it will likely be out of fashion anyway. Now wait right here."

A few minutes later, she was back with a glistening length of black fabric draped over one arm.

"It's going to be magnificent with your coloring," she said, holding it up in front of me. "I shall be ashamed to wear it after you."

At her urging, I went behind the screen and emerged a moment later. The dress was like something out of a fairy tale. But not one the princess would have worn. No, this was more suited to a villainous queen. It was black satin, fitted bodice to hip with a long skirt that was both loose and form-hugging all at once. Two black satin straps originated on the right-hand side, one going over the right shoulder, the other crossing my chest to go over the left shoulder. The two wide straps crossed to form an *x* across an open back.

I did a turn in front of the mirror, admiring how the black satin hugged my figure, the liquid darkness of the skirt against my legs. I hadn't liked my curves as an adolescent girl. I'd wanted to continue fitting in with my cousins, not be ogled by their friends. A couple of them had even been so brazen as to get handsy before Colm and Toby had knocked the stuffing out of them.

"Are you certain you don't mind if I wear this?" I asked for the third or fourth time, still observing myself in the mirror.

"Not at all. It looks wonderful on you. I'll be glad someone can get some use of it. I won't be wearing evening wear for some time when I get back to Cumberland. Everything is so very dull there."

"Thank you," I said. "I'll be careful with it."

She waved a hand. "Don't fret about that. Now, let me help you with your hair."

My unruly hair had always been my adversary, but it conformed readily enough to Noelle Edgemont. Even my curls bent to her will. She crafted an elegant and fashionable coiffure, wielding pins with ease until she'd secured the style just as she wanted it.

She stepped back to observe her work. "Perfection. Now, on to the makeup."

I powdered my face, darkened my already black lashes with mascara, and chose a dark red lipstick to complement the ensemble. I looked at myself for a moment in the mirror and was satisfied. I looked rather glamorous, I had to admit.

Glamorous was one of the last words I would normally use to describe myself, so I found the change amusing—and a little bit exciting.

Noelle had gone out of the room for a moment, and when she came back, she had a small box in her hand. "To complete the ensemble," she said.

Before I could reply, she opened the velvet box to reveal a glittering diamond bracelet. "You don't need a necklace with that neckline," she said. "But this will give you a bit of sparkle."

"Oh, no. I couldn't."

"Yes, you can. Give it to Gibby when you're finished with it. He can keep it for me until I'm back in London."

She put the bracelet on me, and I felt a strange little tug of emotion at the fact that she so easily trusted me with it.

"Gabriel's in the foyer with that profligate Frenchman," she said. "You should go down now and make an entrance."

I let out a little breath. I was not especially keen on that idea, but I did need to go downstairs. So I turned to Noelle. "Thank you so much for everything."

Impulsively, I gave her a little hug. She was cool and elegant like her brother, but it didn't stop her from hugging me back. "Good luck tonight, Ellie. And, if I don't see you again before I leave, I hope I see you again next time I'm back in London."

I nodded. "I hope so, too."

I took my handbag and left the room, walking to the top of the stairs. I could hear the men below, conversing in French, but when I started down the stairs the conversation stopped.

The black satin glided across my legs as I made my way down the stairs.

For just one moment, my gaze caught Major Ramsey's, and I felt a flush spread through me at the look in his eyes.

I looked away. I didn't want him to think I had been flaunting my appearance for his sake. Ramsey said nothing as I reached the foyer.

Aristide, however, had enough of a reaction for both of them.

"Ellie, you are a dream! A vision! A temptress and an angel!" He came to me as I reached the bottom of the stairs and pulled me into his arms. "I shall have to remind myself it is all an act, or I shall fall at your feet."

I laughed, pushing back from him. He was ridiculous in his flattery, but it was nice to be flattered all the same.

Only then did I look again at Major Ramsey. His expression was now carefully neutral, but his eyes had gone the flinty gray color they turned when he was annoyed. Was it annoyance at me or at Aristide? Perhaps both.

I smiled at him. "Your sister played fairy godmother and now I'm ready for the ball."

"I don't think you'll have any problem fitting in," he said.

"Thank you."

"I disagree," Aristide said. "She will not fit in. She will stand out, shine above all the women there. We ought not to have put you in that dress if we wanted you to escape notice."

I frowned playfully at him. "That's quite enough of that."

He shrugged. "I am yours to command. I am at your complete disposal." His eyes flashed and he leaned closer, lowering his voice so that only I could hear him. "In any way you should choose to use me."

Despite myself, I felt a little flush at his outrageousness.

"Dupéré has the map in the pocket of his dinner jacket," Ramsey said tersely. "When you're ready to get into Lazaro's safe, he'll give it to you."

I nodded. "I think we're ready, then."

"Wait a moment," Noelle called. She came down the stairs with a fur coat draped over her arm. "Put this on, Ellie."

"Oh, I don't think—"

"I will not take no for an answer. Put it on."

"Allow me." Dupéré took the coat from her and held it up. I slid into it, the soft mink collar grazing the bare skin of my back.

"You can leave that with Gabriel, too. I have no use for mink in Cumberland."

"Thank you, Noelle," I said again.

"Don't wait up for us, Ramsey," Aristide said as he slid an arm around my waist.

A muscle in the major's jaw jumped.

"Wish us luck," I told him over my shoulder as Aristide led me to the front door.

He didn't reply.

CHAPTER TWENTY-FOUR

Truth be told, I was rather excited at the prospect of infiltrating the party in evening dress. It had been a while since I had been to a glamorous event. In fact, the last time I'd been to a party had been in Major Ramsey's company. I had been to a nightclub or two with Felix since then, but nothing high society like this.

It had also been a while since I'd been involved in a good, old-fashioned robbery.

A combination of the two might be almost too much fun.

Not that I was inclined to be flippant about any of it. I was under no illusions about how dangerous this job would be. I knew we were taking risks breaking into Nico Lazaro's safe. Especially during a party. It was possible his guard would be down at the event, but it was also possible there would be even more precautions on his part.

There was a flutter of nervousness in my stomach as I considered this, but I was honest enough to admit that that flutter was also tinged with excitement. I couldn't deny to myself that I enjoyed this type of work.

There was, in the back of my mind, the worry that, when it was time to do the job, I would be scared after what had happened in Sunderland. It had occurred to me that there might be lasting repercussions from what we had endured in that cave, from the close call that we had had. But I didn't feel as though it was going to hinder me in my work. I felt clearheaded and focused. I felt ready to do what needed to be done.

We got into the car, and Dupéré slid close on the seat. "We are going to have fun this evening, yes?"

"Yes, I think so. Perhaps you'd better give me the map now so that I can keep it on me in case I find a good moment to slip away."

He reached into his pocket and retrieved a folded piece of thick paper. I took it from him and, for lack of some better place to put it, shoved it into the bodice of my gown.

"Ah, it has come to this," he said, following the progress of the map. "That I should come to envy paper."

He really was frightfully bold, but I decided that I might as well enjoy it. It wasn't as though Aristide Dupéré was serious about pursuing me. Nor was I interested in him. He was handsome, charming, and amusing, but I did not have the patience for his type of man.

Even if there wasn't the matter of Felix. Even if there wasn't the matter of Major Ramsey. I didn't judge the girls who found comfort in this sort of easy charm, but I knew myself and knew that it would not make me happy. His bonhomie, if that was the right word for it, was just the sort of thing designed to irritate me with any sort of prolonged exposure.

The problem with men like Aristide is that, even though it's perfectly clear that they don't mean any of the outlandish things they say, there is still something flattering about the effort they put into their charm and blarney.

There was a bit of that sort of an attitude in Felix—not that I believed for a moment he was insincere with me. But I had seen that side of him often enough, the way he had dazzled the neighborhood girls when we were younger. The way women still smiled encouragingly at him now.

"Perhaps we will be friends even after this," Dupéré suggested. "You are, I think, the kind of woman I could fall in love with."

I laughed. "I am not going to fall in love with you," I told him firmly. "And, while we are being honest: I am most definitely not going to fall into bed with you."

He gave me what I supposed was meant to be a shocked expression. "I can assure you, my intentions are most *honorable*."

"Yes, well, *honorable* or not, you're wasting your time."

He looked at me for a moment, and then he grinned. "It is not very often that I am unsuccessful."

"No," I agreed. "I don't doubt it. Which is precisely why you've developed this bad habit."

He laughed outright then. "Do you care nothing for my pride, Ellie?"

"I think your pride is healthy enough to survive me."

There was something quite enjoyable about arriving at the party on the arm of Aristide Dupéré. He instantly drew notice, of course. Not just because he was handsome but because he carried himself in the manner of a man who knew he was.

Usually, I found these sorts of men tedious, but, for some reason I had not yet put my finger on, I liked Aristide very much. Not that he wasn't occasionally tedious.

But I thought that, if one knew the right way to handle him, he was essentially harmless and quite amusing.

We entered the apartment without comment from the butler, Cheevers, who let us in. He looked about as miserable as it was possible for a person to be, and I commiserated with him.

Music was playing loudly, and I could hear the underlying sound of conversation, laughter, and clinking glasses.

I gave a friendly nod to the naked lady statue as I passed, and then Aristide and I went into the main rooms of the flat.

"All eyes are on you, the most beautiful woman in the room," he murmured into my ear as we entered. I knew perfectly well that he was lying—no one was paying us any particular notice—but sometimes a girl likes to hear nice things about herself.

I felt glamorous in the black satin dress, as though I belonged at fancy parties like this. Not that I had any desire to be a part of this world, but it was always nice when a disguise did what it was designed to do.

I spotted Nico Lazaro at once. He was the center of attention, a group of women around him laughing as he told them some story, waving his arms expressively. He looked handsome and elegant in a black velvet dinner jacket, his dark hair slicked, but there was that unmistakable aura of lechery about him that kept him from being appealing.

A moment later, he glanced in our direction and, excusing himself from the group, made his way toward us.

"Miss Donaldson," he said as he reached us. "I'm delighted to see you. I didn't think you'd come." He leaned to brush a kiss across my cheek, and I caught the aroma of strong aftershave and several strong drinks.

"And Dupéré. I didn't know you were acquainted with Miss Donaldson."

"We are . . . old friends," Aristide said, inflecting a clear insinuation into the words. I was certain a part of his assignment from Major Ramsey had been to keep Mr. Lazaro at bay, but I wasn't certain this was the best way to go about it. I saw the unmistakable flash of excitement in Nico Lazaro's eyes. He was taking it as a challenge.

I repressed a heavy sigh. Men could be so very tiresome.

"Can I get you a drink, Elizabeth?" Mr. Lazaro asked.

"Not just now, thank you. I think I'll wander around and look at some of your art."

He smiled. "By all means. Please let me know if you'd like me to tell you about any of it. I would be happy to give you a tour."

Aristide's hand landed on the small of my back in a slightly possessive gesture.

Nico Lazaro flashed his teeth at us, and then he turned to greet a pair of new arrivals.

"I do not like the way he looks at you," Aristide said in my ear.

"It's exactly the same way you look at me," I pointed out.

He made one of those deeply affronted faces. "You wound me, Ellie."

"We don't have time for you to be wounded," I said. "Mingle with the guests and try to be a distraction so I can slip away."

I walked away from him and farther into the room, the air heavy with the smell of cigarette smoke and too many perfumes. It would be easy enough to lose myself in this crowd. There were a great many people here, apparently unconcerned with the possibility of a German air raid. So far, we had been lucky this evening, but I wondered where all these people would go should the sirens start.

That was a worry for another time, however. At the moment, I needed to disappear into the crowd, make myself inconspicuous enough and engage with enough of the guests that I could finally slip away without drawing attention to myself.

Aristide, of course, soon made himself the life of the party; he had as many women surrounding him as Nico Lazaro. I realized that the major had made a good choice in sending him along with me. He naturally drew attention to himself, and, as a result, he would draw attention away from me.

After perhaps half an hour, and a few sips from a much-too-strong drink that had been foisted upon me, I set my glass down and moved unobtrusively toward the corridor that led to his office. With a casual look over my shoulder, I slipped down the hallway.

It was unlit, a clear indication that this part of the house was not meant for his guests. If I was caught, I would say I was looking for the powder room. But it didn't seem that anyone had observed my exit from the main rooms of the house.

I made my way quickly down the corridor, the satin of my dress rustling softly against my legs.

As I approached the office, where I had previously seen the un-opened crate of artifacts he kept there, I heard voices. There were two men talking in a room not far from me.

I moved silently forward, listening. If I had the lay of the land correctly, the voices were coming from inside Nico Lazaro's office. I hadn't noticed if he was still in the room when I had slipped away, and now it seemed that he had stepped out of his party to conduct a bit of business.

I would have to come back when the office was unoccupied.

I was about to turn around and go back to the party when a statement caught my ear.

"We have the buyer ready?" It was Nico Lazaro. He could, of course, be talking about a buyer for any number of things. He dealt in art, after all. But he seemed more interested in buying art than selling it. What he might be interested in selling, however, was the map he had acquired.

I took a step closer so I could better hear.

"Yes, we have the buyer lined up," the other voice said. "He'll meet you at the club in the morning. There are rumors that those Germans are still looking for it, so the sooner it's off your hands the better."

They were definitely talking about the map, then.

"It's safe," Lazaro said. "I put it in my safe at the club. Few people will think to look there."

The club? I tried to figure out where he must mean, and then I realized suddenly that it was the nightclub in which he owned a partial stake. In all likelihood, the thieves would never have thought to look there.

Well, this certainly put a crimp in things. We were going to have to rethink our entire plan now, and we didn't have much time to do it.

I realized then that there had been silence inside the room for a moment too long. Were they aware of my presence?

As quickly and quietly as I could, I turned back toward the sound of the party, toward the laughter and lights and sloshing liquor.

"Elizabeth, wait a moment."

I stopped at the sound of Nico Lazaro's voice. He had seen me. Well, I would just have to play it off.

I turned as the man he had been talking to moved past me with a brief nod and disappeared back into the crowded party.

I was alone with Mr. Lazaro.

"I was looking for the powder room," I said. "I remembered where it was from the last time I was here."

"Don't rush back to the party," he said, his voice low and warm. "Come and talk to me for a bit. In my office. We'll have more privacy there."

My instincts told me this was not a good idea, but I could think of no good excuse. I didn't want to put him on his guard. Besides, he had already come to me and slipped a hand around my back, shepherding me in the direction of his office.

"Well, I'm sure Aristide will be looking for me before long," I said. "But I suppose he can wait for a few minutes."

He smiled down at me. "Aristide Dupéré can wait for you all night as far as I'm concerned."

I laughed as he guided me to his office door. I glanced over my shoulder down the hall. There was no one in sight. And, whatever I might have said to Mr. Lazaro, I doubted very much Aristide would be looking for me. After all, he expected me to be working on the safe.

"If I'm honest, I was a bit surprised to see you with the likes of Dupéré," he said. "Do you know him well?"

"Not, I think, as well as he would like."

"I'm glad to hear it, my dear. He's not the kind of company you should be keeping."

Mr. Lazaro led me into his office, where I stepped away from him and his warm hand on the bare skin of my back. He shut the door behind us. The sound from beyond immediately silenced. It didn't escape my attention that he had not closed the door with his associate but had done so with me.

It was a large enough room, but it was so crammed with objects that it seemed much smaller. There were more boxes and crates stacked up here than the last time I had been in this room. Apparently, he'd been able to collect more art from displaced persons.

There was a lamp on one corner of the desk, and he moved to it, pulling the chain to turn it on. Then he beckoned me closer. "Come and see this piece."

I moved to the desk and looked down at the piece on the corner of it. There was a very nice miniature there, clearly an expensive piece, though I didn't recognize the artist.

"It's lovely," I said politely. "Who painted it?"

"Nicholas Hilliard. It's late fourteenth century. He was a goldsmith as well as an artist. Did many paintings of the Elizabethan court."

I looked down at the miniature. "Her face is striking."

"A beauty with an eye for art. You impress me, Elizabeth." His hand landed on my back again, his warm fingers brushing the bare skin.

I hadn't expected him to be this fast of a worker. The major had warned me, of course, so I shouldn't be surprised. But I'd never had a man try to undress me after giving me a one-minute art lesson.

"Thank you for showing it to me," I said, turning and causing his hand to fall away. "Now I suppose I'd better be getting back to the party."

But he had moved to put himself in my path. I was now between him and the desk.

"Don't play hard to get now, Elizabeth," he said. "We'll have a lovely time, you and I."

"Really, Mr. Lazaro, I didn't come here for this."

"No? You seemed interested enough when you were here with Ramsey."

I felt my anger growing along with my alarm, but I pushed both down and tried to remain calm. "I apologize if I gave you the wrong impression, but I'm not looking for romance."

He stepped closer, close enough that we were nearly touching. "Sometimes romance finds us when we aren't expecting it."

"If you'll excuse me, Mr. Lazaro . . ." I made a move to step around him, and his expression grew darker and lost the pretense of pleasantness. With a suddenness that caught me off guard, he grabbed my upper arms and pushed me backward. I hit the edge of the desk hard and then he was leaning over me, his arms braced on either side.

"Don't toy with me, darling," he said. "You'll find it won't work in your favor."

And then he tried to kiss me. I turned my face away, and his mouth hit my neck, which seemed to suit him just fine, as he began pressing hard kisses into it. I struggled against him, but his grip on my arms tightened painfully and his body pressed hard against mine.

He was a good deal bigger than me, but he had failed to take one thing into account.

There was a very sharp letter opener sitting within reach on his desk.

"Let me go," I said, giving him one last opportunity.

"Stop struggling," he murmured, his breath hot on my skin. "You may as well admit you like it, and . . ."

He stopped mid-sentence as I pushed the edge of the letter knife into the flesh above the general vicinity of his kidney just hard enough to make him realize I was serious.

"Back up, Mr. Lazaro," I said.

He stilled, swore.

I pressed the letter opener a bit harder. Naturally, I hadn't had time to test the point, so I wasn't sure how sharp it was. For his sake, he'd better hope that it had been dulled by opening letters. Even dull, I could get it into his guts if I needed to.

"I'd appreciate it if you'd back up a bit," I said again. My tone was still pleasant, but I knew there was no way he could miss the hard undertone or the look in my eyes. I wasn't playing games with him, and he knew it.

He lifted his hands and eased back slightly. "All right, all right. There's no need for all of this."

I eased myself up from the edge of the desk, pressing the letter opener a bit harder as I moved forward. "Yes, well, you didn't seem to understand me before. I thought perhaps this might improve your hearing."

He offered me a smile, trying to ease the situation. But his eyes were blazing with fury. He was used to having his way, it seemed.

I started to move around him, the letter knife still held up, and he made a sudden lunge, grabbing my wrist. So, with my left hand, I hit him in the nose as hard as I could. I wasn't naturally left-handed, but I'd been in enough scrapes with the boys over the years to know how to use both my fists.

There was a disturbing crunch and immediately blood began pouring from his nose.

He called me a name that was mostly unintelligible due to the fact he was clutching his face in his hands, but I caught the gist of it.

"As lovely as the evening has been, Mr. Lazaro, I think I'll take my leave."

I turned and left him dripping blood on his Persian carpet.

CHAPTER TWENTY-FIVE

Back in the main rooms of the house, I spotted Aristide standing in a corner, leaning close to a young woman who was making a great show of letting him peer down her décolletage, while pretending not to.

I made my way over to them. "Aristide, darling," I said, with the feigned coolness of suppressed jealousy. "May I speak to you for a moment?"

"Of course, *chérie*." With an apologetic look at the woman, he took my arm and led me over to another corner of the room.

"Try to look as though I am scolding you for flirting outrageously with that woman," I said.

He made one of his expressively innocent gestures that I was certain would give the right impression to anyone who happened to be watching us. "I was not flirting with her," he protested. "We just happened to share an interest in art."

I didn't have time to argue the point. We needed to move, and fast.

"We have to go," I said.

He was instantly alert, a kind of sharpness in his gaze I had not seen there before. I wondered if I had underestimated him. Perhaps he was not just a pretty face.

"What's happened?" he asked. I noticed that his accent seemed remarkably less pronounced now that he was not playing the seducer. I supposed being excessively French had worked in his favor on more than one occasion.

"We must contact Major Ramsey. The map isn't here. It's at Lazaro's nightclub."

"There are marks on your arms," he said, looking down at the bare skin. I followed his gaze. Sure enough, the marks of Lazaro's fingers were slowly appearing in a pale purple against my fair skin.

"It's nothing," I said. "Let's go."

Understanding flashed in his eyes, and I saw indecision there. He was wondering if he needed to address this situation. Ultimately, though, he acceded to my wishes. After all, the mission took precedence over the slight I had received.

He led me through the crowd to the front door and we collected my coat while he used the telephone in the foyer. I didn't understand the French, but I expected he was asking Ramsey to meet us. We'd sent Jakub and the car away, not knowing how long the job would take.

Cheevers held up the coat for me, and I slipped it on, glad to cover up the bruises on my arms. I thought, perhaps, he had noticed them, for there was sympathy in his gaze as he opened the door for me.

I wondered how many other women had left this flat with bruises—or worse.

Back in the frigid air, I breathed a sigh of relief. We might have a long night ahead of us, but at least we were free of the party and of Nico Lazaro.

"Are you all right?" Aristide asked me.

"Yes," I said. "He didn't hurt me."

"You're bruised."

"So is he."

Major Ramsey arrived in record time. We had been standing outside, a bit down the street, for perhaps ten minutes before he arrived. I was extremely glad of the warmth of Noelle's mink coat.

Almost before the car had pulled to a stop, Ramsey was getting out and coming toward us. I expected him to demand information about what I had overheard regarding the map in the safe, but it appeared Aristide had also told him about my encounter with Lazaro.

"What did he do?" he demanded, his gaze intent.

"It's nothing."

"Tell me." He was using his commanding officer voice, and I'd learned it was better not to argue with it.

"He tried to kiss me. I'm fine."

He knew that wasn't the whole truth. "And what else?"

I sighed. "He pushed me against his desk and wouldn't let me go until I stuck a letter opener into his kidney. Then I broke his nose. I know how to take care of myself, and it wasn't . . ."

My words trailed off as the major turned and stalked down the street in the direction of the flat. I hurried after him. "What are you doing?"

"I'm going to have a word with Lazaro."

"No. Major, wait."

He ignored me, and I had to increase my pace to keep up with him. I caught his arm before he could reach the building.

"You can't do that," I said.

"Let go of me, please."

"Ramsey . . ."

He turned to look at me, and his eyes were steel gray. "That man cannot be allowed to go on treating women that way. If you hadn't had the wherewithal to do what you did, you know what would have happened."

"But it didn't," I said.

I felt the tension in his arm beneath my hand, like a steel cable that was ready to snap. It was always a bit surprising to me to see this side of the major. Normally, he was so cool and controlled. But this was not the first time I'd seen this more volatile side of him.

There'd been several times when he'd had to keep himself in check. It was the military discipline that prevented him from letting his temper have free rein, but that discipline was holding on by shreds at the moment. And we didn't have time for this.

"We've got a job to do, and you are not going to put everything in jeopardy," I said. "So pull yourself together."

It seemed my sharp words were enough to cool his temper because I felt the tension in his arm lessen ever so slightly, and I dropped my hand from it.

He looked down at me, his expression unreadable. "I don't want you to be harmed because of me, Electra."

"Well, you did try to warn me."

"That doesn't matter. I knew his reputation, but I didn't think he would go so far. Not in the middle of a party."

"All's well that ends well," I said lightly, though I was, in all honesty, a bit shaken by the situation. I'd never had a man be quite so physically aggressive with me before. I knew it happened, of course, but I had never imagined it happening to me.

I wondered again if there had been other women who had not been so fortunate as I had and had been unable to make an escape. It seemed likely; Mr. Lazaro had been very comfortable with the entire thing, as though it was something he had done successfully before.

It was a good thing for Mr. Lazaro that Colm and Toby weren't in London. If they heard of this, I wouldn't have been able to stop either of them from demonstrating their protectiveness to Nico Lazaro in an extremely violent way.

"Let's just get the job done," I said. "We can deal with Lazaro later."

He let out a breath, nodded.

"I do appreciate the sentiment," I said as I slipped my arm through his and led him back to where Aristide was waiting for us near the car.

"You've got blood on your hand," Ramsey said.

"It's all right," I said. "It's not mine."

We discussed our options on the way to the nightclub. Somehow, Ramsey had been able to acquire the plans to the building, and he spread them out on his lap, Aristide and I on either side of him looking them over.

"I've been there," Aristide said. "The office is on the second floor of the building, here." He pointed to a place on the plans. "The ground and first floors are part of the nightclub itself. The office will be where they keep the earnings in the safe, so it's likely well guarded."

"If I recall correctly, there's usually a guard posted at the stairs," Major Ramsey said.

Aristide looked at me and winked. "We could send Ellie to lure him away. I'm sure she'd manage it."

"We will not be sending Miss McDonnell to lure him away," Major Ramsey said, his voice tight.

"No, because then who would open the locks for you?" I asked. "You'd be lost without me, Aristide."

"I tell you this, and still you rebuff me," Aristide said with a wounded expression, pressing a hand to his chest. "When this is all over, Ellie, how will I go on without you?"

"I have a feeling you'll make do."

"If we could continue with the plan . . ." Major Ramsey said tersely.

I pointed on the plans to what appeared to be a set of French doors leading to a balcony. "Can't we go in here? It looks as though it faces the back garden and not the street."

"We could," Aristide said. "But the balcony doesn't connect to any other rooms. You'd have to find a way to get up to the second floor."

"That's a long way down," I mused. "Is there anything that might make the outside scalable?"

"You're in evening dress," Major Ramsey pointed out. I hadn't remembered that little fact, but it was something to consider. There wasn't any spare time for me to collect more suitable clothes and change.

"I can climb a tree in a skirt, if need be," I said.

Aristide's eyes flashed, but I shot him a look before he could make some sort of inappropriate comment.

"There aren't any trees on that side of the building," Ramsey said.

"Ivy?" I suggested flippantly.

"A Rapunzel to let us in, perhaps," Aristide said.

"Focus, if you please." Ramsey was clearly losing patience, and I realized it was time for me to stop jesting with Aristide and formulate a plan.

"What about some sort of ladder? Is there a garden shed on the grounds? We may be able to find one there."

"It would be too obvious on the outside of the building," the major said. "I imagine the garden will be deserted in this weather, but I don't think we should take the chance of such a blatant entrance."

"What about a rope ladder or something of the sort?" I asked. "We could toss up a grappling hook, and Aristide could climb it and lower the ladder for us."

"There are both a grappling hook and embarkation ladder in the boot," Major Ramsey said. I was not entirely surprised. He was the sort of man who liked to be prepared.

"But Aristide will not be accompanying you," he went on. "It will be you and me going into the office."

"Can you climb a rope?" I asked. "Your injuries . . ."

"Are healed," he said, though I knew he was stretching the truth. It could be that his wounds had healed outwardly, but it was clear how much they still pained him. Especially after his violent encounter with that assailant. Major Ramsey climbing a rope to scale a wall before helping me up seemed risky.

"I think I can climb it," I said.

Major Ramsey looked at me dubiously, and I felt the familiar irritations I'd always had when Colm and Toby had doubted I could do something they could.

"You don't think I can do it?" I challenged him.

"I think it will be difficult in a gown," he replied carefully.

"I have no doubt you could do it if you needed to," I said. "But you don't. I'll do it."

He was going to continue arguing with me, but I didn't give him a chance. "Ingress should be easy enough. Then as long as they don't come into the office, we should be able to get in and out fairly quickly."

"Some sort of distraction in the nightclub would be even better," Major Ramsey said, with a glance at Aristide.

Aristide grinned. "I'll take care of that."

I had no doubt that he would find a way to call enough attention to himself that Ramsey and I could get in and out.

"How long shall I stay inside?" Aristide asked.

"Not more than an hour, I should think," I said. Inwardly, I hoped the safe was not one of the more difficult varieties. There was no sense worrying the men about this possibility.

Major Ramsey next unfolded a map of London. "Once you leave the nightclub, meet us here," he said, tracing a path to what looked to be a side street about half a mile from the nightclub. "Jakub can wait there, out of the way, and we can get away without being seen."

And, just like that, our plan was set.

CHAPTER TWENTY-SIX

This was the second time I'd been forced to open a safe in an evening gown in the presence of Major Ramsey, and, despite how glamorous I had felt earlier in the evening, I didn't think it was entirely fair that I was drafted into service while wearing uncomfortable clothes.

Jakub dropped us off down the street, and we made our way toward the building, as casually as we could with a grappling hook and rope ladder tucked beneath the major's arm.

It seemed the nightclub was a popular spot, even in wartime, for there were several couples making their way down the blacked-out streets toward the entrance, and I could hear the sound of music from within.

Just before we reached the building, the major's arm on my back guided me to the shadows at the side of the building and around toward the back garden. Everything was dark, of course. Even the nightclub had blackout curtains, but there was a quarter moon, and it was enough to see by.

Cautiously, we made our way into the back garden, where we stood still for several moments, listening. It seemed whatever entertainments the club offered happened inside the building, as the garden was entirely dark and quiet.

The major motioned for me to follow, and we moved to the spot where we could see the iron railing of the balcony two stories up. Taking the grappling hook in his hand, the major swung it upward. It hit the railing with a little clatter and then dropped back to the ground.

He swore beneath his breath.

He took it in his hand again, visually gauging the distance and angle he needed. He would not have admitted it, but I suspected just throwing the hook was painful. There was no way I was letting him climb the rope.

The second throw was good, and there was again a clatter and then a scrape as the hook caught the balustrade. Ramsey gave a little tug, and it held firm.

Before he could attempt the climb, I stepped in front of him and grasped the rope. "Give me the ladder," I whispered.

"Electra, I don't think . . ."

"We don't have time to argue," I said. "I'm climbing it. But if I ruin this dress, you must buy Noelle a new one. I can't afford it."

With that, I removed the fur coat and set it carefully on the ground. The sleeveless, backless satin dress was no match for winter weather, let me tell you. It felt for a moment as though I'd jumped into ice water. But I could tune almost anything out when I was focused.

Ramsey reluctantly handed me the little rope ladder, but I found that it was too wide to easily drape over my shoulder.

"I'll go up," he said, attempting to take the ladder back from me. I held firm.

"Nonsense." I considered for a moment, and then I realized what would work. I rested it in the skirt of the gown at one side and tied up the hem to create a little sack. Now my legs were free to climb, and the ladder was secure. It wasn't heavy, just unwieldy, and this had been the perfect solution.

"Won't be a moment," I whispered. Then I grasped the rope

and began to climb. It was much easier with my legs free. The going was not quite as effortless as it had been when I was a child, but I managed the first floor easily enough.

Major Ramsey watched my progress for a moment, but, the next time I glanced down, he had averted his gaze. I thought at first he was just keeping guard but then realized I had probably been flashing him my drawers.

I pushed aside any embarrassment I might have felt. Modesty was of secondary importance on a mission, and it was dark anyway.

Besides, I was confident they were not the first pair of knickers he had ever seen.

I reached the balcony and carefully pulled myself over the railing. Untying the sack I had made of the dress, I quickly secured the rope ladder so Major Ramsey could climb it. He did it so quickly, it felt as though I'd barely had time to drop the ladder to the ground before he was beside me on the balcony.

He pulled it up behind us and then gave me a little nod to proceed. Moving to the French doors of the office, I pressed my ear against the cold glass. Naturally, the blackout curtains were drawn, so we would have to trust that Aristide had been able to make enough of a distraction that no one was in the office.

I listened for several moments and heard nothing. It was entirely possible, of course, that someone was working quietly in the office, and we would be caught as soon as we came in.

That was a risk we were just going to have to take.

I pulled a pick out from where I had secreted it in the bodice of my dress along with the map and moved to the door. It took only a few seconds for the lock to give. Locks on second-floor balcony doors were generally not intended to withstand much resistance.

Slowly, the major pushed the door open a crack. There was a small alcove behind the curtains due to built-in shelves on either side of the French doors, and he stepped into it and pushed one of the curtains aside ever so slightly. The room was dark. The coast was clear.

He motioned for me to enter, and I hurried inside, glad to be out of the freezing wind.

I moved directly to the safe in the wall. A quick inspection told me it wasn't one of the more complicated varieties. It was, in fact, an easier model than I had anticipated. We might even get out of here ahead of schedule.

I put my hand to the dial and began turning it, ready to go to work. The major stood quietly a little ways away while I worked, moving the dial to feel for the internal contact points. I found one and then two.

Suddenly, there was a sound at the door. We both stopped and looked at each other. Surely no one was coming in. Aristide was meant to be downstairs causing a distraction.

I looked over toward the French doors. Ramsey had closed them behind us, so they wouldn't cause alarm in themselves, but I didn't think there would be time enough for us to get out of them before the door opened.

Ramsey jerked his head toward the balcony, and I hurried in that direction with him hot on my heels.

His hand on my elbow, he hustled me into the little space between the curtains and the French doors just as the office door opened. There was no time to get out onto the balcony, so we both froze. My back was pressed against the cold panes of glass with the very warm major pressed against the front of me.

He likely couldn't move without jostling the curtains, so we stood still.

I tried not to think about how close we were, tried not to notice the way I could feel the rise and fall of his chest against me.

Instead, I forced myself to focus on the sound of movement inside the room. Someone was moving around, though it seemed to be only one person as there was no conversation. He was also whistling to himself, which seemed to indicate that there was no cause for alarm.

"Ah," a voice said after a moment, as though he had found what he was looking for. The footsteps retreated. Then the door inside the office closed and there was silence.

I let out a breath.

But I had not yet begun to breathe easy because Major Ramsey hadn't moved. He was still standing so close I could feel the press of each of his jacket buttons through the satin of my bodice.

I looked up at him.

He looked down at me.

"They're gone?" I mouthed.

He nodded. But he still didn't move.

The attraction was electric, zinging through me. I felt drawn to him, like there was a magnet preventing us from moving apart. I clenched my hands at my sides to keep from putting them around his neck. He'd made it very clear how he felt about a romance between us; if he wanted a step in that direction, he was going to have to take it himself.

He let out a slow breath that caused a loose curl to dance against my neck. He reached up to touch it, his fingers warm against my chilled skin. My breath caught in my throat. Our eyes met.

Then he blinked, and he stepped back. I was left with only the cold glass for comfort.

"All clear," he said.

I followed him from behind the curtains, feeling that my head was not at all clear. But I understood as well as he did that the job needed to be done, and we didn't have time for distractions.

We went back into the room, and I marshaled my focus and moved quickly toward the safe as the major moved back toward the office door. He leaned close, listening, and gave me a quick nod.

I went back to work, thinking only of the numbers and the feel of the dial beneath my fingers. Major Ramsey stayed very still and very quiet, and I blocked him from my mind. I didn't have the luxury of addressing those emotions now.

After perhaps half an hour, I had the combination, and the safe lock gave a click as it released.

Ramsey moved to my side as I pulled the door open. He reached inside, sifting quickly through the papers as I drew the map as unobtrusively as I could from my neckline.

"Here," he said, after a moment, unfolding a map. "This is it."

I unfolded the map that Felix and Archie Blandings had drawn up and compared them. It was good work. It wasn't a map of the same area, as the goal had been to give them bad information. But I doubted anyone who had given the map a cursory glance would notice they had been switched.

I quickly folded the map back up and put it inside the safe, the major layering the other documents inside over it in the order in which he had found them.

Then we closed the door, and I spun the dial.

"Good work," he said. "Now let's go."

We hurried back out onto the balcony, and Major Ramsey helped me climb over the rail. My dress rode up my legs as I went over, once again giving him a bit more of a view than I'd intended, and I didn't dare look at him as I began my descent.

Once I reached the ground, he unfastened the ladder and dropped it, then looped the rope around one of the rails so he could lower himself down.

He dropped to the ground beside me. I was always amazed at how soundless he could be for a man his size.

He pulled the rope down after him and quickly looped it so he could carry it conveniently. With a glance around to be sure the coast was clear, he nodded.

I grabbed up Noelle's fur coat from the ground, not taking the time to pull it on until we were safe, and we hurried away.

There was a small garden down the street that was suitably secluded, and we stopped for a moment to catch our breath. The major consulted the luminous dial of his watch. "We have a quarter of an hour before we rendezvous with Dupéré. It will be best to wait here, I think. We have little chance of being observed in this spot."

"All right."

"You did well," he said. "That went off without a hitch."

It had almost been too easy, really.

The wind gusted, and I shivered.

As though without thought, his hands moved to my shoulders, rubbing up and down my upper arms, warming me. He seemed to realize the intimacy of it a moment after he'd done it, but though his hands stilled on my arms, he didn't pull them away.

He was looking down at me, his gaze hard to read. It was softer than usual, somehow, but more closed off at the same time. It was the same way he had been looking at me as we were pressed together behind the curtains.

One thing was obvious: he wanted to kiss me badly. And I wanted him to. I'd been longing for him to do it ever since I'd first gone back to his office a week ago.

But his self-control won the day again, and his hands dropped from my arms. He was still looking at me, though, as if trying to decide what to say.

I began to pull on Noelle's coat, which had been draped over my arm. He moved to help me, but I didn't let him hold it up for me, putting it on myself instead.

"Noelle's coat is much warmer than mine," I said, because the silence was growing excruciating.

"She had a lot to say to me after you left," he said.

I didn't look at him. "Oh?"

"She's quite taken with you." I couldn't tell how he felt about this from his tone, but I realized there was a reason he was telling me.

"I like her very much, too," I said.

Another drawn-out moment of silence. He was debating on that invisible line between us, the one he had told himself he could not cross again. Now he was standing with his toes on it.

"She's . . . noticed there's something between us," he said.

"Yes, she mentioned that. I told her there couldn't be." My voice sounded tight and breathless to my own ears. Because what we were saying was entirely at odds with what I knew we were both feeling.

"Perhaps if things were different . . ." he said.

I looked up at him, the meaning of the words crystallizing in my mind.

"If I were different, you mean." It had always been clear that I would never be up to snuff in the major's world. At least now it was out in the open.

"No."

I smiled, though I felt a bit sick to my stomach. "It's all right. I understand. We'd better go." I turned away, began to walk from the garden.

He gently caught my wrist, stopping me. "Electra. That's not what I meant . . ."

I turned back, looked up at him. "I'm not the kind of girl a man like you romances," I said without bitterness. "It's just the way things are. And we're both practical enough people to realize it."

He swore, his eyes flashing silvery in the darkness. "It isn't your past, Electra. Or your family. You've proved what kind of woman you are when it counts."

My heart began to hammer at the words, and my throat tightened as tears threatened to spring to my eyes. Was it possible he meant it?

I was so elated that it took me a moment to remember this was not a declaration; he was still listing his reservations.

"But you know better than anyone how all-consuming my work is. I'm not in a position to make promises at present. There are . . . so many things to consider." He sighed. "If I could just forget this bloody war for one minute . . ."

"What would you do?" I asked. Suddenly, I felt bold enough to want to press him. To make him acknowledge his desire for me, if nothing else. Nothing would happen after tonight—we'd both go back to our separate lives, no promises given—but perhaps I wanted to go back to my life with a few romantic memories.

Our eyes caught, and I could feel the weight of the air shift around us.

"If you could forget the war . . ." I pressed softly, leaning ever so slightly closer. "For just one minute . . . what would you do?"

His hand, still on my wrist, slid up my arm. His gaze met mine, and I felt the spark zag through me.

"Electra." I didn't know if the warning note in his voice was meant for him or for me.

"War's a difficult thing to forget, of course," I said as casually as I could manage. "But, after all, a minute isn't very long."

"I told you in Sunderland it wouldn't happen again," he said in a low voice, though his gaze flickered to my mouth and his fingers closed around my arm.

"Forget that, too," I whispered. "Just for one minute."

His eyes on mine, his other arm moved around me, and he drew me closer. I felt as though all the air had left my lungs, as though my body melted into his as I rested my hands on his chest and tilted my mouth to his.

He kissed me. It wasn't a fiery kiss like the one in Sunderland had been. It was slow, languorous, and it melted me just as effectively. I slid my arms around his neck, held on to him as though I could catch on to this moment and make time stand still.

For a few breathless moments, I didn't think about any of the things that separated us. I thought only of the warmth of him, of the slow, simmering passion of his kiss. Of the romance of embracing a handsome man in the moonlight.

All too soon, he pulled back slightly, though he didn't release me. "That was longer than a minute," he murmured.

"I wasn't counting," I replied, breathless. "Perhaps we'd better start again."

He kissed me again, the intensity of it increasing as one hand slid into my hair and the other moved inside the fur coat and around my waist, pulling me more tightly against him. I clung to him, every inch of me tingling.

I understood then the recklessness of passion, why people were willing to risk so much for it, why it was so dangerous.

He understood it, too. And that was why he stepped back suddenly, his hands once again grasping my upper arms, as though to steady us both. "Dupéré will be waiting."

I nodded.

Our eyes held for just a moment longer, savoring the magic of that moment that lingered.

And then he let out a breath that was almost a sigh, released me, and motioned for me to precede him out of the garden.

CHAPTER TWENTY-SEVEN

We reached the rendezvous point just as Aristide was approaching from the opposite direction. He had clearly come in a slightly circuitous route to escape detection.

"Alas, I was, perhaps, too good an actor," he said as he reached us. "I got myself ejected from the nightclub within twenty minutes."

I was not at all surprised.

"Were you successful?" he asked.

The major gave him a nod.

Aristide smiled. "*Bon.* Then let us get out of this wretched cold."

The major led the way toward the street where Jakub was waiting for us, and Aristide fell into step behind me.

"The safe must have been a challenge," he said in a low voice. "It looks as though you've been pulling your hair in frustration."

I didn't answer. The laughing note in his voice made it perfectly clear he knew what had happened.

My own head was still in a whirl from it. Had Ramsey and I really been locked in a passionate embrace only moments ago? It seemed almost like some sort of dream.

We got in the car and drove back toward the major's house. I tried not to sit too close to him, but it felt as though I was drawn closer with each corner we turned until I was nearly leaning against his side, the warm length of his thigh pressed against mine. He made no move to shift away.

Constance was still at the office when we arrived and helped divest us of our outerwear. Aristide, of course, flirted shamelessly with her, but she wasn't entirely annoyed by it.

"We have had a great success tonight, Constance. Kiss me in celebration, will you?"

"I will not, Monsieur Dupéré. Major Ramsey, Captain Blandings and a . . . companion are here to see you."

I glanced over at the major, wondering if he had been expecting Archie this evening. I assumed his companion was Anna Gillard, as I knew Ramsey had told Archie to make contact with her. I hoped he would let me in on the conversation.

"Thank you, Miss Brown." Ramsey turned toward the former front parlor that now served as a little waiting room, and I followed, Aristide trailing behind.

Archie Blandings rose to his feet from where he had been sitting on a chair. There was a young woman on the yellow sofa. She, too, rose when we entered.

"Good evening," Major Ramsey said to her. "I assume you're Anna Gillard?"

She nodded.

"My office doesn't have a good deal of comfortable seating," he said. "Let's sit here, shall we?"

He motioned for them to resume their seats, and he indicated a seat on a sofa facing them for me. Then he sat beside me, not too close. But close enough.

I tried not to think too much about it and looked across at Anna Gillard, the woman we had assumed had been murdered at the Valencia.

She was young and pretty, and she looked terrified. No doubt, after all she had endured in fleeing her country, being questioned by another man in uniform—no matter which insignia it held—was disconcerting.

She had thick dark hair and liquid dark eyes that glistened as she looked first at Ramsey and then at me and then back to him. She was thin, her body giving evidence of the hardships she had endured over the past months, but there was a set to her chin that told me she was beaten down but not defeated.

"Can I get you some tea?" Ramsey asked. I knew he would be impatient to get down to business, so I thought it kind of him to offer.

"Miss Brown has been so kind as to go and prepare some for us, I believe," Archie Blandings said.

"Then let us tie up loose ends while we wait, shall we?" he said, in a more pleasant tone than I was accustomed to him using. "I know it's late. It won't take long. I just have a few questions for you."

She nodded. "Yes, of course."

I was, to some degree, uncertain why he still wished to speak to her. After all, we had the map. And, no doubt, there would be repercussions for Lazaro for having taken possession of it. But I also knew Ramsey was not one to leave a stone unturned. He no doubt wanted the full story.

"Captain Blandings has explained to you that someone was killed in the hotel room you vacated?" he asked.

She nodded, her eyes glistening. "He told me as much. I was so sorry to hear it. I knew the people who were after me were dangerous, but I did not think they would do such a horrible thing . . ."

"You knew you were being pursued?"

"Yes. I was told by . . . an acquaintance that I was to deliver an important package. I knew very little about what it was, but I was warned it could be dangerous."

"Let us start from the beginning. You are originally from Belgium?"

"Yes. I fled in June, and, after much hardship, I reached Lisbon."

"Did you bring any luggage with you?" he asked. "Trunks, suitcases, things of that nature?"

She shook her head. "I left my home with just a small pack. I had to balance any objects I wanted to keep against the importance of food for the journey." I noticed as she spoke that she played with the gold necklace around her neck, a medallion of some sort on a long chain. I supposed it was one of the few things that she had been able to carry with her from her homeland.

"The food was gone long before I reached Lisbon. As for the objects, there is nothing that would be of much value to anyone but me."

"What is on the necklace you're wearing?" Major Ramsey asked. The question had come out of the blue, but it was asked in such a conversational way that it seemed almost natural. It always surprised me, the ease with which he could converse with people, because— until tonight, at least—he was always so very formal with me.

He was not an easy man, but he could occasionally be an understanding one.

"It was a gift from my husband," she said. "It has the dates of our meeting and our marriage on it."

I felt a pang of sadness. Would she be reunited with her husband someday? I hoped desperately that she would, but there was no guarantee that any of us would be reunited with the ones we loved.

Then I frowned, something nagging at me.

Beside me, Major Ramsey continued with his questions. "So what happened when you got to London?"

"I stopped at the Valencia. I intended to stay there until I could hand off the map, but I noticed people following me when I would go out for meals. It made me worried, and so I snuck out the back entrance one day. I left the map at the agreed-upon place, and I have been hiding ever since."

"Why did you leave the hotel with all your things still there?" Ramsey asked.

"It seemed safer that way. If people assumed that I had disappeared without notice, they might stop looking for me."

There was a certain sort of logic to it. Add to that the body we had found in her bed, and it had been rather an effective method of throwing us off her trail. It seemed to have worked for the German agents who were pursuing her, as well. She was still alive, after all.

"And since then you have been in Aylesbury?"

She nodded. "I have been unsure where to go."

And then I realized suddenly what was nagging at me. When we had gone to see Germaine Arnaud, she had told us the woman touching her necklace had referred to a sister, not a husband.

Why the change in story? Had Germaine Arnaud been mistaken?

"We spoke to someone else who mentioned you and your sister wore matching necklaces," I said.

There was a long moment of silence, and I sensed a shift in the room. Something in Ramsey's posture, something in the change in Anna Gillard's face, told me we were at a moment of crisis.

And then, to my horror, she reached into her handbag and pulled out a gun.

Being raised among criminals, I had never had a fear of weapons—though I certainly regarded them with a healthy respect. But the sight of the gun, after what had happened in Sunderland, made my blood run cold.

"You are very smart, mademoiselle, but perhaps not smart enough. I heard this one here," she said, jerking her head in Aristide's direction, "mention that you had been successful. I assume you have found the map you are searching for. I will take it, if you please."

I looked over at Ramsey, but he wasn't looking at me. His gaze was trained on Anna Gillard. I imagined he regarded facing down a weapon with even more distaste than I did. After all, he'd been shot four times only recently.

But, aside from a slight tensing of his bearing, which I understood to be a focusing of readiness, there was no change in him.

"You never had the map," he said.

She shook her head. "I was sent from Lisbon to try to retrieve
it. I thought, perhaps, it was in the possession of the Frenchwoman,
and so I engaged her in conversation on the flight. I tried to make
her sympathize with me, hoping she would confide in me if she had
a secret, but she is not a woman with sympathy in her."

She wasn't exactly wrong about Germaine Arnaud, but I didn't
think there was much sympathy in this woman either.

"What about the dead woman in your hotel room?" I asked.

"I had just received a message that Lazaro was likely in possession of the map. I was burning the message when she walked into the
room. It occurred to me that a body being mistaken for mine would
buy me more time in case I was followed." She shrugged. "And so I
killed her. Then I hid until I could contact my compatriots."

I felt a chill at her casual words.

"Your compatriots," Major Ramsey said. "That is the group
of thieves, I assume?"

"Yes. We were sent separately with the same aim: retrieve the
map. They had their methods, and I had mine. We see which has
been successful."

Not successful yet, I thought. Though my vision may have blurred
for just a moment at the sight of the weapon, I had gathered my wits
about me. There were four of us in this room to just one of her.

The weapon counted for a lot, for though I knew Ramsey was
wearing a gun, he would not have time to remove it before she
could shoot him.

It was then that Constance came into the room bearing a tea
tray.

"I think I've got everything," she said, looking down at the tray,
oblivious to the little scene playing out. "I've brought some biscuits,
too. I know it's late, but I thought you might enjoy a snack."

She moved into the room and toward the table that sat before Anna Gillard. Constance was normally so very attuned to what was going on around her that I couldn't believe she had failed to notice the gun in the woman's hand.

And then I realized she hadn't.

She reached the table and, instead of setting the tray on it, dumped the entire contents on Anna Gillard, who screamed and dropped the gun as the water scalded her.

It would be a long night of questioning for Anna Gillard.

The instant the tea had hit her, she shrieked, and then Archie Blandings, who had moved like a flash, was on her. Aristide had not been far behind.

I saw only part of the action, as Ramsey had moved on the sofa to push me behind him.

She had been handcuffed and led to the cozy little interrogation room down the hall.

Constance was briskly cleaning up the mess on the carpet as Ramsey walked me out to the front porch.

"Are you all right?" he asked.

I knew from passing a mirror on my way out the door that I was still white as a ghost. "That was rather frightening . . ." I admitted. "After what happened to you in Sunderland. I didn't know what to do."

"You don't always have to know what to do, Electra," he said. "That's why we have a team."

I turned my face to him. It was dark, but his eyes were clear and silvery as he looked down at me.

"We make a good team, I think." His voice, low and warm, sent a little shiver through me.

"Yes," I said softly. "A very good team."

"I may be tied up with this all day tomorrow," he said. "But I'll ring you soon. We should talk."

I nodded, feeling a little surge of excitement rather than dread at the words. There was a feeling that things had shifted between us. Our kisses in the garden weren't going to be able to be swept under the rug.

"Oh," I said, before I turned to go. "Take this."

I removed the diamond bracelet Noelle had loaned me from my wrist and pressed it into his hand. He looked down at it.

"Give it to Noelle."

He nodded and dropped it into his pocket.

"I should give you her coat, too."

He shook his head. "She'll manage without it. It'll keep you warm on the way home."

And then he gently clasped the fur lapels and tugged me closer, lowering his mouth to kiss me again.

The memory of that kiss did a lot more than the mink to keep me warm on my ride home.

CHAPTER TWENTY-EIGHT

I was glad Ramsey was tied up the next day because I still had my job to do for Pony. Even the cloud I had been floating on since I left the major's town house had not been enough to make me forget that little task.

Before I'd left our last meeting, Pony had told me he'd send someone along with me to do the wiretapping. I was only required to get us in and out of the building without detection. That was simple enough. It was dusk the next evening when I slipped out of my flat and made my way with one of Pony Peavey's men toward the target destination.

I hadn't told anyone about this job, and I thought that was for the best.

I didn't like hiding things from Uncle Mick, but it seemed that ever since the war had started there had been more and more things it was necessary to keep from him. I hated this war, hated the secrets it created.

There was also the nagging realization that what I was going to do for Pony was illegal, and if I were caught I would have a devil of a time explaining it to the police. Technically speaking, I hadn't broken the law since that night we had been "arrested" by Major Ramsey and drafted into service. I'd broken into Peter Varney's flat to retrieve Julia's letters, it was true, but I didn't count that as a crime, not when he was blackmailing her.

While I was justifying things, I supposed I could say that what I was doing tonight was a part of my work for Ramsey. In order to get the information we needed, I had agreed to do this favor for Pony. All the same, I felt doubts about it.

Not enough to back down, of course. Pony Peavey wasn't the sort of man you reneged on an agreement with.

I would be very glad indeed to close the books on my dealings with Pony Peavey. It wasn't just that the man had a bad reputation, even among criminals. It was that I had finally begun to acknowledge that I might be ready to walk away from my life of crime.

It had been a scary thought when it first began blooming in my mind at the beginning of all of this, the idea I might diverge from the family business into a more law-abiding career when the war was over. But now I was almost certain that I could not go back to being a thief. It wasn't just Ramsey—though, admittedly, he was part of it. His dismissal of my past had reminded me that my future was entirely up to me, that my own choices determined what kind of woman I was. Whether or not Ramsey would be a part of that future, I was a different person now than when the war had begun.

Uncle Mick would, I knew, support me in this decision as he had always supported me in whatever I did. In fact, it would probably be a relief to him that I wanted to go straight.

There was still the matter of my father to be resolved, of course. Perhaps I would tell Ramsey the truth, after all. He had said my family history didn't matter to him, and I believed him. He wouldn't hold whatever my father might have done against me. It was also possible he would be able to find out something about my father's movements during the Great War, whether or not he had been suspected at the time of espionage activities. I could tell him about the Chambers Flower Shop and show him the letter to see

what he might make of it. To my surprise, I felt the weight of the
secret lift at just the thought of confiding in him.

A cold gust of wind blew flecks of icy snow into my face, drawing me back to the present. I had better focus on this job. There
would be time for daydreaming about Ramsey later.

The fellow accompanying me gave his name as Bert, and he
seemed to speak mainly in monosyllables. He didn't even say many
of those as we took the Tube to Pimlico and then walked to a street
consisting mainly of office buildings. It was fairly quiet at this time
of evening. There was never any knowing when the Germans would
decide to pay us another visit, and only idiots hung around in places
they didn't have to. Idiots and people who were up to no good.

Bert motioned me to the back of an office building, where there
was a door set into the brick wall. I glanced at the doorknob. It was
standard stuff, wouldn't take me more than a minute or two.

"No guards in this building?" I asked as I took my tool kit out
of my pocket.

"No."

I worked the back door open with no trouble, and in a blink,
we were both slipping inside the dark building. I closed the door
behind us.

Bert took a torch from his pocket and flipped it on. Then he led
the way. He'd cased the building beforehand, that much was clear.
He knew exactly where we were going and moved ahead without
hesitation. Well, so much the better. It made things easier for me. I
would be relieved to have this job over and done with.

We took a dark stairwell rather than the lift and then went
down a long, dark hall. I walked silently as I had been trained to
do, but Bert's footsteps echoed in the quiet. I hoped his confidence
in the emptiness of the building was not misplaced.

He stopped at the second door from the end. "This one."

Again, I went to work on the door. I was surprised Pony hadn't
had someone capable of doing this easy sort of work. Surely he

knew a lockpick or two. Then again, I owed him and he didn't have to pay me. Besides, we McDonnells were known for our ability to get in and out without leaving a trace. Less experienced lockpicks might leave telltale scratches to show someone had broken in.

If they were going to tap his phone calls, it made sense they'd want not even the smallest hint that someone had been here.

The office door, too, was the work of only a minute, and then the lock clicked.

"Wait here," Bert told me.

I was glad to. I had no desire to wait in the dark office with him while he did whatever he needed to do to the telephone. Besides, it felt a bit less illegal on my part to not actually enter the office.

I didn't know anything about tapping into someone's telephone wires, and I had no idea how long it would take.

I wondered what sort of information Pony might be collecting and what he might use it for. A momentary and unaccustomed sensation of guilt assailed me at what I was helping him do, but I pushed it down. Like Julia, I'd been forced to do a bad thing for a good reason. When it was over, I would put it all behind me.

The minutes stretched. I could hear Bert moving quietly around inside, hear the occasional movement of his tools. And then he was back in the doorway.

"Done," he said.

He didn't have to tell me twice. I relocked the door, and we made our way from the building.

We parted ways outside, and I was glad to start back toward Hendon on my own.

As I sank into my seat on the Tube, I breathed a sigh of relief. With any luck, the last of my criminal days were now behind me. Frank Doyle and Pony Peavey had both called in their markers, and now my debts were paid. I could begin again with a clean slate.

CHAPTER TWENTY-NINE

The telephone call I'd been waiting for arrived the next morning during our breakfast.

"The major asks if you would join him here this morning," Constance said.

"Certainly. I'll start that way now," I said, careful to keep the eager note out of my voice. I would be glad to see him again.

I had hoped he would come here, that we could have a less official place to discuss what I anticipated might be some sort of understanding, but I wouldn't quibble.

"Important meeting?" Uncle Mick quipped with a wink at me across the table.

I felt myself flush. "Something like that."

Uncle Mick had spread the word, given to him by an "unnamed source," that the false map had been sold by Lazaro. The buyer's name had been passed to the band of thieves, and they had gone on their way, presumably to relieve him of it. I hoped the map would cause the Germans a hundred times the trouble it had caused us—and then some.

I arrived at the town house in record time, and Constance helped me off with the mink coat. I hoped I would be able to convince Ramsey to drive me home. It would give us a bit more time together, and then he could take the coat back with him. The dress I'd cleaned and folded carefully in a box, which I handed off to Constance.

"I didn't get much time to talk to you the other night," I said. "But I admired your quick thinking so much. You might have saved us all from a very nasty outcome."

She smiled. "I only did what anyone would do. I made the most of the materials available to me."

"Well, it was a jolly good show," I said. "I'm glad to be on a team with you, Constance."

"I feel the same way, Ellie."

She went back to her desk, and I drew in a little breath and made my way down the hall to the major's office.

I tapped lightly on the door and heard his call to enter from the other side.

I went in, closing the door behind me as I always did. This time, however, I felt a new awareness of being alone together. What was he going to say? Would he kiss me?

I turned from the door to look at him.

Something was wrong. He didn't come to take me into his arms. He remained behind his desk. His face was unreadable, never a good sign.

"Good morning," I said brightly, trying to gauge his mood.

"Have a seat," he said.

I did as I was told, with a sinking feeling in my chest. The day since I'd been here had been long enough for him to change his mind. He was going to tell me that there could be nothing between us, after all.

My mind was running along counterarguments to this stance, so I was caught off guard by what he said next.

"Where were you last night?"

For just an instant, I was confused. Had he been to visit me and been irritated to find I was not at home? No, this was something more than that. And then I felt the lurch of alarm in my stomach.

He knew.

My brain spun, trying to figure out how to play it off. What could I tell him that he would believe?

While I was trying to think, Major Ramsey reached into his desk and pulled something out. He dropped it on the table between us.

I didn't know exactly what it was, but I could guess. It was the components of the device Bert had used to wiretap the telephone in that office building.

"Explain yourself." His tone wasn't angry; it was cool and controlled, which was somehow almost worse.

It seemed there was no choice but to tell the truth. That was generally the best option with Ramsey anyway, as he seemed unnaturally skilled at finding things out.

"How did you know?" I asked, as lightly as I could manage.

"I've had your house watched as a precaution since we were attacked."

Of course. He'd done it before, but it hadn't even occurred to me that he might do it now. He could be protective to a fault, but I felt too anxious to be angry with him. There was something in his manner that set the alarm bells off in my head, and years of finely tuned self-preservation skills told me to tread carefully.

"I didn't know you were accomplished at wiretapping." The emotionless tone of his voice was chilling, and I wished he would shout at me instead.

"I'm not," I said. "You know I'm not."

He waited.

"I owed Pony Peavey a favor. When he found that man for us, I told him I would do something in return. And this was it. You haven't complained about me using my skills to help you in any other circumstances. Why is this any different?"

"Do you know whose office these were put in?" I realized suddenly why his manner upset me. It reminded me of the first time we had met, when he had questioned me in that empty interrogation room down the hall. When I hadn't known him at all.

"No," I said. "Pony showed me a picture, but I didn't recognize him."

"His name was Nathaniel Gregory. Do you recognize that?"

The sinking feeling deepened, because I did. I'd seen it in the papers often enough. "He's a member of Parliament, isn't he?"

"Yes."

I'd helped bug an MP's office. This must look very bad indeed.

"I didn't know," I said. "Really. I was only concerned with paying off my debt to Pony."

"Why didn't you come to me?"

"It didn't have anything to do with you," I said honestly. "We needed information, Pony got it, and so I owed him. It's as simple as that."

"It's not simple at all," he said.

Then he reached into the desk again and pulled something else out. That was when my heart fell.

He tossed it on the desk between us. I looked down at it and schooled my face not to react. It was the blue glove I'd dropped in Peter Varney's flat.

When I was sure that my features were expressionless, I looked back up at him. I said nothing but waited for him to make the accusation.

"There was a break-in reported a few days ago at another government official's home. He said that his desk had been tampered with, documents disarranged. The thief left this behind. I was consulted, as it was an intelligence matter. Imagine my surprise when I recognized this glove."

"That glove could belong to anyone," I said.

"Your fingerprints were found at the scene."

I hadn't worn gloves; they'd been in my pocket. I hadn't needed them for such a simple job. Or so I'd assumed.

"My fingerprints aren't on file with the police," I said, trying to find my footing in this conversation. "I've never been arrested."

"No," he agreed. "But I have them on file, and I told Kimble to make the comparison."

I wasn't surprised. He was nothing if not thorough.

There was nothing to do but come clean.

"He was blackmailing a friend with her love letters," I admitted. "I got them back. That's all. I didn't look at any other documents."

"You could go to prison for this."

"Then call the police, if you must."

He slammed his hand on the desk and swore, his eyes flashing. "This is not a time to be flippant with me."

"I don't know what you want me to say," I said. "I'm telling you the truth."

There was a long silence.

I knew perfectly well that Major Ramsey was not one for niceties, and there were none to be had here.

"You committed felonies," he said, his tone once again even and cool, impersonal. "Broke into the offices of not one but two government officials, conspired to wiretap a telephone, and stole personal documents from a desk containing sensitive information."

I said nothing.

"These could be construed as espionage activities," he said. "Do you understand that? You could be arrested and potentially hanged as a spy."

I was cold all the way through now.

Silence held heavily in the air.

At last, he spoke, and this time his tone was neutral, horribly professional in tone. "I'm removing you from duty effective immediately."

Somehow, I had not expected this, hadn't even considered the possibility, and it was impossible for me to hide my shock. I'm rather afraid my mouth dropped open.

"You're what?" I whispered.

"Here is what is going to happen," he went on in that same flat voice. "You are going to return to your house, return to working with your uncle in the locksmithing profession. If you wish to continue contributing to the war effort, I suggest the Women's Voluntary Services."

"You want me to go from spying to doing clothing drives and serving coffee to soldiers?" I asked. I knew that work was important, of course, but I was accustomed to doing dangerous work. I was accustomed to working with *him*.

He didn't answer what he clearly deemed a rhetorical question.

"You can't do this," I said. I was angry at the tremor in my voice, but I was shaking with emotion, my insides warring between sorrow and fury. Strangely, my temper, which had always been so difficult to control, was wilting under growing despair.

"You'll be paid for your services for this job, but I'm afraid we will no longer be keeping you on the payroll in the future."

It was maddening, the way he went on as though all the work I had done meant nothing, as though I meant nothing to him at all. Perhaps I didn't. Perhaps those kisses in the moonlight had been only one minute of forgetting, as I'd suggested.

But my services were valuable. I'd been instrumental in the capture of more than one spy ring. And now I was to be swept aside so easily.

"You don't have to do this," I said. "I've told you my reasons for what I did."

"Yes," he said, his eyes meeting mine. "And I believe you. Which is why I'm not turning you over to the authorities."

He would have, I realized, if he hadn't believed me. My future had hung in the balance more than I had realized during this conversation.

"If you know I'm telling the truth, why are you doing this?"

"Your motives are immaterial. The problem, as I'm sure you can see, is that I cannot trust you. You gave me your word you would not commit robberies on your own while working under me."

The accusation, however true, was like a slap across the face.

"I've put my neck on the line from the beginning to employ you," he went on. "And it could very well have brought us both down if you had been caught or discovered during the course of these robberies. You endangered yourself and my entire operation with your inability to follow instructions and your propensity for rogue behavior."

My lips parted as if in preparation to argue, but I pressed them closed again. What could I say?

He was not finished. "Again and again, you ignore my instructions, hide things from me, and do what seems best to you. I understand that you are not a part of the military hierarchy, and that sometimes, in our line of work, improvisation is called for. But I cannot allow you to work for me if you won't keep to your word."

It was as thorough a dressing-down as I'd ever received, and what made it particularly awful was that I was fairly sure it was deserved. While it hurt to consider it in those terms, I had broken his trust. I'd told him I wouldn't pull any jobs on my own, and I'd done two. That didn't mean, however, that I would go easily.

"I've done so much to help. I could do more. You know how valuable I've been." Annoyingly, I felt a lump in my throat, and I had to stop before my voice cracked. Already it was an effort to keep the tears at bay. But if he was dismissing me from service, I was not going to cry.

"No one is questioning your capabilities," he said. "Or the value of your contributions. You saved my life. And there's nothing I can do to adequately thank you for that. I will, to some extent, be forever in your debt. But that is outside of the bounds of this operation. I have to do what is best for everyone concerned, and so that is why this is going to have to be your last assignment."

It was clear he had made up his mind.

But there was one more thing I had to know.

"And what about what happened between us?" I asked softly.

For one horrible moment, I was afraid he was going to ignore the question, but then his eyes met mine and he let out the faintest breath, the first hint of yielding in the entirety of this conversation. Again, I could sense that he was trying to think of the best answer, weighing his words carefully.

"That, unfortunately, was another aspect of what led me to this decision."

This I had not expected.

"Why?" I whispered.

"In short, you've become a liability. To the work, to the operation. When you act impulsively, you become a distraction."

"To whom?" I demanded.

"To me," he said.

The words hung in the air between us, open for interpretation. Then he clarified: "Clearly, there is a strong connection between us. I had hoped, after Sunderland, we would be able to put it behind us, but I found myself incapable of it."

I looked at him, wondering what sort of declaration this was. Something told me it wasn't the happily-ever-after sort.

"I owe you honesty," he said, "and the truth is that I can't do my best work when I am constantly concerned about your safety because you will not do as you are told. I cannot afford to have my focus compromised."

"That's not fair," I whispered.

"Perhaps not," he said. "But it's how it is."

I felt rather as though my world was unexpectedly crumbling around me, and I didn't know how to react.

I gave a short nod, unable to meet his eyes. He'd as much as confessed that he had feelings for me, but there was not a hint of joy in it. It was costing me my work, and I was gaining nothing. After all, it was clear that he intended to send me on my merry way. Out of sight, out of mind, it seemed.

"What about Uncle Mick?" I asked. "It's a shame for his skills to go to waste because of me."

"If another job comes up that requires safecracking services, I know where to reach him."

I nodded again, drew in a breath. There was no sense in dragging things out.

"Then I suppose this is goodbye," I said briskly, rising from my seat. I'd recovered myself now. My voice was steady, and the tears had somehow been pressed down deep until I had the leisure to let them out. My pride was too strong to let him see how much this hurt.

He had risen with me, though I think my abruptness had caught him a bit off guard.

I forced myself to look up at him. His eyes were on my face, and I didn't intend to let him see any of the inner turmoil I was feeling. I drew in a slow breath through my nose to steady myself and then spoke.

"Thank you for the opportunities you've given me, Major Ramsey. I've enjoyed the work very much." I ought to have said something about being glad to know him, but I was angry and hurt, and, besides, I wasn't sure I could say it without crying.

"Your country thanks you for everything you've done."

I couldn't stop the cynical little laugh that sprang to my lips.

There was nothing more to say, so I turned and walked out of his office for the last time, closing the door behind me.

Constance was gone from her desk, and I was glad. I didn't think I could have managed to say goodbye to her. I was barely holding myself together as it was.

I went, coatless, out the front door, and the cold air hit me in the face.

It was in that moment, of course, that I realized the horrible truth of it.

I was in love with him.

CHAPTER THIRTY

One might say that the Irish are, on the whole, a romantic people. But what we really love in our romances is a good tragedy, and so it seemed fitting that I realized the depths of my feelings now that it was too late.

I held myself together all the way home, a strange sort of pre-serving numbness stealing over my mind, encapsulating all the thoughts within so tightly that I couldn't turn them over and over as I took the Tube back to Hendon. I didn't even feel the cold.

A neighbor stopped to chat, but I later had almost no recollec-tion of what we talked about. It was as though I was in a daze. It sounds rather dramatic, and I suppose it is. Isn't heartbreak usually?

It was just so stupid of me not to have realized it before now. I supposed it had been obvious for the longest time, but I had been ig-noring it. Oh, I'd known that I was attracted to him, that I admired him, valued his opinion, that I trusted him with my life. But I hadn't tied all those elements together into what they clearly were: love.

That he didn't feel the same was patently obvious. He had admitted that he cared about me—otherwise he would not have been so worried about my safety that he dismissed me—but he hadn't cared enough not to say goodbye.

He had let me walk out the door, and he had made it very clear that I wasn't likely to be seeing him again.

And so that was that.

It wasn't until I was back in my flat that that dam burst, and I sank with great heaving sobs upon the sofa.

It was perhaps only half an hour later when there was a tap at the door.

"Ellie?" a voice called. It was Felix.

I didn't really want to see him, not now. But I got up anyway and went to open the door.

He started when he saw my face. "What is it, love? What's happened?"

I tried to pull myself together. I couldn't share this with Felix. But I couldn't stop the tears either.

"Everyone's all right," I said to assure him there had been no sudden deaths or anything so dire. I wiped at my face. "It's just . . . it's something else . . ."

He came in, closing the door, and gathered me into his arms, his free hand gently stroking my hair as he murmured soothing noises. "It's all right, Ellie. Whatever it is, it'll be all right."

I pressed my face against his jacket, unable to look up at him. I couldn't tell him. I simply could not tell him I was in love with Major Ramsey. Not now. Not like this.

"It's nothing so very earth-shattering," I said at last. "I'm just rather in a muddle at the moment."

"It seems it must be something pretty important."

I pulled back, wiping at the wet patch on his coat from my tears. "I've got your coat all soggy."

"Don't worry about that, sweet. Why don't we sit down, and you can tell me all about it."

I drew in a shaky breath.

"Or you needn't talk, if you don't want to," he said. "We can just sit. But let me stay with you awhile."

I nodded, sniffed. "I'd like that."

We went over to the sofa. I sat, and Felix sat close, his arm around me. It felt so right to lean on him when I needed comfort. But it felt wrong, too, because my heart was broken over another man. This wasn't fair to Felix. It wasn't fair of me to accept his support when I knew now for certain that I wasn't in love with him.

Another involuntary sob escaped me at the thought.

"Why don't you tell me what's wrong, love?"

I took a handkerchief out of my pocket and realized it was one of the major's that I'd neglected to return to him. I wiped my eyes with it.

"It's silly, really," I said, trying to make my tone light. "Major Ramsey sacked me today. Dismissed me like . . . like I mean nothing at all."

Felix said nothing. I wondered if he was waiting for me to continue or if he was trying to decide how he should reply. I knew the fact I was no longer working for Major Ramsey would not hurt Felix's feelings in the least. He had never really liked my doing it. His feelings for the major aside, he didn't like the danger it put me in.

"I . . . the work was important to me. And now I'm at loose ends. I don't even know what I'm going to do next."

"We could get married."

At first, I wasn't sure I had heard him right. I turned to gape at him.

"I know this is sudden," he said. "I don't have a ring. I hadn't really thought this out, to be honest. But I've been known to win big on impulsive gambles, so there you have it."

"I . . . I . . ." I felt absolutely frozen. I could not have formulated a sentence at that moment to save my life.

His warm brown eyes searched my face. And then he smiled. It was an easy, comfortable smile. "That's a no if I've ever seen one. All right, then. No harm done. One can't win them all."

"No, Felix," I said quickly, grabbing his arm. "Please don't . . . it's just that I . . ."

The weight of all the emotions hit me, and I started to cry again.

He gave a little affectionate laugh but pulled me into his arms, leaning his cheek against the top of my head. "It's all right, love. I usually have much better timing than this. It just occurred to me, and I came out with it. Just put it from your mind. We don't ever have to talk about it again."

"We have to talk about it, Felix." I drew in a steadying breath. "I need to talk to you about . . . several things."

"You can talk to me about anything, Ellie. You know that."

"Some things are harder than others," I whispered.

"Do you want to tell me?" There was something in the words that caught my attention.

I looked up at him. "Tell you what?"

"Whatever it was that happened between you and Ramsey in Sunderland."

I could feel the heat creeping up my neck, and it was difficult to meet his gaze. "What do you mean?"

"Things haven't been quite the same between us since. You'll forgive me for bringing it up, but you've put a distance between us . . . physically."

I felt my flush deepen as I struggled to find the right words.

"You can tell me, Ellie," Felix said. "I'm not entitled to ask, of course, but I want you to know you can talk to me."

"I want to talk to you, Felix. It's just . . . This is different."

He was silent for a moment, and I thought how loud the ticking of my clock seemed.

When he finally spoke, his voice was neutral, careful. "It's none of my business, Ellie, not really. But if he seduced you and then tossed you aside . . .”

"No," I said quickly. "It wasn't like that."

Felix's voice was still calm, but I could feel the tension in his body now. "No matter how you felt about it, if he took you to bed under the assumption that there was some future for you and then . . ."

I shook my head against his chest, unable to look up at him. "No. He didn't . . . we didn't . . . We've kissed. That's all."

It felt good to admit it. To lay my cards on the table. Beside me, Felix's posture eased, and I felt him let out a breath at the knowledge that I hadn't been cruelly compromised.

Now that the dam had broken, I didn't feel as though I could stop the words. "But I have feelings for him, Felix. I didn't realize until today how strong they were, not until I realized I won't be seeing him again." I forced myself to look up into his face. No matter how hard this was, I had to be honest with him. "I care for you so much, Felix. You're my best friend. But I don't . . . I can't . . ."

"I understand," he said, shifting slightly away and taking his cigarette case from his pocket. "After all, the two of you have been engaged in all this top-secret work, and there's something rather sexy about secrets, isn't there?" His tone was light, but there was an edge to the words.

"Felix . . ."

"I don't blame you, Ellie. If anyone's at fault, it's him. He knows better, but he trifled with you anyway. I worried from the beginning he would turn your head and hurt you in the end."

My instinct was to defend the major, but I knew it wouldn't do any good. Not when Felix was angry and upset.

"I'm sorry," I said, fresh tears welling up. "I wouldn't have hurt you for anything."

He looked over at me and let out a sigh, his expression softening.

"Don't cry, sweet," he said, brushing the tears away with his thumbs. "Like I said, a man can't win them all. I know how to take my losses and shoulder on."

I knew him well enough to know he was crushed, but for my sake, he was putting his own feelings aside for the time being. He was the truest friend I could have asked for, and I felt wretched.

"We'll still be friends, won't we?" I asked, clasping his hand. "I couldn't bear it if you hated me."

He looked into my eyes. "Nothing on this earth would stop me from being your friend, Ellie McDonnell." Quiet settled between us for a moment, as Felix smoked.

And then he said, "I came here to make my own confession to you."

I turned to look at him.

"I'm going away again, and this time it could be months, maybe longer."

I felt a sinking feeling at the idea of losing him.

"Back to Scotland?"

He hesitated. "No. To France."

I gasped, as shocked as if he had slapped me. "Felix, no," I breathed.

"I told you I've been doing some work related to the war effort. Well, an opportunity has come up for me to do more of it in France."

I knew how dangerous the situation was in France. Knew that there was no mercy for spies. And whatever Felix was doing there would be considered espionage by the Nazis. If he was caught, he would be tortured and killed.

All of these thoughts must have flashed across my face, because he reached out and caught my hand. "Don't look like that. It's going to be all right."

"But, Felix. You've done enough for the cause. Your leg . . ."

"My leg may prove an asset," he said. "Who expects a one-legged spy?"

I was too miserable to even smile at his levity. "Oh, Felix. Is there anything I can do to change your mind?"

"I'm afraid not. It's all set. It's been in the works for the past few weeks, in fact, but I was trying to find the right time to tell you."

I wondered suddenly if that was why he had asked me to marry him, because he was worried he wouldn't be back. I had turned down his proposal, and now there was a chance I would never see him again. "I'm scared, Felix."

"You know I'm a lucky fellow, Ellie. You don't have to worry about me."

I would worry about him every second of every day, of course.

"Just promise me you'll make it home, Felix."

He squeezed my hand. "I promise."

CHAPTER THIRTY-ONE

It was five days later when there was a knock at our door at dinnertime. Uncle Mick got up from the table and went to answer it. A moment later, he came back into the room.

"Ellie, someone to see you."

I could tell from his careful expression that he wasn't sure how I would feel about the visitor, and then I knew instantly who it must be. I had confessed to Uncle Mick about my side jobs and the trouble it had got me into with Major Ramsey.

I had not told him that I was in love with the major, but Uncle Mick had always been adept at reading between the lines.

I *had* confided my feelings to Nacy and cried on her shoulder while she patted my hair and tutted sympathetically. It was, after all, the first time I had really been in love. The first wrenching heartbreak I had experienced as a result of it.

I could see the warring emotions in her face now, as I looked across the table at her. She was glad that the major had come, optimistic about what it might mean, but she was also indignant on my behalf. Major Ramsey had lost some of her favor when he dismissed me.

I was really tempted to tell Uncle Mick that he might relay to the major that he could go to the devil, but I knew he likely wouldn't be here without a good reason. And, if I was true to myself, I could acknowledge that I hoped deep down that the reason was he had realized he couldn't live without me.

As soon as I walked into the parlor, however, I could see that was not what had brought him here.

"I need to speak to you, privately," he said without greeting.

I waved my hand at the empty room. "There's no one else here."

He hesitated, and I sighed, going to close the doors so that we could have privacy. This house was old, and the doors were thick. Even if Nacy and Uncle Mick were inclined to try to listen—which I knew they wouldn't—I doubted that they would be able to hear much.

"Well," I said. "What can I do for you, Major Ramsey?"

"What else are you involved in?" he asked.

I frowned. "What do you mean?"

"Is there some other job you haven't told me about?"

I had no idea what he was talking about, but I felt a sudden surge of irritation that he had come here to question me. "My work is no longer your concern," I said.

He swore. "I don't have time for this, Electra. Someone is trying to kill you."

I blinked, certain I had misheard him. "What?"

"We caught the man who attacked us with the knife that night, tracked him down from the fingerprints on the knife you collected from the scene. We questioned him, and he confessed he wasn't after me. He was after you."

I felt a cold chill run through me, fear warring with confusion. I had assumed that assailant had been connected with the missing map.

"He wouldn't tell us why," Ramsey said. "But I had a feeling you would know."

I shook my head. Why would someone want to kill me? I didn't have any enemies.

And then the realization struck. It had something to do with my father, with the information I was gathering about his espionage activities. My visit to the Chambers Flower Shop had kicked a wasp's nest, it seemed. I was getting too close to something someone didn't want me to know.

I couldn't tell the major this, of course. Perhaps I had been a fool to ever think that I could. No matter that keeping things from him was what had come between us, I could never be open with him now.

If he knew that my father had been spying for Germany, he might change his mind about the nature of the work he'd caught me doing. He might not believe that my intentions had been good. He might believe I was a spy.

And so I shook my head again. "I don't know anyone who would want to hurt me. He must have been lying to you."

He looked at me, his eyes on my face. They had taken on a steely cast. I had always noticed that the violet drained out of them when his emotions were strongest.

He knew I was lying, but he also knew he couldn't force me to tell him the truth. He no longer had the privilege of my confidence.

As for someone trying to kill me, I had to believe it was an exaggeration. I might have been killed several times throughout the past week. No, it had only been meant to scare me off. A warning that I should stop asking questions.

Unfortunately, threats often had the effect of making me do just the opposite of what whoever was threatening wanted.

"That's not the only reason I've come," he said.

I waited. Despite everything, there was still the teeniest flicker of hope that he might make some kind of personal confession.

"This cannot go beyond this room."

I nodded.

"Captain Blandings came to see me this morning. We were seeing to a few loose ends, but he also wanted to share an intercepted

German missive he received yesterday. As you know, a great many refugees are making their way to Portugal in hopes of making it out of the Continent. There has also been work setting up an escape line for POWs through the Pyrenees to Lisbon."

My heart thudded heavily at the words, as though it already knew what they meant.

"Blandings told me the intercepted note spoke of three escaped POWs who were en route, and one of the names caught his attention: T. McDonnell. The description the Germans gave fits your cousin."

Toby. I gasped, my body stepping toward Ramsey of its own accord. "Does Archie know when he escaped? How far he might have come in this time?"

My legs felt limp with relief, and he must have sensed it, for he reached out to support my elbow.

"We don't have any more information than what I've given you, but it does seem possible your cousin is making his way to Lisbon with the Germans on his trail."

I felt a dizzying wave of emotions. Elation, relief, fear. "What can be done to find him?"

He hesitated, his expression grim.

"Blandings is working to get in touch with his informants. The escape line is, of course, closely guarded. It would be disastrous if information about it fell into German hands."

I nodded. "But Toby may be close to Lisbon already. The information could be old."

"Even if your cousin does make it to Lisbon, there will be danger. The Gestapo isn't going to let a little thing like Portuguese neutrality thwart them. If they catch him, they'll do everything in their power to get information about the route and anyone who helped him."

If possible, I went colder. He was talking about torture. There was no telling what Toby had endured already, but the thought of his suffering any more made me sick.

"What can I do?" I asked. "Surely there's something I can do to help him."

He didn't look happy about what he was about to say, but he said it anyway. "Blandings went over my head to Colonel Radburn. Radburn feels it is imperative for you and I to go to Lisbon."

I was shocked at the suggestion. So shocked I said nothing.

"With your cousin's help, we can help Blandings build up his information about the escape line and do what is possible to help future escapees." The major's eyes met mine. "Radburn doesn't know, of course, about what has happened between us. And I'm afraid this doesn't change what we discussed. This is not technically my mission. You'll be working for Blandings."

In other words, he was here against his will, and he still wanted nothing to do with me.

"Radburn, obviously, cannot order you to do anything," he said, when I still didn't answer. "The decision of whether to go is up to you."

So things were not quite over with Major Ramsey yet. I held out no hopes about romance—he could not have made his feelings on the matter any plainer—but my first focus was on Toby. If I could find a way to help him, if I could find a way to get him back to London, it would go a long way toward putting my shattered life back together.

I had been dismissed by Ramsey; Felix was going to be risking his life in France; but, perhaps, I could get Toby home.

"Yes," I said without hesitation. "Yes. I'll go to Lisbon."

ACKNOWLEDGMENTS

As always, the conclusion of a book gives me the opportunity to reflect on all the truly excellent people who contribute so much to the writing process and to my life. My sincerest thanks:

To my astute and amiable editor, Catherine Richards, for her thoughtful input and valuable insights.

To Kelly Stone and to the team at Minotaur for all their efforts. You take a simple document and turn it into a sparkling new book, and that will always be magical to me.

To my friends and family, who are always there to offer encouragement, suggestions, and humor. And especially to Larson and Anders, my Lolly and Binx, who make my life as an auntie the absolute best.

To everyone at the Allen Parish Libraries for their support and for daily laughter.

And last, but certainly not least, my thanks to the wise and witty agent who started it all: Ann Collette, to whom this book is dedicated. This is our eleventh and final novel together, but I look forward to many years of continued friendship!